Welcome

Hello readers new and old. This book
in the Izzy Palmer Mystery series. I want   ...one so
that anyone who reads these books at an   ...ic of year isn't forced
to get all Christmassy and anyone who wants to feel Christmassy can
dive in without discovering the secrets of the other books.

Apologies to my existing readers who have to wait until the spring
to find out what happens with boyfriends, businesses and (not Izzy's)
marriage proposal, but I promise the time will just fly by.

Prologue

I try so hard not to think about Christmas all year round, but, when October arrives, I can't hold it in anymore. That festive feeling grips hold of me and I find myself singing "Rudolph the Red Nose Reindeer" in the shower, making a mental list of potential presents and dreaming of mince pies and Christmas pudding.

By the time I open the first window on my Advent calendar, I'm a full-on kid again; twitching at all the warm-spirited adverts on TV, bursting into song at the faintest note of a jingled bell and spending every last minute of my free time either producing or consuming baked goods.

I don't care what anyone else says about it, Christmas is magical.

And, no, I don't think that's too strong a word for it, or that, at thirty years old, I should grow up and start pretending that I don't like it. What else in life has the power to make your whole body get so tingly and excited?

I can think of one thing, my brain said, but I chose to ignore myself. I zipped my bright green suit up and stepped outside into the knee-high snow.

It was Christmas Eve and I was five hundred miles from home, about to enjoy my first ever white Christmas. The chirpy nine-year-old who was buried not nearly deep enough inside me was humming a happy tune as I came to a stop in the middle of the winter village square and looked around at all that snow. It had come down heavily the night before and the roofs of the colourful chalets were repainted for the season.

There was a huge bank of the stuff at the entrance to the crescent of houses and it was incredibly difficult to resist running over and diving in.

It's time to make a snow angel... No, a snow man. Ooh, what about building up a store of snowballs and then ambushing everyone? My brain was even more fired up than I was, but I managed to stay focused as I started my morning trek. Thirty feet out of the village and it already felt like I was in some isolated wilderness. I entered a forest filled with evergreens and a glorious, fresh scent, which I would

7

always associate with Scotland, hung in the air.

There was a feeling inside me that this is what I should have been doing every Christmas since I was born. A real Christmas had snow, every kid knew that. So what had my parents been thinking keeping us in drizzly old London year after year?

I followed the path out of the forest as it began to slope upwards. My boots crunched beneath me and I realised that there are few sounds on this earth that are quite so musical. Not even the steepness of that hill could kill my joy and I soon arrived at the top, out of breath but elated.

The view was absolutely worth the climb. I was high above the trees now and, with their red and green woodwork and chains of dangling fairy lights, the houses looked like toys. In the distance, I could make out the flashing sign at the entrance to the park, welcoming us to 'Santa's Glen'. The elves' workshop and grotto were tucked away in the copse of birch trees at the edge of the village and, beyond them, there was nothing but white, stretching out across the horizon and up the Cairngorm mountains.

Well, white and a strange patch of red, like a wine stain on a tablecloth. I stared at it for fifteen seconds to make sure my eyes weren't playing tricks on me, then sprinted back towards the forest. I almost lost my footing once and imagined myself rolling down, accumulating snow along the way until I was one great ball.

But this wasn't a children's cartoon. It wasn't even a holiday. I was supposed to be working and a very real, physical fear had materialised in my stomach, like I'd swallowed a boulder.

"Please don't let it be her," I prayed, and whispered it five more times as I reached the village square to cut between two of the houses. The blood was easy to find, it stuck out as brightly as any of the light sculptures which illuminated the park. I don't know if it was the snow or the cold temperatures, but it hadn't turned rusty brown as I'd normally expect and had kept its Christmassy lustre.

There were great dabs of the stuff, like someone had been painting with a giant brush in a strange, jerking path. I couldn't see where it led at first and hoped that it was from a wounded animal, but then I saw the body, tucked in between two pine trees.

I immediately recognised the outfit of course; the red suit, with white trim and fluffy bobble on the hat. As much as I didn't want to find my client stabbed to death, I also couldn't stand the thought of the rosy-cheeked old man who played Father Christmas lying there. I hesitated, practically inching towards the poor soul who, face down in the snow, wouldn't be getting up again.

I felt truly cold for the first time that morning. In my gloves, woolly hat and three scarves, it wasn't the temperature that was cutting through me but the reality of what had happened. I crouched low to turn the body over and, even before I saw her face, something told me who it would be.

"I see now," I said, out loud for some reason. "It is you after all."

This wasn't what I'd had in mind for a Christmas present.

Chapter One

"We wish you a merry Christmas,

We wish you a merry Christmas,

We wish you a merry Christmas and a happy New Year!" It was the seventeenth time that my best friend Ramesh had sung this.

"Ra, don't you know any other songs?"

"Like what?" he was putting the final touches to the Christmas tree in my office and didn't look at me as he expertly threw slivers of shiny plastic onto the tree.

I'd given him permission to decorate on the condition that he didn't go overboard. Sadly, *overboard* is Ramesh's natural state and I should have known that he'd turn up the next day with a tree taller than the ceiling. He'd spent half that morning sawing off branches with a kitchen knife, singing as he did so. I may act like a kid at Christmas, but my friend has the perpetual demeanour of Buddy the elf.

"How about a song you know more than eleven of the words to?" I suggested.

He paused what he was doing to straighten a wonky snowman. "Stop being such a Scrooge. Sing along with me and it will make you feel better."

"I'm not a Scrooge," I bit back, feeling thoroughly hurt by such an insult which, in a sensible world, would rank alongside the very worst swear words in existence.

"Good." His whole face, from his floppy brown fringe to his dimpled chin, turned into a smile. "So get that box of silver unicorns and help me finish the tree."

The truth was that, for the first time in my life, even Christmas couldn't perk me up. Not only would my boyfriend be away for months still, it had been almost two weeks since The Private I Detective Agency had any new clients.

If only more people were murdered in London. Is it too much to hope for an abduction or something?

That's a disgusting thing to think! I thought back to myself.

"I said the silver unicorns, Izzy," Ramesh reprimanded me as I'd been daydreaming. "Not the golden ones."

I grabbed the correct box from my desk. "What have unicorns got to do with Christmas anyway?"

He looked at me like I'd told him that Santa Claus wasn't a real person. "How dare you, Izzy Palmer! How dare you suggest that there is any line of demarcation between the magic of Christmas and the magic of unicorns…" He held up one of the silver horses. "…fairies…" He pointed to the top of the tree. "…and dragons?"

I realised for the first time that, nestled amongst the reindeer and elves, were any number of mythical beasts. There were orcs, centaurs and a golem mixed in with the baubles and beads. As this was Ramesh, I could be pretty sure this was only the tip of the frosted iceberg.

"You're just grumpy because you think you're going to be lonely this Christmas when actually it's perfect. Patricia will be away so you and I are going to have the most fabulous Noël since Saint Nick picked up a sack and decided he should wear more red."

Ramesh's girlfriend Patricia was far too busy to remain in one place for more than a few hours and was constantly disappearing off on business trips or family emergencies.

"You do know that's not how Christmas started, right?"

He'd gone back to his tree-primping (his term) and didn't look at me as he replied. "Yes, thank you. Unlike some people, I had a proper religious upbringing. I'd go with Dad to mass on a Sunday morning and pray at our shrine at home with Mum straight after. But I am willing to accept that Christmas in a Hindu-Christian household can get a bit muddled sometimes. You should see the Ganesh decorations I've got."

"Is he the elephant one?" I asked, as I got busy distributing the unicorns.

He once again looked offended. "Ganesh is not *just* an elephant, Izzy. He's a four-armed, warrior god with an axe and a bunch of tasty snacks. He's a super elephant."

"Four arms?" I replied with feigned shock in my voice, as this was not the first time Ramesh had told me about his family's favourite deity. "Imagine how fast he is at decorating!"

He stuck his tongue out at me and went to get another ton of stars, balls and shiny trinkets.

"Have there been any calls today?" I shouted towards reception.

Ramesh isn't actually my secretary, but he does enjoy putting on funny voices and answering the phone, so he normally knows what's going on better than I do.

"Nope." He walked back in, swaying slightly under the weight of the box he was carrying. "Just like there weren't any yesterday and, if you don't do anything about it, there won't be any next week either. I still say you should have taken that missing person case."

"It wasn't a missing person, Ra. It was a missing rabbit and it turned up the next day anyway. I'm a real detective now, I want real cases." I was saying this for myself as much as him. I'd only opened the agency a couple of months earlier and my confidence was still a little wobbly. "It is the eighteenth today, right?"

His face lit up. "That's right! Only seven more sleeps till Christmas."

I glanced up at the clock on the wall and realised it was past closing time. "I was expecting someone to call by."

"You mean your phantom client?" He'd taken a string of green tinsel and wrapped it round his neck like a feather boa.

"If you mean the woman who wrote to me as she was afraid for her life, then yes."

"What I don't get is why she'd send you a letter and then wait so long before coming to see you? Sounds like a wind up if you ask me."

"Ra, we've been through this. Maybe she had to go away somewhere or she had a lot of work on." I let out a sigh. I'd been pinning my hopes on this case. "It doesn't look like she's coming anyway." I said this slowly, in case it would trigger the sound of the office door opening and my mystery client walking into the room.

Sadly, it wasn't to be. Despite a promising start to the agency, including a bunch of press interest when I solved a murder live on international television, the offers of work had shrivelled up and died.

By this stage in our friendship, Ramesh had developed the ability to read my mind. "Don't worry so much. Perhaps it's just the wrong time of year." He frowned sympathetically. "Perhaps murderers need a break at Christmas like the rest of us."

He'd managed to cheer me up, as he usually does. "It's funny you should say that. I normally feel like murdering my family more at Christmas than the rest of the year."

He stopped inflating the giant Father Christmas he'd taken out of the box and looked at me through narrowed eyes. "Izzy, try to cheer up a bit. I thought you **LOVED** Christmas?"

"I do. I **LOVE** Christmas. This just wasn't how I imagined spending it this year."

He looked at me the way that an owner looks at a naughty puppy. "How about you come over to my house tomorrow night and we can watch 'It's a Wonderful Life' together? Would that make you feel any better?"

I managed to keep my face sullen for about four seconds before I relented. "Yes, it would. It really would."

I had already seized my bag and was heading towards the door. "Are you sure you don't want to catch the train home with me?"

He looked about at the sparkly debris all around him and shook his head wearily. "I'd love to, Izzy. But I've got a lot of work to be getting on with here."

I smiled at my lovable friend and exited the office through a Narnian corridor of fake snow and fairy lights. I really hoped that a client would show up soon, if only so that Ramesh's effort wouldn't be in vain.

I shot down the four flights of stairs to the street and emerged in yet another winter wonderland. My office is in Leicester Square, right in the centre of London, where a temporary funfair had been set up with bright flashing lights all over it. Tourists mingled with lifelong Londoners in the queues for big wheels and death-defying towers and, above my head, a giant claw was tossing people across the sky.

The air was filled with children's laughter and the scent of mulled wine. Not far from my door, a German market was selling gingerbread hearts and wooden Christmas decorations. Merely stepping out of my building at the end of each day should have pumped enough Christmas cheer into me to last until the New Year.

The longer I spent working in London, the more I loved it. People had begun recognising me, not just the folk working in the neighbouring cafés as I wandered past, but random strangers who'd seen my television appearance a month earlier. I can't say I was famous exactly, but it felt good that some people knew who I was, even if it had never put a scrap of gold or silver in my pocket.

I'd been shut up in the office all day and I needed to stretch my legs before packing myself into an underground train, then packing myself into an overground train to return to my mum's house in the south of the city. I decided to take my time and walked against the crowds over to Covent Garden. Shoppers tumbled out of every shopfront on Floral Street, and, though only just gone five in the evening, the sky above me was pitch black. Luckily, an impressive display of Christmas lights made up for the absentee sun.

I turned towards the market, and had that uncanny sensation that someone was following me. Rather than continue walking like some stupid girl in a horror film, I stopped and looked back up the crowded street. Of course, the problem with crowded streets is that there are a lot of people on them and I couldn't make out which sinister individual had given me this feeling of unease.

I kept walking. Alongside Covent Garden market, people stood watching a street entertainer, who promised he would soon be juggling the three live chainsaws he had arranged at his feet, just as soon as more members of the public turned up to see. It was a Friday night and the pubs were filling up. Late lunchers and early diners were muddled in together in the restaurants I walked past, laden families shot along on their way home and I had the definite feeling of someone walking far too close behind me.

This time, I instantly spun on my heel and came face to face with a group of startled teenage girls who looked like they wanted to scream.

"Sorry," I said as we all stood there, unsure what to do next. "I thought you were someone else."

They glanced at one another, perhaps more scared now than before I'd offered my feeble explanation. I stepped aside like an eighteenth century dandy and they wandered off, chattering to one another and casting further suspicious looks in my direction.

"Izzy Palmer?" Whispered hoarsely into my ear, the words made me jump out of my oversized winter coat.

"2197," I yelled. This is a reflex I have sometimes when I'm scared. You don't need to worry about it. I promise.

"Are you Izzy Palmer?" The woman in front of me asked once more. Her eyes were as wild as a wolf's and she appeared to be shaking. She didn't wait for an answer, but hurried out of the square and down an alley beside the church. As she retreated, she kept glancing back over her shoulder. It was clear that she wasn't just making sure that I'd go with her, but worried about who else might be following us.

"I think it's okay," she told me, her voice full of pride as I caught up with her. "I'm sure there was someone, but I lost them in the underground."

"That's nice," I said inappropriately. I've never been good at talking to nervous people.

With her anxious smile still flickering across her face, she seemed content to stand there in silence. Broad, strong and eye-catchingly attractive, she was dressed in an expensive burgundy cashmere coat and it crossed my mind that, if she was trying to go unnoticed, she hadn't planned ahead. From October to March, blending into the crowds in London requires little more than a long black raincoat and an umbrella.

"Is there something I can do for you?" I asked. I'm a good enough detective to work out that she needed help.

"I wrote to you." A flashing snowflake light on the church illuminated her intensely black hair. Her contrasting pale skin made me wonder if she had Irish blood, but her accent was markedly English. "I told you I'd be coming to find you today."

I smiled, warming to her in some way, despite her strange behaviour. "I assumed you meant that you'd be dropping by the office." I was worried that my tone might scare her off so I tried to sound more cheerful. "I'm glad you're here now at least."

She looked even more worried then. "Oh no, I couldn't have gone inside. They might have seen me." She began to laugh as if I'd said something truly witty.

"Right. Of course not." Some people have the gift of the gab, I have the gift of running out of words at awkward moments in the middle of important conversations. I really didn't know where to go from there so decided to take the bull by the horns. "And when you say, 'them', who exactly do you mean?"

"I haven't the faintest idea." She laughed again and, as the light caught her face once more, I tried to work out how old she was. She was pretty but tired, natural yet glamorous and I desperately wanted to know her story.

"You said in your letter that you think your husband may wish you harm. Is he the one who was following you?"

She peered back down the alley before answering. "No, it couldn't be Howard. But, perhaps he paid someone to come after me. I can't think who else would have done it. Perhaps he's doing it to drive me mad."

Each new comment she made triggered another question in my mind. "Why don't we go to a café and I can buy you a hot chocolate?"

She rolled her eyes excitedly. "That would be lovely, but I couldn't possibly. You don't understand. I'm not safe." Her voice was suddenly more urgent. "I only have a few minutes before I have to run home again. But you will come, won't you?"

Her nervousness had crept inside me. "Where to? You haven't told me anything. Please explain what's going on."

She came a little closer. "There've been letters, you see? They say I'll be lucky if I make it through the year. I think that means he'll try to kill me at Christmas."

"Why would your husband have warned you what he was planning to do?"

She was getting more exasperated. She placed one insistent hand on my arm. "Please, I'll explain everything soon. Just promise you'll come with us. I've got it all planned out. We'll say you're the nanny, he's been going on at me for months about getting help."

"I don't understand what you're talking about. You have to try to slow down."

"I'm sorry, there's no time." She reminded me of the White Rabbit in Alice in Wonderland and, though it was tempting to find out what crazy path she would lead me down, I held myself back.

The sound of boisterous passers-by at the end of the alley made both of us jump and she pleaded with me again. "Just say you'll come and I'll explain everything the next time we meet."

I tried to reason with her one last time. "It's the police you should be talking to, not me. I can't help if someone tries to-"

"No. Not the police." This was the most agitated I'd seen her get. She wrapped both arms around herself and hugged them tight. "Howard would find out. I'm sure of it. But if you're with me, I'll feel safer. I saw you on TV." She blushed then, like she was about to tell me she was my biggest fan. "And I know you'll be able to work out

17

what he's planning."

I had a million more questions but she was already walking away. I went with the only one that really mattered right then. "How can I contact you?"

"My address is in your pocket, I put it there before I spoke to you. Come to my house on Monday at ten o'clock, Howard will want to meet you. He makes all the decisions, you see." She held me in her desperate gaze and I knew she had so much more to say but, five seconds later, she was swallowed up by the crowds of people and sight.

I wanted to shout after her, I wanted to do something to make it better, but instead I just stood there with all those unanswered questions ricocheting about my brain.

Chapter Two

I practically floated back home to south London and still hadn't broken out of my daze when I opened the front door to my house an hour later. The place was filled with the smell of baking, the sound of carols blasting from my stepdad's stereo and the hustle and bustle that I associate with my house at Christmastime.

"Lovely to see you, darling," my mother yelled as she tugged a large suitcase up the stairs. "I can't stop now, bit busy, you see? But I'm sure your fathers will fill you in."

I was still too hazy to question what she was doing with her luggage and wandered into the kitchen to see what was cooking. My stepdad Greg and my biological father Ted were singing 'O Come All Ye Faithful' and had got to the harmony part which they took it in turns to perform. With the chorus completed, they fell about laughing.

"That was wonderful, Ted." My normally restrained stepfather had presumably been at the sherry as he was giggling like a baby in a YouTube video.

"How did you hit those notes?" my father responded. "That's quite the range you have."

I sat down at the table and they finally spotted me.

Greg's laughter died away. "Izzy, is everything all right?"

"Sweetheart, what happened to you?" My father sounded like he wanted to run out of the house and give a good hiding to whoever had made his daughter sad. "I've never seen you look so pale."

I'd been trying to work out what I could do to help the poor woman who had accosted me in the street but I realised I didn't even know her name.

"I'm not sure how to describe it," I began, and they maintained their fearful looks just as Mum came back in.

"Oh, darling. Don't look so down," she said, with all of her usual pep and charm. "It's only a few weeks away and we'll celebrate Christmas when we're all back together in January."

Two of my three fathers (there's a third who retired to the seaside somewhere) suddenly looked guilty, but it was Daddy number one who spoke up. "Um, Rosie, we haven't told her about that yet."

The normally invisible lines on Mum's forehead crumpled together. "Then why does she look so miserable?"

"We haven't got to that either, my love." Greg should give online masterclasses on how to perfect the driest, most sarcastic voice in England.

I finally found my words. "You're going away for Christmas? Without me?" It was almost enough to make me cry. In fact, my brain had a definite sob in her voice.

But who will make us smiley pancakes on Christmas morning if Mum and Dads aren't here?

"Don't be so glum." Sitting down beside me, Mum had skipped any attempt at sympathy and cut straight to the hard truth. "You're a grown up now, not a child."

How dare she suggest such a thing!

"But... I've never spent Christmas alone before." I certainly sounded like a child. "That means Dad won't be here to make Christmas dinner!" In my defence, Dad's roast is beyond delicious.

He sat down on the other side of me and I had flashbacks to when I was a teenager and they attempted to explain why they were getting a divorce.

He took my hand in his. "It's not that we want to leave you, Izzy. But an opportunity came up and..."

"That's right," Mum joined in to rescue him. "I've got a gig singing on a cruise across the Atlantic and Eddie had some spare tickets for Greg and Ted to come along. 'The Bu-Bu La Mer Festive Revue' is about to set sail. The ocean won't know what hit it."

Mum's alter ego, Bu-Bu, was taking her first steps on the path to theatrical stardom and had signed with a big London talent manager called Eddie Vanguard. It had already caused me no end of embarrassment, but then, what else would I expect from my exuberant mother?

"Wait a second." Something had just clicked in my head. "Are you saying you invited your ex-husband ahead of your current daughter?" For two divorced people, Mum and Dad spend far too much time palling around together and I'm still not entirely used to the idea.

I could see Mum's brain ticking over, looking for a way out of this one. "But, darling, I didn't think you'd want to be stuck with a bunch of old fogies on a cruise when you could be here-"

"…All alone, crying into my Brussel sprouts?"

Mum looked at Dad, Dad looked at Mum and, as neither of them had any idea what to say, they both looked at Greg. My stepfather, in his usual sensible way, had decided that his best strategy was to fade into the background, like a well-dressed floor lamp.

"We would have loved you to come too…" Mum ground to a halt like she'd run out of batteries.

"Yes, we'd have loved you to come, but…" My father began positively enough and then searched for a way to explain their cruel abandonment of their only child. A look crossed his face that suggested he had struck gold "… but then there'd have been no ticket for Fernando."

That really set me off. "Fernando is going and I'm not?" It was hard to decide who to direct my anger at, but Mum's usually to blame for this sort of thing so I settled on her. "You invited your hairdresser before me?"

"Darling, I'm doing eighteen nights on the Princess Anastasia mega-liner. Not the warm up show at the Mecca Bingo in Clapham. I need someone to do my hair." My mother has an incredible way of making everything she says sound entirely reasonable.

Thanks to his sweet, innocent manner, Dad never knows when it's best to keep his mouth shut. "And besides, Fernando has never been to New York and he's desperate to go."

My jaw was dangerously close to coming off its hinges and my eyes grew three sizes that day. "You're going to New York? At Christmas? If you tell me that you're going to hang out with Justin Timberlake you can dash all my teenage dreams in one go."

My mother has a way of addressing her mistakes without admitting that she's ever in the wrong. "We're dreadfully sorry you feel that way, sweetie. Honestly we are."

Dad just nodded and they both waited for me to give in. "Forget about it. Go away and have a nice time together. I doubt I'd be good company anyway."

With a carefree laugh, Mum stood up to get back on with her packing. "That's the spirit, darling. I knew you'd come round. Anyway, I'll have a show booked in London before long and you'll be able to see me perform every night." She'd somehow understood that my real issue with their winter escape was that I'd be missing out on seeing her sing.

She put her hand on my cheek and looked into my eyes. I was helpless before her bright and bubbly positivity. I felt like a mouse, coming face to face with a smiley, retired snake.

"That would be nice, Mum. I'll still miss you though."

She didn't answer as, right then, Dad jumped up from his seat to run to the oven. "Blast! I forgot about my Christmas biscuits."

Mum used the distraction to slip away upstairs and so I was left alone with Greg. He's generally less distracted than my biological parents and remained at the table to check on me.

"Is everything okay?" He has a slow, careful voice which always does a good job at calming me down. "You seemed worried about something when you got here."

I paused before replying, unsure if I wanted to kill his buzz with my sorry tale. "A woman came to me today to ask me to protect her from her husband but something doesn't add up about her story."

Sitting across from me, Greg put his fingers together like an evil genius in a spy movie. "Go on."

"Well, she says she's received letters threatening her life. She thinks that someone will try to kill her over Christmas."

He didn't reply at first. He sat looking contemplative then pointed across the table at me. "That's very interesting. Perhaps it wasn't sent by the would-be killer. Perhaps someone wanted to warn this woman of the danger she's in."

I thought about the possibility but it still didn't fit. "That's not how she made it sound. She says they told her she'll be lucky if she survives the year. It's hardly the most supportive way to get the message across."

"Unless…" For all his brains and composure, this appeared to be one mystery too far for Greg and he never finished his sentence.

"Come along, you lot." My mother had returned to break our pensive silence. "We don't leave for a couple of days. I'll forget about the packing for the moment and we can have ourselves the most Christmassiest Christmas weekend together before we go."

Dad had rescued a good number of biscuits and appeared at that moment with a plate full of warm, crumbly stars, bells, snowman heads and Santa Claus shapes. "I'll make my roast!" he suggested and, apparently by magic, Wham's "Last Christmas" started playing in the background. Their smiles had infected me and we beamed back and forth to one another like a family on an advert.

That weekend was everything my mother had billed it as. The following morning, the four of us drove to the farm to pick out a real Christmas tree. It was good to lean in to the festive spirit and I could already feel it warming the cockles of my icy heart. If anything in the world can perk me up it's decorating a Christmas tree – though preferably one without axe-wielding fantasy beasts hanging from it. We binged on mince pies, sang along to Frank Sinatra and even enjoyed a fake snowball fight using the fluffy white decorations my mother had bought from IKEA.

Dad's roast dinner was somehow better than I'd remembered. A huge side of beef, perfectly crisp roast potatoes, soft spongy Yorkshire puddings and delicious homemade gravy filled the house with their unmistakable aroma and I was truly glad that my mum and dad got on well after all. It was getting a bit much for my brain, and she'd started to get emotional.

I just love beef so much!

But what about the environment? You're always going on about how cows create more pollution than trucks or something. Not to mention all the trees in the rainforest that get knocked down each year to make way for grazing herds.

Yeah, but… it's Christmas, isn't it? A time for eating too much, ripping open presents and forgetting all the high morals we have the rest of the year.

I wasn't in the mood for an argument and decided not to lecture myself on the true meaning of the season.

We all went to Ramesh's house that night and I was unsurprised to discover that he'd outdone himself once more.

"Evening, guv'nors," he said, popping up in full Victorian regalia as we set foot in his tiny front garden. "What can I be doing for yas?"

His Cockney urchin impression wasn't up to scratch but he made up for it with the transformation he'd carried out on his ugly maisonette. I can't be sure whether he'd totally repainted the front of the property or it was some kind of projection, but he'd make it look as though he lived in a rundown, nineteenth century townhouse. A grey brick finish had been added and there was a dummy in the upstairs window begging for change. As an overture to the season, he'd decorated the place with green boughs of holly and ivy, their berries visible among the foliage.

"Well hello there, to be sure," my mother joined in. Her accent was less convincing than my friend's and for some reason she ended up sounding Irish. "A top of the evenin' to ya."

"There better be a TV in this Victorian hovel," I warned Ramesh. "I didn't come here to sit staring at an unlit fireplace all night."

"Right you are, Gov. My humble abode is fitted with all the mod cons a young gentleman could ask for. Enter, enter, come in do. Grab a chair - take off your shoes." He flapped one hand regally to usher us inside.

I should have known that the interior of his house would take things to the next level. As we walked along the corridor towards the lounge, Marley and the three ghosts from Dickens' 'A Christmas Carol' visited us. Presumably triggered by motion sensors, they descended from the ceiling one by one, like ghouls in a fun fair.

"Ahhh," my fathers shrieked from the front of the procession as the Ghost of Christmas Future popped up at the end of the hall to point us towards the lounge.

On stepping inside, I was presented with an even more unexpected sight.

"It's so…" I couldn't find the words to express the shock I was feeling.

"…Understated." My mother came to my assistance as we tried to make sense of the muted colour palette and limited range of decorations on display.

Ramesh took his top hat off and frisbeed it through the air to land perfectly on his coat stand. "Yeah, well I didn't want things to get O.T.T., did I?"

There was a small Christmas tree in the corner with plain white lights on it, candles burned on a wreath on the dining table and the only sign of Ramesh's typically outrageous sense of style was in the cat basket beside the television where his two Persians, Kiki and

Elton, were napping peacefully in their full reindeer costumes.

"Interesting development in your new case," Ramesh said as we took our coats off. "It turns out your client does exist after all."

"How do you even know…?" I began to ask, but it was a stupid question anyway.

"Your mother and I are Instagram buddies, Izzy. We talk. Get over it already." He set about pouring everyone steaming-hot flagons of mulled wine, so I decided not to get huffy at him.

"What I'm wondering," Mum began, like she was the detective and I was her clueless assistant, "is why any killer would send letters telling their victim what they'd got planned."

"Especially weeks in advance," Dad added. "It increases the possibility that they'd get caught."

Greg looked over at me, before replying with his usual composure. "The letter could just be a decoy? A way of distracting from whatever else is going on."

With the mugs distributed, we settled down on the sofa and Ramesh put in a theory of his own. "There's nothing to say her husband's got anything to do with it. It could be a member of her family." He looked across suspiciously at my mum as if weighing up her potential as a murderer.

"Or a lover," Dad suggested.

"An old friend perhaps?" Mum had delivered her suggestion and everyone turned to my stepdad.

"What?" He looked back, confused. "Oh, right, you want me to make a guess… well… Her former driving instructor maybe?"

Not wanting to throw cold water on their fun… No, wait a second, that's exactly what I wanted to do. "Before you get carried away, can I just point out that no one has been murdered and we don't even know the circumstances this poor woman is in? It's probably better if we wait until we're familiar with the suspects before you start picking a culprit."

Dad looked across at me with his typically warm-hearted smile. "That's why you're the professional detective and we're just amateurs, Izzy."

Professional? Who's he kidding? You're Pro-am at best!

Shut it, brain! You're always putting me down. If it wasn't for my fathers saying such nice things about me, I'd have terrible self-esteem.

I hadn't gone to Ramesh's to talk about the case so I took my chance to move things along. "Right, it's clearly time to stop talking about a murder that might never happen and get stuck in to the movie."

Ramesh clapped his hands then raced out of the room and reappeared a few moments later with a little trolley with a small gadget on it. "Who wants popcorn?"

We watched "It's a Wonderful Life" and it was just as moving as I remembered. From the moment the film started, to "Atta boy, Clarence" in the final scene, I was a teary mess. My companions took turns to comfort me but that only made me cry harder. I could feel all my stress and worries dissolving like a puddle in the sunshine. For two whole hours, I wasn't worried about my nearest and dearest all deserting me. George Bailey's incredible life, unfolding in black and white before my eyes, was an emotional detox. It was just what I needed.

When the film was over, we spent the rest of the evening camped out around the stereo, listening to eighties Christmas hits. Mum led us in the singing, making good use of her full vocal range on Band Aid's 'Do they Know it's Christmas?' and putting the rest of us to shame. Ramesh and Greg had a competition to find out who could catch the most popcorn in their mouth (the result was a nil - nil draw, though Ramesh claimed victory as one piece hit his tooth). And Dad finished up the evening with a surprisingly faithful, word-for-word rendition of rap legends Run DMC's 'Christmas in Hollis' complete with dance moves and whole heaps of attitude.

He is a man of extremely well-hidden talents.

When the night was over and it was time to go home, perhaps it was the wine, but I felt confident that I'd be able to deal with whatever my strange year had left to throw at me.

Chapter Three

Monday morning was so cold I thought it might snow. I knew that it couldn't because it never does in London in December – except in movies. It's constantly snowing in London in movies but a real London winter consists of short days, grey skies and the odd burst of fleeting sunshine to remind us what we're missing.

My potential client lived in a large, expensive house overlooking Clapham common. The dark-brick, Georgian façade was rather intimidating as I climbed the front steps to ring the bell. The front door was painted glossy black and a lion door knocker looked at me with hungry eyes.

"You came," the woman said, filling those two words with so much relief. She stood there examining me, just as she had when we'd spoken in the alley in Covent Garden. Once again, I noticed the fragility underlying her heavy-set frame and it seemed an effort for her to even stand there. I could hear a baby cooing and wished she'd let me in for the sake of the poor child (and my cold fingers).

"Of course. It's no trouble."

She studied me for a few more seconds then turned to walk into the house. It was dark inside and I could see no sign of any decorations. The corridor we'd entered was lined with old photographs of some old, rich family and I wondered if they'd come with the ancient house or were ancestors of my mystery woman.

Mixed in amongst the photos was a series of contemporary paintings in bright colours on each wall. They looked completely out of place in the ancient space and my client must have noticed me looking at them as she smiled shyly and said, "Terrible aren't they? I should never have studied art in the first place."

"No, I like them." I was being honest, there was something rather mesmerising about the sharp zig-zagging lines and fiercely contrasting shapes. I thought they summed up the enigmatic woman in front of me rather perfectly. "Are you a professional artist?"

She paused for a moment, as if the question needed careful consideration. "Yes... Well, I was. Though, perhaps you should define professional. People paid me for my paintings if that's what you mean."

There was something on my mind and I couldn't stand it any longer. "I'm sorry, I don't know your name."

She pointed me into a sitting room, where a tray of tea things was laid out on a coffee table, then waited until we were both sitting down before answering my question.

"Katharine, my name is Katharine Taggart. My husband will be here any minute to meet you so I'd better fill you in before he arrives."

I assumed this meant that I was about to find out exactly what I was doing there, but she once more hesitated. She looked around the dark reception room as if she was the visitor and I was the host. The suite of furniture we were sitting on must have been a hundred years old and the room clearly hadn't been decorated in all that time.

Still, there was nothing shabby or threadbare about it. Though the glamour was faded, it retained its opulence. All the place really needed was better lighting, and the gold-leaf woodwork and opulent fabrics would have shone. But then, something told me that wouldn't happen any time soon.

"He's taking us away for Christmas." She glanced down at her outstretched fingers like she wanted to make sure they were perfect. Unlike the first time we'd met, I could see that everything about her was neatly manicured. Her hair was long and glossy, her skin free from the slightest imperfection. She looked like one of the ghostly figures from the old family photographs.

"Your husband's planned a trip?" I asked to hurry her along.

"Yes, Howard. He says it will do me good to get away from here. He says that, since Amelia was born, I haven't been myself." She gestured towards an antique crib at the end of the chaise longue she was sitting on. On cue, its occupant gurgled cheerfully. It was the first suggestion of happiness I'd encountered there. "It's just for one week. We fly to Inverness on Wednesday and we'll drive from there to where we're staying."

"Scotland? You want me to go to Scotland?"

"You don't have to worry," she tried to reassure me. "We won't be alone. Our friends and my family will be coming too. But I know that, if Howard is going to try something, that's where it will happen. He'd never get away with it down here. But, perhaps up in the snow, he could make it look like an accident."

Now I was the nervous one. It wasn't just the news of her dilemma that set me on edge. The thought of leaving behind the world I knew at Christmas brought out an involuntary infantile reaction in me. I was scared just thinking about it.

"I know it's a lot to ask at such short notice," she continued. "But I have money of my own and I can reward you handsomely." The way she spoke fitted in well with the out-of-time scene she was part of. As if suddenly remembering it was her responsibility, she smiled and went to pick up her daughter. "This is Amelia, she'll be no trouble. She never is."

She turned the child to look at me as if she were a doll. I couldn't deny that the little creature was incredibly cute. Strawberry blonde and perfectly chubby, she peered around the room with a knowing smile on her face. A moment later she'd been deposited on my lap and I could tell that, though my role as detective was confirmed, her mother wanted to check on my childcare skills.

I was still coming to terms with the idea of spending Christmas with a bunch of people I didn't know, in a place I'd never been to. Looking after a child on top of that was even more terrifying.

"I'm afraid I haven't spent much time with kids."

"Just look at her; she clearly adores you already." Katharine beamed across at me with motherly pride. "And I'll be looking after her most of the time anyway. The nanny thing is just a way to explain you coming with us."

I have to admit, Amelia did look very comfortable on my knee. She was a gorgeous distraction and so I tried to focus on the case once more.

"Can you tell me why you think your husband is trying to kill you?" I whispered the question as if this would prevent the baby understanding.

She didn't reply but looked out of the window, perhaps wondering when Howard Taggart would arrive. Reassured by the dim, lifeless view, she reached between the cushions in her seat and pulled out a letter. It was a classic ransom note from any number of movies. The words had been cut from magazines, their fonts dramatic and bold – all blacks and reds in heavy block capitals.

We exchanged the baby for the letter and I read the short message out loud.

"'ENJOY THIS TIME WITH YOUR CHILD. YOUR DAYS ARE NUMBERED. YOU'LL BE LUCKY IF YOU MAKE IT THROUGH THE YEAR.'"

Katharine shook as I spoke and her eyes fell down to the mosaic floor. "That was the first note that came a few weeks ago. I'm afraid I burnt the most recent one. It was so violent; I simply couldn't bear to have it in the house."

"Who do you think could have sent it?" I asked. "Surely, if your husband wanted to hurt you, he wouldn't have told you in advance."

"I've thought about it over and over. It's the only thing that makes sense. I don't see anyone except my two brothers and sister-in-law these days. Howard says he worries about me when I go out, but I think that's just another way for him to keep tabs on me."

I felt the paper in my hand and tried to extract something from its casually violent message. "And do you have any other reason to believe that he wishes you harm? Is there anything that would explain why he'd want you dead?"

She hid the letter away and then stroked her daughter's soft, round cheek. "Howard has been different this year. Since Amelia was born, it's as if he doesn't love me anymore, but I'm still the one with the money. This house belonged to my parents and, when we got married, they pleaded with me to get him to sign something but I laughed it off. I couldn't imagine Howard marrying me for my wealth." She let out an exhausted sigh. "It's hard to describe, but the way he treats me has changed. All I can say is that I don't feel safe here when he's around. I just-"

At that moment, her words ran dry and she turned to wax. She was a Madame Tussauds dummy, fixed in position for tourists to marvel at. It took me a few seconds to realise why, but the sound of a key entering the front door told me everything I needed to know.

A tall man with curly red hair and a strong, square jaw came to a stop in the door to the lounge. He was broad and muscular in a way that clearly came naturally to him. I could tell that he was no gym bunny but that his bulk had been handed down to him from past generations.

How? Are you psychic?

"Is this the girl?" he asked. Though years living in England had sanded away the rough edges, his deep voice had an unmistakable Scottish undertone to it. His face was serious and he was handsome in a slightly too brawny and intense way.

I held my breath, waiting for his wife to reply, but I could see that it wasn't going to happen.

"My name is…" It suddenly occurred to me that he might have seen me on TV, or in the paper, and I raced to think up a convincing alias. "Sally Starmer."

Seriously?

"I thought your name was Clare." He took a few steps into the room then paused and I was sure that he'd seen through me.

"That's right, my name's Clare. But people call me Sally for… short." I stood up so that we were eye to eye. He was almost exactly as tall as I was. My heart thudded loudly in my chest and if he didn't recognise me – or see through my pathetic story – I thought he would at least find the tribal drumbeat booming out of me suspicious and work out what was going on.

Instead, he smiled and offered me his hand. "Howard Taggart, but I imagine that Katharine has already told you that much."

There was something quite impressive about him. It wasn't just the firmness of his near-excruciating grip, but the confidence he exuded. I'd pictured some vaudevillian rogue with a long, pointed beard coming to do away with his wife under the cloak of darkness; the reality was far more complex and alluring.

"It's nice to meet you." I sat back down as he went to embrace his wife and child.

Amelia was ecstatic to see him and let out a squeal of joy as he picked her up from his wife's lap and lifted the little person high above his head. Even Katharine smiled at this. The tension in the room had diffused and she had come back to life.

"I was just telling…" She paused and I thought she'd forgotten my fake name but caught herself just in time. "Sally about our holiday."

He sat down on the chaise longue beside Katharine and, with Amelia on his knee, it looked like they were posing for a family photograph. "I thought the wee bairn might like the chance to meet the big man."

I understood every word in the sentence he'd uttered, but I couldn't make sense of any of it.

"Santa!" he explained. "Father Christmas, or whatever you want to call him. Didn't Katie get to that part?"

His wife put her hand on his shoulder. "No, darling. I was just telling Sally that we're going up to Scotland and that it would be great if she could join us."

He smiled widely and his eyes brightened. "I love Christmas. I know I'm a bit of a kid at heart, but I can't help it. I booked us in for a week in the snow in a rather exclusive Christmas village. There'll be reindeer and elves and all that sort of thing. It looks incredible on the videos online. And the friends who we're going with have got older kids so I'm sure they'll really get into it too."

"Oh, that's nice. How do you all know each other?" Before the words were out of my mouth, I realised that I was in detective mode, not meek and innocent wallflower-nanny mode.

"We were at university together," he replied all the same, but shot a glance to his fellow interviewer. "Katharine lived with the girls, didn't you darling?"

"Um, that's right." She was nervous again. "But they're all Howard's friends now." She spoke as if she no longer had any right to call them her own.

I cleared my throat and tried to sound professional. *Trying* to sound professional is something I've had plenty of experience at, but haven't quite mastered. "Is there anything else you'd like to know about me?"

"I don't think so," Howard quickly replied. "I've seen your CV and it all looked very impressive. Where are your folks though? Shouldn't you be spending Christmas with them?"

"No, sadly not. My parents die…" I began before, out of her husband's view, Katharine frantically shook her head. "I mean, my parents are dying to get away from it all this year. They're away on a cruise, so I'll be alone."

She could have given us a head's up for the exact type of nonsense we're supposed to be spouting.

"And I saw that you did equestrian studies at university?" His cheerful tone lifted higher.

"Yep, that's right. Equestrian studies. I love… equestrians."

Horses, Izzy. It's the study of horses.

You could have told me that five seconds earlier!

Howard didn't appear to have noticed that everything I was saying was complete tosh. "Aye, there's little I like more than going for a hack. I look forward to hearing about what you got up to on your degree."

An idea popped into my head right then and it occurred to me that, if I was going to spend Christmas with these two loonies, I should probably bring some backup.

"Katharine told me that she was planning to bring a chef along too," I said, hoping I wouldn't cause her any trouble. "I know someone who'd be perfect."

The air between us suddenly froze and the big man turned to his fragile wife. "We haven't discussed this, Katharine."

The poor woman looked nervous again and even baby Amelia could sense that something wasn't quite right and let out a cautious burp.

"You said you wanted me to rest, so I thought that might help." She put one hand on his shoulder in a display of apparent affection. "I only mentioned it in passing, but Sally here says she knows an excellent candidate."

Howard's brow unfurrowed and he seemed to accept this explanation. "Yes, that sounds like a good idea. But, whoever it is, they'll get Christmas Day off as you know I like the way you roast my tatties, Katie." I believe there is an unwritten law that Scottish people have to mention potatoes at least once in every conversation.

"I'll send you my friend's contact details. His name's Ramesh Khatri."

"Ah, Ramesh. Is he Indian?" Howard asked, his brow now shooting skyward.

"British," I replied, as what difference did his ethnic origin make?

He coughed softly and tried to backtrack. "Sorry, I didn't mean to sound racist or something. I just love a curry."

Oops! Awkward!

"Well, if there's one thing Ramesh knows how to make it's Rogan Josh." This was true. There was only one thing Ramesh knew how to make and it was, indeed, Rogan Josh.

Amelia laughed to break the silence that had descended and her parents started making a fuss over her to finish the job.

"She's adorable," I said as I was the one who'd made them uncomfortable in the first place. I walked over to the pretty family with all the dark secrets and knelt down to talk to the baby. "Are we going to have fun together in Scotland?"

"She likes you," Katharine said again and Howard smiled his approval.

Seeing them together right then was a marked contrast from the picture she'd painted of her life and I wondered which version was closer to reality.

"We leave first thing on Wednesday morning," Howard added, to bring us back to business.

"Fantastic," I said, like it was no big deal whatsoever that I'd just agreed to spend Christmas in some isolated spot in the northern Highlands with two weirdos and their no doubt weirdo friends.

I really think we should have discussed this. What if it's a plot to get us up there and… and… Actually I have no idea why they'd want to take us on holiday with them. Fine, a Scottish Christmas it is.

With Katharine sitting quietly once more, Howard sewed up the proceedings. He gave me his mobile phone number and led me to the front door.

"You don't have to worry about a plane ticket," he told me on the way out and I could tell he wanted me to be impressed about something. "I've rented a plane and I'll be flying us all up there."

"Oh, wow." I was annoyed at myself for fulfilling his expectations, as I did actually find this quite impressive. "Are you a pilot then?"

"No, I'm in the police." Even this made him look a little smug. "But it's another one of my hobbies."

Katharine draped herself self-consciously over her husband. "Howard is a chief superintendent." Her voice was cold, as if to say, *now do you see why I couldn't call the police?* "He's very good at his job."

I hovered on the front step, eager to find out more about the odd couple but perfectly aware that this wasn't the moment for questions.

"I'll see you Wednesday." I turned and, with a wave, raced down the steps and along the road.

As I walked away from the common towards the centre of Clapham, I suddenly realised how cold I'd got sitting in that icy house. I moved faster and my body began to warm up, but there was something uncomfortable about the experience that I found difficult to shift.

Chapter Four

"How can you do this to me, Izzy?" Ramesh wasn't happy about the news. "Seriously, did you stop and think about my needs for one second?" It wasn't the sudden trip north he objected to. "I mean, is it too much to ask for a little consideration?" And he wasn't upset about the thought of pretending to be someone that he wasn't. "You've really landed me in it!"

The problem was that, for my beloved friend, packing a suitcase was at least a three-day operation which required careful planning, preferably with a series of sketches to maximise potential space and, at the very least, time for colour coding of his possessions.

"I normally take two days just to choose the clothes, let alone fit them to my very high standards into my luggage."

"I'll make it easy for you," I told him as I sat on the floor of his lounge trying to get one of his feline-reindeer hybrids to chase a piece of cotton. "Take all the warmest clothes you own. You'll freeze to death if you don't."

I wasn't looking at him as he stormed back and forth in front of the TV, but I could tell from the sudden fall in volume that he'd come to a dramatic halt. "That's easy for you to say. Swanning about with your 'jeans' and 'jumpers' like you've never heard the word fashion in your life. Some of us have to work hard to look this good."

I still wasn't looking at him because I knew it would only make him tetchier. Elton John – the cat, not the classic rocker – had no interest in chasing the thread and was savaging my hand instead.

"Ra." I tried to huff every last molecule of breath from my body to show him that I really didn't want to say what was coming next. "Are you telling me that we have to take a trip to your wardrobe?"

He clapped his hands and let out a sound like a drunken seal. "It's a Christmas miracle!"

I have very little interest in clothes but they mean the world to Ramesh and this was reflected in the walk-in wardrobe which he'd built when he and Patricia moved in to the property. It had originally been two spare bedrooms but, in a rare display of just how macho he can be when he tries, Ramesh had taken a sledgehammer and knocked the partition wall down to create his dream space. He'd allowed his girlfriend one corner for her small clutch of largely work clothes, but the rest of the room was dominated by mirrored wardrobes which were full to bursting with Ramesh's own unique collection.

It was a commitment of our friendship that we had to go in there twice a year for him to strut about showing off his newest purchases.

"I've got the perfect velvet snow suit I bought just for such an occasion," he announced as we stepped inside and high-energy Christmas music automatically started playing.

How does that keep happening?

I sat down on my designated pink satin pouf in the middle of the room and waited for the show to begin. I've often tried to get to the bottom of how Ramesh's passion for fashion developed, but the most I could get from him was that he really likes the shopping scenes in 'Pretty Woman'. In fact, most things in Ramesh's life appear to have been influenced by 1990s romantic comedies.

He popped out from behind his bejewelled dressing screen wearing, what I can only describe as, an overgrown Christmas jumper.

"What on earth is that?" I was taking in the scene of extreme festivity that was emblazoned across his chest and down each leg. It had all the usual Christmas icons – a blazing fire, a Christmas tree, stockings and mistletoe – but also displayed a carefully knitted depiction of Bruce Willis' bald head, David Bowie and Bing Crosby together beside a piano and Ramesh's cats Elton and Kiki singing karaoke whilst dressed in their own matching Christmas jumpers.

"It's a funsie! Like a onesie but more fun. It's real wool. I had it custom knitted."

He took a turn on his catwalk to show off the workmanship and then disappeared once more behind the screen for a quick change. His next three outfits were made exclusively out of tinsel.

"Haven't you got anything a little more subtle?" I asked as the sound of his shiny plastic jumper rustling against the matching silver trousers nearly deafened me. "We're supposed to be undercover."

He looked at me like I'd punched him in the guts. "More subtle, Izzy? Is that really the sort of language you think it's appropriate to use around me? I have struggled with subtlety my whole life and you think it's acceptable to just throw out a question like that?"

"Sorry, Ra. But-"

"No, let me finish." He took a deep sigh and adjusted his spangly, shooting-star-framed glasses. "Do you really think I want to spend half my money each month on haute couture? Don't you think I'd like to wear muted colours once in a while? Well, I would, but I can't." There was a surprising amount of emotion invested in his words. "Some people are addicted to drink or alcohol, Izzy. Well I'm addicted to being me. It's not easy being this fabulous, but I give one hundred and twenty per cent each day to achieve it. So, if buying a leopard skin gilet or combining three kinds of waistcoat in a single outfit is what gets me there, that's the sacrifice I have to make."

He was crying by this point, but I knew they were his stage tears and I wasn't falling for it. "Okay, good. So finish up your fashion show and then we'll get to the real reason I came round today."

"Ooh." His face perked up. "Did you want me to help you pick out an outfit for Christmas Day that says, *I'm a nanny, deal with it?*"

I glanced at the piles of discarded party wear and, without even considering the fact that he was a man and half a foot shorter than me, I doubted he'd have anything to my taste. "Not exactly. But I'm worried that someone will recognise me. It was a close call already this morning. What if one of their friends saw me at the royal wedding? What if they work out I'm there investigating and it backfires on poor Katharine?"

Without saying a word in reply, he walked towards me, turning his head from one side to the other as he looked me over. "Okay, Izzy. I'm going to try something a little bit drastic so don't freak out."

He came to stop right next to me and slowly moved his hands towards my face like he was about to pick up a bar of uranium or some ancient relic. Instead, he removed my glasses. "There. That's perfect. They'll never recognise you."

I glanced at myself in one of the thirty seven mirrors we were surrounded by. I looked exactly the same, but a little blurrier. "I look exactly the same! They'll know it's me."

He assessed the result once more but appeared to be content with the transformation. "No, chance, Izzy. You're reverse-Supermanning them. It's a proven disguise!"

"I don't think you can use anything that happens in a comic book as proof, Ramesh."

He made a dismissive tut. "Celebrities do it all the time too. Do you think Bono really needs glasses? And what about Mahatma Ghandi? Would he pop along to the opticians whenever he was on a hunger strike? Of course not, they both discovered the power of blending in. Honestly, if you see Bono without his specs, you wouldn't recognise him. He's just some bloke called Paul."

"Ramesh, I'm pretty sure that Ghandi didn't worry about being recognised in public."

He laughed at me smugly. "Think what you like, Iz, but, just so you know, old Mahatma was actually the one who invented it."

"I guess this means I'll have to wear my contacts then." I looked in the mirror and tried to believe what he was telling me. "Well, whatever. Short of putting on a fake moustache, I don't know what else I can do anyway. Let's finish your packing then I should go home and get ready myself."

"Ha! Finish up my packing! Izzy Palmer, you really are too cute. If I'm done by Wednesday morning, it will be a Christmas miracle." He did a twirl on the spot so that his baggy jumper swished outwards and we cut to a scene at my house (by which I mean, I sat through another two hours of him talking about clothes and then took a slow, cold bus back to mine).

My folks were setting off on the cruise that afternoon and their bags were piled up in the hall.

"Daaaaaaaaaarling," my mother yelled, running down from upstairs as soon as she heard the door bang shut. It was not the first time it had occurred to me how much she had in common with my best friend.

Well, they do say that you're most likely to marry someone just like your mother.

I'm pretty sure that's only for men and Ramesh and I... Actually, never mind.

"I'm going to miss you so much, my sweet." In a flowing woollen coat that looked like a winter wedding dress, she launched herself from the bottom stair to cuddle me. "I feel awful that we're leaving you behind. If you tell me to cancel, I will. I'll do it right now."

She waited for my response and even though it was unnecessary – and I knew she was only bluffing – it made me feel better.

"Don't worry about it, you go away and have a wonderful time. Ramesh and I have got a case to work anyway. We're going to Scotland."

Her sympathetic tone disappeared. "You're going to Scotland, without me?" She sounded even more put out than I had. "How on earth do you think you're going to solve a case if I'm not there to hold your hand?"

It took me about three hundredths of a second to realise she was acting. "I'll miss you too, Mum."

She smiled and looked at me for a moment, before pulling me back in for another hug. As I'm six foot three and she's a bit on the short side, I ended up squeezing her head as always. Greg turned up just then but wasn't much of a hugger.

"Come along, Rosie." This was pretty much my stepfather's catchphrase. "Ted just messaged that he's about to arrive. We mustn't be late."

He gave me a pat on the back as he passed and then seized Mum's heaviest bag. I could see he was struggling so I gave him a hand. When we got outside, there was no sign of Dad but there was a car pulling into the road with its horn beeping out a melody. A black stretch limo came to a halt with my Mum's hairdresser Fernando poking out of the sunroof.

"Miss La Mer," he shouted across to us, as my father in the driving seat wound down his window. "Your carriage awaits!"

Mum adopted the stage name Bu-Bu La Mer after... you know what? It's a long story. We loaded up the limo with her endless selection of bags and there was time for one last goodbye.

"Izzy," my stepfather said, like he had something important to impart. "Have a very merry Christmas." He got into the passenger seat and turned on a rather subtle classical piece which my father immediately replaced with pumping pop music.

"Feliz Navidad," Fernando shouted through the sunroof, as the car pulled away.

With a bottle of champagne in one hand and two glasses in the other, my mother soon joined him. "Joyeux Noel!"

"Fröliche Weihnachten," Fernando came up with.

My mother gazed blankly at me down the street as she clearly didn't know how to say Merry Christmas in any other language. "Have a great one, Izzy. Missing you already!"

"Nadolig Llawen!" I called back, as this is the only phrase I know in Welsh.

The limousine turned on to the busy main road and disappeared into traffic. I was alone in my house for the first time in ages and, though I missed the busy energy that Mum always provides and my two fathers' generosity, it was nice to have some time to myself.

I put a Hawaiian pizza in the oven, brewed up my frothiest hot chocolate and set aside the evening to call my boyfriend.

Chapter Five

I got a text from Howard telling me to be at Wandsworth Town station at eight the next morning. I didn't understand where we'd be going from there, considering that it was nowhere near an airport, but I didn't have to wait long to find out.

"I made it by seconds, Izzy. Seconds!" Ramesh turned up with three large suitcases, just before our client. "It took me an hour to choose which funsies to bring with me and, if I'd gone for the fluffier ones, I'm pretty sure I'd have missed the flight."

A discreet black Audi pulled up in the road in front of the station and a driver climbed out in a neat blue livery and cap. Without a word, he took Ramesh's bags and placed them in the boot of the car then came to collect the backpack I'd stuffed with clothes an hour earlier. There was something rather nervous about the way he took the bag from me, using only his fingertips, then peered up at me like he thought I wanted to eat him.

Howard and Katharine remained in the car and I forced Ramesh into the front to make sure he didn't get too chatty with them before we were up in the air and they could still change their mind about paying for the fake chef I'd recommended.

Once the greetings and introductions were out of the way, Howard looked as cheerful as he had two days before and Katharine was suitably apprehensive for a woman who feared for her life.

"Isn't there supposed to be a baby?" Ramesh pointed out and both parents made a panicked face.

"Only joking," Howard said and Katharine laughed for the first time. "She's gone on ahead with her uncle. We're meeting them at the airport."

"I assumed we were going from Heathrow or somewhere," I told them but, before they could answer, we'd pulled up in front of London Heliport.

We got out of the car and, after a moment of panic, it clicked that this was only the first stage of the journey and that we would not be travelling all the way to the Highlands of Scotland in something which looked like a child's toy.

"How rich are these people, Izzy?" Ramesh asked as we were waved through security in the terminal.

"Clearly far richer than I realised."

The Taggarts' luggage was already on board the helicopter and so we boarded and flew off; it was as simple as getting a taxi. Neither of my employers looked particularly impressed by this, but Ramesh's face was stuck in a massive grin and could no longer relax.

"I'm basically a celebrity!" he managed to squeak out through clenched teeth.

Personally, I spent the journey to the airfield in a state of terror. Helicopters may be expensive and exclusive, but they are not a pleasant mode of transport. I was convinced – CONVINCED! – that we were going to fall to our deaths at any moment or that the pilot would turn to us and say, "I have no idea how to land this thing!"

And I'd have to scream and say, "What the hell do you mean? You're supposed to be a pilot!"

To which he'd roll his eyes and say, "Yeah, but not really. I just gave them a phony CV and they told me I was hired. I thought I'd be working in an office or something."

Then Ramesh would start screeching his lungs out and ask, "What kind of person would pretend to be a pilot?"

And the guy in the pilot's seat would look put out and, just before we crashed to earth in a giant fireball, say, "That's rich coming from a fake nanny and a fake chef!"

Except, thank goodness, none of that happened. We landed safely at Biggin Hill and were free to dance across the tarmac to our patiently waiting jet.

Now this was something I could get excited about. The pearly white Bombardier Learjet was a thing of beauty. I just wished that we'd all dressed up in period clothes so I could pretend I was in an Agatha Christie novel.

"It's just like 'Death in the Clouds'!" Ramesh said it before I could, but then we caught sight of our fellow passengers and he wouldn't say another word for the next two hours. "Oh my gosh, that's…"

An incredibly well-dressed man in Harris Tweed and a matching flat cap was lingering at the foot of the fold-down steps. Beside him stood a woman in a svelte, pencil skirt and high-necked blouse. He looked like he was about to set off on a hunt and she looked like she was there to report on it. Except of course, they weren't. In fact I knew exactly who they were and I couldn't get my head around it. It was Lady Penelope and Rupert Gravely-Swans.

"You didn't know?" Howard asked as he walked past us. We'd come to a dead stop on the runway and I'm pretty sure that our mouths were hanging open. "Katharine is Rupert's sister. She was a Gravely-Swans before I sullied her good name!" I had to keep reminding myself that he was a potential wife-killer as I couldn't help finding Howard rather charming.

There were other passengers boarding the plane then but I didn't notice them because we were in the presence of a (sort of) princess. Lady Penelope was actually only the daughter of a princess – the queen's cousin – but the British public had adopted her as a makeshift substitute, as none of the real princesses would be getting hitched any time soon.

If I was struggling not to run up to the recently married couple and tell them how beautiful their wedding had been, I can only imagine what Ramesh was going through. They waved to us regally, presumably used to such reactions, and turned to board. As they did so, a chubby man dressed identically to Rupert, but with none of his style, bumbled down the stairs with his arm threaded through a baby seat.

"Katie," he shouted inappropriately loudly, even over the sound of the engine. "Little Amelia made a terrible pong, but I couldn't work out how her nappies work so I just wrapped a towel around her and that seemed to do the trick." He stood smiling proudly, waiting for the child's mother to thank him.

"It's hardly rocket science, is it, Bertie?" She pulled her child from him in one aggressive tug. "And it's not like I haven't shown you five times already."

With an embarrassed laugh, the man moved aside. As the other guests pushed past to board the plane, I felt a bit sorry for him. He was still doing his best to smile when we drew level.

"Hullo!" he said in a drippingly posh accent as he cast a hungry glance up and down me. "I'm Katie and Rupert's big brother, Lord Bertrand Gravely-Swans. And you're a lovely tall girl, aren't you?"

My sympathy quickly vanished for some reason. "I suppose you're the nanny they talked into coming with us. Poor you. Many a nanny has passed through the Gravely-Swans family and regretted it."

I tried to sound like a nice, sweet, ordinary person as I replied. "I'm only here for the week. I'm sure we'll have a great time together."

"That's right, that's right." He laughed and his tummy shook like a bowl of jelly. "A very merry Christmas and all that."

With his pale skin and dark features, he was clearly a Gravely-Swans, and yet it was hard to see how such an artless man could be related to Katharine or Rupert.

A curious look passed over his face. "You know, you remind me of that detective girl. What's her name?"

"Bertie, will you get on the damn plane, you old fool?" his brother called down to him and I was relieved that Lord Bertie had lost his train of thought.

Rather than waiting for me to board, he squeezed past and I pushed the still shell-shocked Ramesh up the steps. Once inside, I had another moment of silent wonder as I took in the interior of the plane. It was like a gentleman's study, with oak panels, green baize and dark leather running the length of the cabin. The lighting was low and choral Christmas music filled the air.

I would have happily stood there in my trance for a while longer but a loud-voiced American woman with fine, Japanese features broke me out of it. "It's always like that in this godforsaken country," she was telling Katharine. "Why I ever married a Brit, I'll never know."

Sitting in a plush reclining seat opposite, her diminutive husband smoothed down his beige tie but said nothing. In the seat beside him, a teenage girl sat staring at her phone. This was the second of the three families on board. On the other side of the aisle, there was another with two sons, but I didn't have time to take much more in as, at that moment, the door clunked shut and it was time to sit down.

I prodded Ramesh to two free spaces at the back of the plane and he stumbled along, in full daydream mode. His eyes were a compass and Princess Penelope was his magnetic north. They didn't leave her for one moment, even as he turned to collapse into his seat.

"This is your captain speaking," Howard said once we'd started taxiing towards the main runway. "Our destination today is the North

Pole, home of Father Christmas himself. Our sleigh will be pulled through the air by a pair of TFE731 jet engines." He was clearly enjoying himself and laughed at his own silly joke, before filling us in on the weather and flightpath.

I was relieved when bumbling Bertie emerged from the cockpit. For some reason, I couldn't imagine him doing a particularly good job co-piloting the plane.

The petite American woman hadn't stopped complaining about Britain. Despite the fact she was dressed in an elegant silk dress and looked like she'd spent a small fortune having her hair styled, her voice was pure Mall of America. "I mean is it impossible to find someone who knows what the hell they're doing in this place? I just hope Howard knows how to fly this damn plane."

The Brits in the audience smiled politely and the mother of the final family sitting in front of me, who'd been overseeing her younger son's reading until now, looked up disapprovingly. She had a teacher's voice and a pointy face, which I felt sure I'd seen on TV.

"I hear there's going to be a lot of snow up in Scotland," she said to change the topic. It wasn't clear who she'd addressed the comment to but, landing down in the free seat beside the American, Bertie was happy to respond.

"I bloody hope so, Suzanne. Wouldn't be much point going all this way if all we got were dark skies, cold winds and midges now, would it?" He snorted out a laugh and his neighbours feigned amusement.

Dressed in a formal naval uniform, the woman's husband looked unimpressed by Bertie's comment and returned to his task of staring out of the window. Beside him, a teenage boy sat playing a handheld computer game. His mother was once more struggling to think up something to talk about.

Well, we're British, so… the weather? Wait! No! She's already talked about that! Ahhhhhhhhhhh! Now what?

Luckily, the PA system went Bing and Howard interrupted. "We are ready for take-off so please fasten your seatbelts and keep them attached whenever possible throughout the flight."

The teacherish woman, Suzanne, looked relieved as she settled into her chair to prepare for the g-force. In some ways, she was rather out of place there. She was the only one in normal, everyday clothes.

Her hair wasn't incredibly well coiffed or styled and her features were plain. The others looked like they could have been cast as the unrealistically attractive group of friends in a classic Hugh Grant comedy, but she would have only made it as an extra.

I suddenly felt overwhelmed by the sheer number of new faces I'd have to learn. Normally my cases have a bit more variety and diversity to them but, with the exception of the outspoken American, the whole lot of them were rich and very British and they all looked rather similar. To aid my memory, I called up an old tool of Dame Agatha Christie's and sketched out a little diagram in my head.

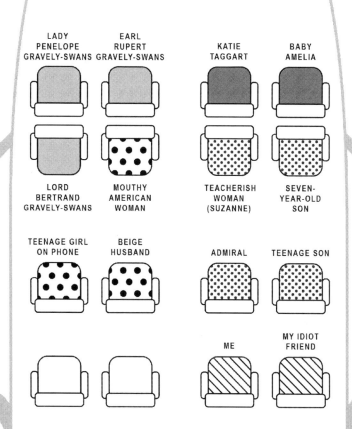

Three families, a lord and a famous royal couple. I was yet to find out all the names but I was sure I could pencil them in as the holiday progressed. To help me tell one from the other I focussed on the colours of their chic attire. The Gravely-Swans had their family-mandated tweed, the American woman's dress was a sunny yellow that was blinding beside her dull beige husband and the admiral, his wife Suzanne and their two sons all wore complementing shades of blue, as if they'd planned their outfits using a colour chart.

"Are we going to tell jokes or sing Christmas carols?" the admiral asked once we were up in the air and the cabin was still quiet. He was a lot more striking than his wife. With his thick dark hair, blue eyes and the four stars on his uniform, he had the look of a romantic lead. "It's going to be an awfully long journey if no one speaks."

"Great idea, Toffee. I know a good one," Bertie inevitably answered. "What do you call a fat woman with no bottom?"

Rupert jumped up from his seat to give his brother a slap round the side of his head. "Bertie, if you continue with that joke, we'll throw you out of the plane with no parachute."

"It's just a bit of fun, Rupee! When did a harmless joke ever cause any problems?"

The American woman's short, tanned husband was the one to answer this time. "Never. But not every joke is harmless." He had a posh country accent – from Dorset or Cornwall maybe. With his bland clothes and everyman face, the only remarkable thing about him were a pair of sparklingly bright green eyes.

For once, being ridiculously tall had its advantages and I had a good view of most of the passengers. I noticed that, as everyone started to bicker, Katharine remained quiet. Her hands gripped the armrests tightly and she pushed back against her seat like she was afraid she might fall out. I was coming to see that her moods came in waves. She could be relaxed or uptight, paranoid or calm and it was hard to say which version of her we might get.

Perhaps she doesn't like flying?

Then she shouldn't have married a pilot.

Perhaps she didn't. Perhaps he's only learnt recently.

Oh, you're so clever!

I thought I'd better check on Ramesh as he was looking oddly pale.

"Are you okay, buddy?"

He nodded, so I knew he was alive at least, but he was still staring at the back of Princess Penelope's head. It was probably a good thing he'd lost his voice, he'd only have bombarded everyone with questions, demanded a seat beside the pilot and then led us in a medley of his favourite TV theme tunes. Bless him.

"That's not what you used to say, Astrid," the admiral told the American woman and I wished that I'd been paying attention as, right then, a hush fell over the plane. "Oh, lighten up, will you? It was only a joke."

The silence held and Lady Penelope was the only one brave enough to sneak a look at her fellow passengers as all other eyes fell to the floor.

"I know a joke! Does anyone want to hear it?" Bertie tried again.

"No!" several voices called back with conviction.

"It's not a rude one. Promise!"

No one replied and Bertie had the sense to interpret this as a further refusal.

"Mummy," a small voice eventually whispered and Suzanne's spectacled, seven-year-old son sat forward to ask a question. "What *do* you call a fat woman with no bottom?"

Chapter Six

"It's like a joke, isn't it? An admiral, a professor, a lord, a lady, an earl, a policeman and…" Bertie didn't seem to know how to finish this sentence. Presumably he had no easy signifier for the other members of our party.

We were standing outside the terminal in Inverness, waiting for our car to arrive. Bertie had been dispatched by the others to wait out in the cold and, so I'd felt bad and agreed to join him. I couldn't get a handle on the man. He inspired in me a mix of mild amusement, pity and outright revulsion.

"No, it's not. It's like a murder mystery," I corrected him. "The question is, who's got it in them to be a killer?"

He looked impressed by my comment and let out a whistle. "You've got a point. And I'll give you a hint." He leaned in close to whisper. "They all have."

I laughed. "Even your brother and sister?"

"Especially those two. They're rotters. They never mean to be, but it's in their nature. They got it from Daddy. He was a born rotter and he passed it down to the pair of them."

"But not you?" I jumped on the spot to keep warm.

"Oh no, not me. I'm alright really. I always say the wrong thing, but I'm nice enough underneath, Mummy made sure of that."

We both stared into the distance to where the car would be coming from. After all the luxury we'd enjoyed that day, we were overdue a hiccup in our travel plans.

"And what about the others?" I asked, trying to get as much information as possible from my loose-lipped friend while we were alone. "What's the scoop on them?"

He frowned like he didn't think much of his friends. "Well, they're all rich and ambitious types. Katie met them at Oxford and they've been buddies ever since. I can't think why. I swear they can't stand one another."

A thought occurred to me and I decided to keep it to myself but Bertie cottoned on.

"What?" he prodded. "What were you thinking?"

I let out a sad laugh. "That I was right; it's just like a murder mystery."

He did not seem shocked and a wicked smile formed on his face. "So, who's best bet for the killer?"

It was an easy decision, at that point – though I made a mental note to wait until someone was murdered before making my mind up. "Well that American woman is kind of a loudmouth. What's her story?"

"Ooh, good choice. Astrid is a character, that's for sure. She's a high-up director of some pharmaceutical company and rules her family with an iron fist. She's spent her whole adult life trying to keep up with us Gravely-Swans. It's her husband Grantham I feel sorry for though, not to mention their poor daughter Justine. If anyone deserves a longer leash it's those two. She won't let them go to the lavatory without written permission. And yet, for some reason, I rather like her."

We both fell quiet to consider this. The others were still inside the terminal, I'd propped Ramesh up somewhere and stuck a cup of coffee in his hands to see if he'd snap out of his daze but I didn't have much hope. I've never met someone so completely obsessed with celebrities the way he is. Coming face to face with royalty had clearly been too much for him; it was like two galaxies colliding and he was the unfortunate casualty.

When I finally caught sight of a black shape at the end of the road, I waved to Howard to get his attention. A fleet of long black cars pulled up soon after and a sprightly old woman jumped out from the driver's seat of the first limo.

"Aggie!" she hollered at us.

"I'm sorry?" Bertie attempted, speaking slow and loudly in case her hearing had gone after years of hollering.

"Ize Aggie!"

"Nope, I didn't quite catch that." He at least sounded cheerful as he completely failed to understand her.

"Aggie?" I jumped with excitement, like I'd solved a riddle. "That's your name. Agnes or Agatha, right?"

"Aye, so I saed." She looked disgruntled but kept talking. "Are ye goin tae Aviemore?"

Bertie tipped his head to one side and smiled. "No, I'm terribly sorry, that meant nothing to me. Perhaps my friend Sally here will have better luck."

I was on top of it this time. "Aviemore? Isn't that near where the Christmas village is?"

"It is! Hey, you're good at this." Bertie made it sound like we were playing a game. "Aggie, try another one on us."

The wise-eyed old chauffeur looked wary as she went to open the back door. The others came from inside the terminal and Howard handed me baby Amelia to look after, which I was a bit put out about, before remembering it was my job. She didn't seem to mind and gurgled joyfully as I strapped her into the back car of the procession.

"Archie!" the middle-aged driver yelled at me.

"Sally," I called back and he nodded and seemed to approve. "I don't suppose Aggie is your-"

"Aye, that's right. She's ma mam!"

There was nothing particularly unusual about our arrival in Scotland except for the fact that the snow we'd been promised hadn't arrived. There was plenty of rain though, so that was good.

We drove in our motorcade southeast towards the Christmas village. It wasn't a long journey but, as soon as we were up in the mountains, the going was slow. It turned out limousines aren't designed for the Scottish Highlands' winding roads.

It was my first time up there and the scenery was just as vast and impressive as I'd been hoping. We drove through pretty villages and caught sight of an old steam train puffing along in the distance. The land on either side of us was painted green and purple with gorse and heather and a vast loch reflected back the slate-grey sky. There were valleys and vistas and everything was in full widescreen through the car windows as we climbed towards our destination, half-way up Cairngorm Mountain.

It was midday by the time we arrived at the brightly illuminated entrance to Santa's Glen. We went in through an archway of trees beside a large porter's lodge and then took a track around the wooded estate to the Christmas-themed car park where we piled out to be greeted by a troop of elves.

"Merry Christmas," they shouted, jumping up and down like they couldn't contain their excitement. Some leapfrogged over one another, a few had an imaginary snowball fight – they'd obviously planned this based on the now disproven weather forecast – and one came up to sing "Santa Claus is Coming to Town" in its entirety.

Seeing how Amelia was more interested in the shiny car wing mirror and two of the other kids were over fifteen, the performance didn't generate the festive cheer they might have been hoping for. In fact, the only people who seemed impressed were the newly revived Ramesh and Howard, who was every bit the kid at Christmas he claimed to be. Katharine tried to be cheerful for her family's sake and the others looked like they'd rather be checking their e-mails.

"I'm Jing Jing," the head elf announced, going up to the oldest boy in our group. "What's your name?"

The teenager put on a fake smile and I could tell this wasn't going to go well. "My name's Kevin. Did you spend five years at drama school to play an elf, Jing Jing? Are all your dreams coming true this Christmas?"

No one looked particularly impressed by his comment and Jing Jing made the wise decision to move on to a less intimidating member of our party as American Astrid totally lost it at her friend's son.

"We're here to have a good time, Kevin. Couldn't you think of your little brother and try to act like a decent human being for once?"

His mother did not appreciate this reprimand and replied through gritted teeth. "Yes, thank you, Astrid. But I think I can look after my own children. Why don't you worry about Justine?"

The other teenager, a pretty, brown-haired girl who was about the same age as Kevin, had taken her phone out and was filming the light sculptures and wooden figurines we were standing near with a look of supreme distaste. "This place is amazing. It's just so tacky."

"Justine!" Astrid had plenty of rage left for her daughter too. "If you don't get off that damn phone for five seconds this vacation, I swear I'm going to snap it in two."

Ignoring the man with pointy ears who was squishing her cheeks, Baby Amelia laughed at the middle-aged meltdown.

Kevin still looked upset about being told off. "This place sucks, there's not even any snow."

"Kevin," his mother complained. "Try to enjoy it for Aidan's

56

sake." She motioned to the younger brother who looked really quite confused by the whole conversation.

Jing Jing had a second attempt at geeing us up. "Why don't we get you inside? It's not long till Christmas, folks! Who wants to see Santa?"

As a fan of the season myself, if I had to critique our welcome I'd say that I prefer the more traditional term "Father Christmas" over "Santa Claus" and I have no idea why Jing Jing was doing a scary German accent.

Walking as if we were treading through snow and it was incredibly hard work, the troop of elves transported our bags towards the Christmas village. It had started to rain and even Howard was looking a bit blue by this point. It was around zero degrees, there were great icicles hanging from each building, but there was a noticeable absence of the white stuff.

Despite the pretty lights in the trees and the cosy chalets painted in festive colours, without the snow, the supposedly luxurious accommodation looked rather like a cheap roadside hotel. The fact that there were no other guests made it look like a supremely unpopular roadside hotel.

"This is going to be great." Howard tried to sound positive at least.

"Absolutely." If this was Bertie trying to sound positive, he definitely failed.

"No, I'm serious." Howard wasn't giving up so easily. He turned to address the group and Jing Jing looked happy that someone was willing to share his burden. "We have everything we need for a wonderful holiday. We have friends, family, some great bottles of wine and I hear that Ramesh over there makes a mean Rogan Josh curry."

"I honestly do!" Ramesh did not need any encouragement to look on the bright side of life.

"And you know what else we have?" Howard paused and looked across at his wife. "We have music!" He waved to the elves to join him and, just like in a musical, burst into song. "Deck the halls with boughs of holly…" he began, for his little helpers to join in with all the fa-ing and la-ing. "Tis the season to be jolly…"

Katharine looked at her husband like he was the world's biggest goofball and I once again tried to make sense of their relationship.

This feels like the mid-point of a romantic comedy, not the build up to a murder. When are we going to get to the good bit?

"Honey, why do we hang out with these people?" Lady Penelope asked her husband with a warm smile, as Howard plucked his daughter from my arms and began to dance about with her.

"I know, it's tragic, isn't it. But what can we do? They're family." I'm pretty sure that Rupert Gravely-Swans is the poshest person on the planet. Everything he said came out coated in layers of snoot and plumminess.

Howard's gamble had paid off and even the two teenagers had let down their guard. The girl danced a little and Kevin looked at her shyly, perhaps enjoying her company more than he wanted to let on.

At the end of the song, Howard dropped to one knee and held his free arm out whilst holding the last laaaaaaaaaaa. The singing elves formed a semi-circle around him to match the shape of the village and with the song complete, we burst into applause and laughter.

It had brightened everyone up and, suddenly, the wait at the airport and the absence of snow didn't seem to matter. We walked over to the main building, with the guests and elves chatting away to one another happily. All traces of cynicism had disappeared.

"I didn't know you were so talented," Astrid told Howard, without the hint of a smirk or snarl.

"My granda' was known as something of an entertainer in our village and I like to think he passed it down to me. Just don't tell the lads at work about it, a'right?" I noticed that his Scottish accent had become thicker since we landed in his motherland. When I'd heard him chatting to our driver, I could barely understand what they were talking about.

"Oh, wait up," the American said, and nabbed one of her bags back off the porter elves. "You guys go ahead, I'll be right there."

Inside the enormous communal lounge, Christmas had seriously kicked off. It was a yuletide paradise with every last detail, from the ceiling to the furniture, picked out in red and green. A tree bigger than me, and ten times as bushy, was located by the door and another even taller one stood not far from the roaring fireplace. There were some coos of appreciation and Kevin the teenager got his friend Justine to take a photo of him throwing a peace sign. There was a lot of nervous smiling and softly spoken compliments as the girl handed the phone back to him.

Each family had a chalet to themselves and Ramesh and I would be in with the Taggarts. After a glass of mulled wine and a break to unpack, a whole timetable of activities was planned, but my friend would not be partaking.

"We can't eat Rogan Josh every meal, Izzy. I'm going to spend the afternoon watching YouTube videos on how to cook. I've never really tried before, there's always been someone else to do it or a takeaway nearby." He sounded pretty nervous as he lugged a bag of cookery utensils towards the kitchen. "I'm terrified of failure, Izzy. Ab-so-lutely terrified!"

I watched as the smiling families dispersed off towards their homes for the week and tried to understand how anyone could be in danger in such a remarkably happy place.

Chapter Seven

That sugar-sweet cordiality held for a little while longer as the festive activities started in earnest. A parade of horse-drawn sleighs transported us from the chalets on a path through the forest, just as the snow started coming down. It really did feel special and I was a bit sad that Ramesh couldn't be there to once more proclaim *a Christmas miracle.*

By the time we arrived at the reindeer stables even the teenagers were full of excitement – which was in no part due to Bertie's attempts at entertaining them.

"Look, kids." He held up two carrots on his head like antlers and at least baby Amelia chuckled.

"Very mature, Bertie," Astrid chastised him, unable to hide a touch of amusement in her voice. "You know, I thought you were allergic to vegetables."

"Now, now, Astrid." The tubby joker fed one carrot to the animals and took a bite of the other. "You know that I'll eat anything."

"Astrid, darling," her husband interrupted. "Perhaps we should get a photo as a family?"

The curvy American did not hide her irritation. "I was talking, Grantham. I'm sure there'll be a million chances for photos. Do you have to interrupt?"

Clearly used to his wife's bad temper, Grantham waved his camera in front of her and looked hopeful.

"I'll take it." Kevin ran over to grab the device and Justine perked up as she huddled in with her parents. Astrid forced a cheerful look but did not enter into the spirit of the moment, even when one of the reindeer forced its way hilariously into the photo.

I watched Kevin's parents as the scene unfolded. His mother Suzanne was clearly unimpressed by this new outburst from her supposed friend and the admiral was too busy with their younger son Aidan to pay any attention. I could see the fault lines in the group quite clearly already and it made me wonder why they would ever have agreed to come on holiday together.

Katie hung back from the rest of the group but tried to appear happy whenever her husband was near. I took Amelia over to see her, which sadly failed to brighten her grim countenance. Her nerves had clearly got the better of her once more. It made me wonder how much her apprehension about the holiday was boosted by the trials of becoming a mother for the first time.

Once we'd finished petting the reindeers, the elves helped us write up our Christmas lists. I have to say, I was pretty excited for the highlight of the day, when we would all get to visit Father Christmas himself. There was an underground tunnel to get there which sparkled with tiny fairy lights set into a woodland scene. And when we emerged in his grotto there were Lego sculptures of snowmen and elves, giant red and white candy canes (that I like to imagine were lickable) and intricate chains of ice-white garlands, woven around one another on the ceiling. The only thing missing were the stops – as they'd all been pulled out.

*Ha ha, you are **too** funny.*

There was no cynicism as we queued up to sit on the jolly man's knee. Even breezy Lady Penelope and her slick husband Rupert seemed in awe of the moment. The man in the red suit was one of the best Father Christmases I'd ever seen, complete with his own long white beard and patient manner – which he managed to maintain even when Chief Superintendent Howard spent ten minutes taking selfies with him.

In fact, old Saint Nick was so warm and welcoming, in his big comfy, golden throne that, when it was my turn to go up, I got a bit emotional.

"What would you like for Christmas, Sally?" Not only did he somehow know my (admittedly fake) name, but he managed to avoid looking at me as if I was the Creature from the Blue Lagoon, coming to crush him to death.

So perhaps you can forgive me for reverting to a childlike state and replying, "Polly Pocket!"

"Ho ho ho," he chortled and waited for my real, adult answer.

"Oh... fine. World peace I suppose."

He smiled, then whispered conspiratorially into my ear. "I'll see what I can do."

By the time we were back outside, the snow was lying thick on the ground and flakes the size of teabags were falling down softly from the skies. Wrapped up in a fleecy blanket, in my sleigh for two, I cuddled my ward Amelia closer and had a word with my inner child. *Dear nine-year-old Izzy, if you can hear me, there's nothing to worry about. All your dreams will come true.*

That evening for dinner Ramesh made his signature dish and it was greatly enjoyed by all. He would need to work on his serving skills though as, every time he spotted Lady Penelope he'd make a ridiculously deep bow and almost spill whatever he was holding.

"You really don't have to do that, old chap," she said humbly, though the "old chap" slightly undermined the message.

Despite being a group of wealthy aristocrats, it was my own prejudices that I had to set aside as they couldn't have been more welcoming. I had a place at the table and Howard and his admiral friend Toffee (whose real name, I never learnt) made me feel incredibly welcome. Toffee's wife Suzanne, the scholarly woman whose face still looked familiar to me, was friendly and their kids, Kevin and seven-year-old Aidan, seemed to get on well. Grantham and Astrid were the only ones who took a while to warm up but, once the wine started flowing, they were as jolly as anyone and Justine appeared to forget the cold words her mother had directed at her.

Howard even led the group in a reworking of 'We Wish You a Merry Christmas' with the words, "We liked Ramesh's curry very much. We liked Ramesh's curry very much. We liked Ramesh's curry very much and want dessert now!"

I was amazed when our chef emerged from the kitchen with an iced Christmas cake, complete with marzipan snowmen figurines. Everyone cheered with excitement when it was revealed, but I was suspicious.

"Tell me the truth," I said, darting into the kitchen once he'd left his confection behind. "You didn't bake that, did you?"

"Yes, I did." He was very blasé about it as he sat on the counter in his stainless-steel den, swiping away on his mobile. "You can learn anything on YouTube. But it took me five hours to prepare and if I don't get a start on breakfast now, there'll be nothing to eat." Putting down the phone, he retied his apron strings in a way that said I was no longer welcome in his kitchen.

Bertie scoffed half the cake himself and then complained there were no petit fours to go with his coffee. I doubted there was any imminent threat to Katharine right then, so I decided to discharge my duties as a nanny and offered to put Amelia to bed.

I'd never spent much time with a baby before, but this one seemed like a good one. She stayed right wherever I put her, laughed at my jokes and only cried once, during a particularly elaborate game of peepo, when I waited too long before reappearing. The only problem I found was that she didn't appear to have the slightest interest in going to sleep.

"What about a bribe?" I sat beside her cot and looked down at her as she grinned. "If you go to sleep now, I'll make sure you get some cake at breakfast tomorrow. What do you think?"

She gurgled and giggled but did not comply.

"I can respect that. You're young, you're independent; you want to do your own thing." Each cheerful look made me love her a little more and a strange feeling reared up inside me. I'd never felt anything like it before. It was alien and scary and I'm not entirely sure I liked it. "You cheeky little thing. You wormed your way into my heart!"

Having children is one of those things I imagine I'll get around to one day – like reading 'Great Expectations' or visiting the Cotswolds – but I've yet to plan exactly when. It had never seemed particularly urgent before that moment but, all of a sudden, broodiness was upon me.

Is this it then? Does hitting thirty mean we are now a machine with no other function or desire than to pump out sprogs?

It certainly looks that way. I don't know how to confess this, but… I have a definite urge to paint a nursery and I think I want it to be… pink!

I'd barely had a boyfriend for five minutes, and now my hormones were about to hold me hostage until I gave into their demands.

Luckily, at that moment, Katharine came into the room to read her daughter a bedtime story and I was saved from such thoughts for a little while longer.

"How are you doing?" She wore a cautious smile and carried a copy of 'Mog's Christmas'.

"Shouldn't I be asking you the same thing?"

"I've been fine today. Whenever Howard's nice like this, I wonder if I've got it all wrong." She shook her hands out and released a noisy breath. "But I promise that he's not always so sweet. He's been totally different for the last few months. Short tempered, controlling, constantly asking me questions about every single part of my life. I swear, that's nothing like the man I married."

I watched her over Amelia's crib. "You know anyone could have written the letter. It would make more sense if it wasn't from Howard. Perhaps someone was just playing a nasty joke."

Her voice grew more panicked again. "I told you, I don't have much to do with anyone else these days. All the people I care about are here with us. I don't have any other friends or enemies. I've never taken a lover or fallen out with a neighbour. I've been at home in my lovely old house on the common ever since Amelia arrived and that's how I like it. If Howard didn't write the letter, I can't imagine who else would have."

A thought occurred to me then. "I wonder if it could have something to do with your career. Are there other artists you don't get along with who were jealous of your success?"

She closed her eyes for a few seconds like she had to summon the strength to answer. "I quit that crazy scene years ago. Sure, I've made good money from it, but I didn't go in for all the rivalry and backstabbing. I did my own thing and occasionally put on a show. I live in my own little bubble, that's what Rupert always says."

"Okay. I understand."

Her reply was sharper than normal. "No, I don't think you do, actually. Painting was a way for me to fire out all my emotion but for the last year, I haven't been able to pick up a brush. The only thoughts I have in my head are far too negative and no one wants to see them splattered across a canvas."

Ask her what she's angry about.

It wasn't that simple and so, as Katharine gripped the bars of the crib, I tried to find a way to broach the subject. "Don't you think you should tell me what made you feel that way? Maybe it would help me understand who wrote the letters."

She didn't look at me but smoothed the hair on her daughter's little red head. "Oh, that." A pause, a breath, a slight frown. "It's just family heartache, you know the sort of thing."

I hesitated for a moment. "Perhaps it's stupid to suggest but, couldn't one of your brothers have written the letters?"

She took Amelia's chubby hand in her own with great tenderness. "I don't see why. Bertie's the oldest, so he inherited the family estate up in Hampshire. And Rupert is doing just fine after marrying into the wealthiest family in the universe." She smiled down at the child like all her worries were forgotten.

"Keep going, Katharine. Tell me about your friends. They got upset about something on the plane, what was the story there?"

She looked at the red and gold star mobile, which was calmly rotating above the crib. "Old words, old wounds. We've known one another forever. Except for Rupert and Penny, we were all at university together. Astrid Spear, Suzanne Winters and I lived in the same dorm in our first year at Oxford."

A fact clicked into place in my brain.

You're welcome!

"I knew I recognised her. Suzanne is that TV historian, right? She's always on the war documentaries my stepdad watches. I think he secretly fancies her."

"Well, I don't blame him. She's phenomenally clever. She puts the rest of us to shame."

"What about the others?"

"You're right. We can't rule anyone out yet." There was a determined note to her voice and I knew she would give me what I needed. "Astrid wanted Howard when we were younger. She was crazy about him but he only had eyes for me. That's what Toffee joked about on the plane and it was clear she's still sensitive about it." She stopped for a moment to consider this. "I doubt she's ever forgiven me either. But, with Astrid, it isn't a question of friendship so much as her keeping us close to remind everyone how successful she is. We three girls have always been a bit too competitive and it's one battle that she won. If it weren't for Grantham and the boys being such good friends I can't say I'd choose to see her."

"Do your families spend a lot of time together?"

She sucked in what she was about to say, as if she wanted to put a new spin on it. "We used to. I think that Howard likes to think of

66

them as an extended family as he didn't have much of one growing up. There's not a parent left amongst us anymore and so, we sort of club together to make the most of things. They're the family Howard didn't have and I'm not entirely sure I wanted."

Stopping herself again, her face fell once more. "Since my parents died last year, I've felt so much guilt. It's hard to put it into words. Perhaps it's becoming a parent myself but... yes, so much guilt."

I wanted to dig deeper but then she laughed her nervous laugh and swept the hair from her eyes. "I hope that nothing comes of this. I hope I'm overreacting and we'll all go home next week full of Christmas spirit, but..."

She didn't finish the sentence as her expression had become locked into a look of sheer horror. I followed her line of sight to trace what she'd seen. There wasn't much light on in Amelia's bedroom so I hadn't noticed it before, but, just visible between a cuddly Christmas pudding and a red robin at the head of the wooden crib, was an unmarked, white envelope.

It was clear that Katharine didn't have the strength to reach out for it, so I did my job. I took some latex gloves from my bag before grabbing hold of it, then carefully pried the envelope open with the tips of my fingers. I chose not to read the message out loud this time.

THESE ARE YOUR LAST DAYS ON EARTH. DEATH WILL SOON BE HERE.

There was the same dramatic lettering as in the original. Each word was in a different colour but all were in bold capitals and there was something almost violent about the way they looked. The word for death was a pustulant green and I was sure I recognised the font from an advert or something but there was no way of knowing where from.

The envelope was otherwise empty. There was nothing distinctive about the paper, no watermark or insignia that would have provided Poirot with a vital clue and I didn't have anything with me to dust for fingerprints. It wouldn't have helped anyway as, at that moment, Katharine ripped the letter from my grasp and stormed from the room.

I picked up poor Amelia, who started crying as soon as we ran after her mother and out into the falling snow.

Katharine had already made it across to the main building and back into the lounge by the time I caught up with her.

"Who left this in Amelia's room?" Her eyes scanned the group. All of the adults were there but little Aidan had gone up to his room already. "Tell me, right now. Which one of you did this?"

"Katie, what's the matter?" Howard was up on his feet and running over to her. He looked at the letter in her hand but displayed no recognition.

"Did you do this, Howard? Was it you?"

Shaking his head sorrowfully, he wrapped his wife up in his broad arms and she started to sob. I kept my eyes on the other guests to look for signs of guilt.

Astrid and her husband's faces were blank. Rupert had risen to his feet with his hand on Lady Penelope's shoulder but stayed rooted to the spot. I could tell that boisterous Bertie would like to have made a joke to smooth everything over and the admiral and his historian wife's eyes were wide open, though none of them said a word.

"I can't take this anymore," was Katie's muffled cry when it finally came and, just then, Ramesh lumbered in with drinks for everyone.

"Who wants eggnog?" His voice rose cheerfully but then, taking in the dramatic tableau, he shuffled back out the way he'd come. "I'll pop by later to see if anyone's thirsty."

Chapter Eight

Howard took his tearful wife back to their chalet and told me he'd look after Amelia for the rest of the night. This meant I was free to hang out in the lounge, pretending to read 'Hercule Poirot's Christmas' and secretly listening in to everyone's conversation.

"You've always been jealous, Astrid. Why don't you just admit it?" I was surprised to hear this accusation come from Grantham, the woman's own husband. "I think you've gone a bit far this time, though, I must say."

The remaining couples and the two disinterested teenagers were arranged on the sofas around the fireplace with Rupert and Penelope sitting regally on their armchairs nearby. It was a lovely, cosy place for an argument and Astrid was enraged.

"Are you seriously saying you suspect me of threatening to murder one of my oldest friends?"

"I wouldn't put it past you, Mum." Justine delivered the line in just the right abrasive, teenage tone to get under her mother's skin.

"I thought we were going to watch, 'Miracle on 34th Street' tonight." Bertie had retrieved Ramesh's surprisingly good eggnog from the kitchen and was serving it out from a big punch bowl. "I love 'Miracle on 34th Street'. It's an underrated classic."

No one listened to him as there was something far more engaging to watch right then.

"I can't believe my own family would accuse me of plotting a murder." Astrid sunk down in her chair like she was the teenager, causing her daughter to look across at Kevin with an embarrassed shrug.

Her short, unimposing husband let out a laugh. "Really darling, that's not what we're saying. We just think you'd be the prime suspect if anything did happen. You know how competitive you've always been."

"Is that any better?" Her voice went up like a steam train whistle.

"How about a game of something then?" Bertie was like an entertainments manager and was determined to change the topic.

"What about you Suzanne?" Astrid steamed on. "You know damn

well you've always wanted to get one over on Katie."

The professor tried to laugh the accusation off. "Please, we're not kids anymore." Her tone was unconvincing and the expression on her face right then told me that any rivalry between the three of them was still going strong.

"Hey, no eggnog for the girl." Astrid's eyes darted across the lounge. She had found something else to complain about. "It's got dairy in it, right?"

"I think it might be time to cut poor Justine some slack." Bertie was doling out wisdom as well as festive punch. "She'll be sixteen next year. She's practically an adult."

Astrid did not think much of the argument. "Why don't you keep your cake-gobbling face out of my family business?" Her sudden bile drew a loud, "Ooh," from the audience. For a moment, she reminded me of a video I'd seen of a mongoose attacking a snake. "We don't do dairy in my family, it's a personal choice and I hope you can respect that."

Suzanne leaned across to her friend and, in her typically smart voice said, "It's got rum in too, but it's the milk you're most worried about?"

The others laughed once more, causing Astrid to melt back into herself. An awkward silence followed before anyone spoke again.

It was Admiral Toffee who eventually did. "We shouldn't be joking about this letter. It's a terrible thing and whoever is responsible has clearly terrified poor Katie." His voice was cold and serious, his leading-man features drawn into one another.

Astrid saw her chance and pounced. "Well you would say that." Like a good comedian, she paused before delivering the punchline. "If you didn't want us to think you were responsible."

Rupert and Penelope were clearly enjoying the sparring and offered up another, "Ooh!"

Justine had made the most of the grown ups' bickering to take a seat beside Kevin. It was cute to see the shy way in which they interacted. Though they'd presumably known each other since they were kids, it was hard to miss that some new affection was mounting between them. And I wasn't the only one who'd noticed.

"Justine, away," her mother snapped, like she was issuing

70

commands to a dog.

Even knowing her mother's fierce temper, the girl was clearly taken aback by this extreme reaction to two teenagers sitting innocently on a sofa together and jerked away from the boy like he was on fire.

"For all that's holy, cut them a break, would you?" Suzanne said, shaking her head at her uptight friend. "What's the worst that can happen?"

Astrid knew the exact answer to this question and wasn't afraid to deliver it. "The worst that can happen is that she turns up on my doorstep, barefoot and pregnant, and expects me to help raise the damn kid."

No one else seemed particularly afraid of this prospect and it was her husband who jumped in to dismiss it. "And, in that sordid scenario, what happened to her shoes, my angel?"

Bertie let out a snorting laugh at this and gave Grantham a high five.

Clearly not willing to lose face, our sole transatlantic representative doubled down on her anger. "Justine, I told you to get away from that boy. So do what I say, right now."

"Mother, please."

She wasn't one for backing down. "I said, now!"

"I wish you were dead!" The girl's reply was one great scream which bounced around the walls of the oversized cabin. The glass baubles on the Christmas trees vibrated gently, like an opera singer had just paid a visit.

The sound died away, leaving silence once more in control of the room. Justine stayed exactly where she was. She didn't flinch, she didn't cry, she just stared her mother down like a deer playing chicken with an oncoming car.

In the end, neither of them surrendered. It was Kevin who could take it no longer. His face scarlet and on the point of tears, he pulled a coat on and ran from the house. A faint scream reached us from outside and the poor teenager's humiliation was complete. It was hard to know how we could move on from such a scene. I had given up any pretence that I was reading and watched the group of friends, who seemed just as shocked by the violence of it all as I was.

"Okay, that's enough." Lady Penelope got to her feet and, in her crystal-cut voice, admonished the others. "I know there's a lot of history between you, but I didn't come on holiday to have your bad blood ruin my Christmas. If I wanted fights and dysfunction, I'd be at home with my parents."

The way she spoke was mesmerising. She had a confidence which I imagine only comes with a lifetime of public speaking and elocution lessons. She was more than a princess, she was as present and powerful as any queen. "For the sake of the children, you'll act like civilised humans and you'll get on as best you can."

Eyes fell to the carpet or peered out of the window at the storm. No one spoke but it was clear that a truce had been drawn up and, for the moment at least, the terms were agreed. "Good," she continued. "Now, we're going to have a civilised evening and we're going to enjoy ourselves or Mummy will be angry."

A few people laughed at the joke but Astrid did not seem reassured. There was a strange atmosphere as more drinks were handed out and people who, only moments before, had been shouting their heads off attempted to engage in polite conversation. It gave me the impression that such falling outs were normal occurrences in the group and I had to wonder whether there was more lurking in their past than a few ex-boyfriends and broken hearts.

I noticed a particularly stifled atmosphere between the historian and her naval officer husband. Though they sat together and he made every effort to be attentive to her needs, Suzanne seemed to recoil from Toffee every time he attempted an affectionate touch of the hand or brush of the cheek. She smiled through it all, like it was no big deal, but it was clear there was something not entirely right between them.

I sat analysing these strange dynamics for a while, then went up to the mezzanine level above the lounge to do a bit of online stalking of my new companions. I found a bunch of stuff on Katie's art career and the various big prizes she'd won, but her online presence had faded out the year before and there was no sign of any new work forthcoming.

Howard had won a medal for his impact as a community policeman in his first job. Astrid's online business profile made her sound a lot swankier than she came across in real life and Suzanne, who was a professor of war studies at one of the big London colleges, seemed to appear almost exclusively on TV programmes about mass murder and human morality. She was intense to say the least.

I was soon tired of staring at my phone though and took a break to watch the snow falling. I'd never been skiing and London is lucky if it gets more than a centimetre every winter, so this was special for me. I was considering putting my ski suit on and going for a walk when I caught sight of something through the window.

Justine must have snuck out when her mother was distracted by Ramesh's deceptively strong beverage. She was out there in the snow and she wasn't alone. She and Kevin were standing in the doorway to the uninhabited chalet. Face to face, with barely a foot between them, they were framed by an arch of gently pulsating Christmas lights. I could practically feel how nervous Kevin was as he leaned in to kiss her, but he timed it just right. I wanted to jump up and celebrate the moment because it was seriously just about the most romantic kiss I could imagine.

I had my first kiss behind a plastic recycling bin in my school car park with seventeen-year-old Gary Flint – who told me as soon as it was over that he'd only done it because his mates had dared him to. Poor teenage Izzy went home in tears and spent the next forty-eight hours planning her revenge. I wish I'd had Justine and Kevin's first kiss instead. It was practically a Christmas miracle.

I'd started to feel a bit guilty for staring at two kids pashing in the snow when someone appeared at the top of the stairs. I pretended to be very interested in the label of a red gingham cushion, which, as I'd left my book downstairs, was the only thing to hand that could pass as reading material.

"Hello, Izzy Palmer." Lady Penelope crashed down beside me, with a look of mystery on her face. She'd changed out of the formal outfit she'd been dressed in and now wore a fluffy purple cardigan that I could totally have seen Ramesh being on board with.

"Hi, Lady Penelope," I replied as I'd forgotten I was supposed to be undercover. "I mean, what are you talking about? My name's not Izzy Palmer, it's…"

She did not look impressed. "I thought you were supposed to be some kind of master detective? You seriously need to work on your subterfuge. Your acting is atrocious."

I felt a little defensive. I'd never been insulted by a royal before.

"Well, I'm sorry, but that's not where my genius lies."

Ha! Genius?

"Anyway, how did you know it was me?"

She straightened up in her squishy seat. "It's pretty hard to forget the woman who almost upstaged me on my wedding day."

"Only almost?" I laughed sheepishly, not believing for a second that I'd made a dent in her multi-million pound celebration.

She gave a wry smile. "You could have come up with a better disguise than just removing your glasses. Reverse-Supermanning never works these days. I should know, I practically invented it." She looked troubled for a second then admitted, "Well, it was Ghandi who invented it, of course, but I like to think I perfected his technique."

Huh. Ramesh was right about something again. That's at least three times this year. He will be happy when we tell him.

"Besides," she continued. "I couldn't imagine Katharine allowing anyone outside the family to look after Amelia, unless there was an absolute emergency. I'm desperate to babysit that little ball of cuteness and her mother won't let me anywhere near and I'm her sister-in-law."

She was quite different from how I'd imagined she'd be. In interviews on TV, I'd always found her a bit drippy and dull, but she was sharp as a tack in person. I have to admit that, despite the fact she was mega wealthy, owned her own palatial estate in Yorkshire and met her husband at yachting school, she was surprisingly down to earth.

"Please don't tell anyone who I am," I begged, as I have no qualms about such things. "Katharine's trusting me to keep her safe. Personally, I think I'd be better at waiting until she's dead and then working out who did it, but she's confident I can help."

She waved away my concerns. "I'm not going to tell anyone." There was a golden candle holder on the table with little angels on. She struck a match to light it before continuing. "I'm going to help you investigate."

As the heat reached them, the angels flew around in circles, tinging a small bell over and over as they went. It was pretty and Penelope let out a contented sigh as she watched.

"How can you help?" I asked, slightly in awe of the offer.

A mischievous smile curled up her pretty face. "Well first things first, Astrid might be the obvious suspect, but she's not the only one with a grudge against Katie. Suzanne and Toffee have both had their issues with her over the years. They might seem all sweet and friendly on the surface but, I can tell you that, when I started dating Rupee, they were insanely protective of him. It took me years to feel comfortable with this lot."

She stretched her hands out for me to take, like a little girl promising she'd be my best friend forever. "Obviously threatening to murder Katharine means there's a whole new level of wickedness at play, but, tomorrow morning, I'll clue you in on every last secret that nest of vipers has."

She said this in a dramatic manner which suggested we should cut the scene there, but I had one more question for her.

"Why don't you just tell me now?"

"I couldn't possibly!" Lady Penelope looked scandalised and I waited for her explanation. "I've had far too much boozy eggnog and will probably say the wrong thing. But I'm sure that, first thing tomorrow, we'll work out exactly who's got it in for poor Katie."

Chapter Nine

I woke up early the next morning, determined to make the most of the snow before it disappeared. No one else was awake, so I put my contacts in, covered almost every millimetre of my skin in layers of thick fleecy or waterproof fabric and stepped outside.

It was one of those days that winter was invented for. The sun was just rising in a blue sky, the air was crisp and the fresh white snow under my feet was such a unique sensation that I might as well have been walking on the moon. It was as cold as an ice cube out there but I was toasty and warm thanks to the complimentary Christmas-themed snowsuit that was provided to each guest. I'd lucked out. Mine had a giant reindeer head on the front.

I stomped my way through the forest and up the hill, leaving a neat trail of footprints behind me. I didn't really think about the fact that someone had already been walking about in front of our chalet. I figured it was one of the elves, or perhaps old Saint Nick himself paying an early morning visit.

What time do Father Christmases start work these days?

I got to the top of the hill and breathed in that invigorating Highland air – so crisp it felt like it had been filtered through diamonds. I was just appreciating the domed peak of Cairngorm Mountain when I spotted that bright red trail of incongruous splashes between the chalets. At first I thought I was imagining it or that the blinding white snow was playing tricks with my eyes, but no. It was clearly there and it was hard not to conclude that blood had been spilt.

My muscles kicking into action, I ran back down the hill again. I turned on all five senses this time and scanned the square in front of our accommodation. There were tracks leading to the woodshed and another set, trailing off into the open field behind the buildings.

"Please don't let it be her," I said like a mantra, picturing Katharine's body laid out in the snow. Thoughts of poor Amelia growing up without a mother, her father languishing in prison, filled my head, but I pushed them back down again. I tried to keep my footsteps within the existing trail, which wasn't so difficult as the boot prints were massive. There were presents, neatly wrapped in colourful paper, strewn about along the path I was following and I came to my first splash of red. It forced me to a stop but I pushed myself onwards.

This was my job. It was not the first body I'd discovered and I doubted it would be my last. So I tried to think with the cold, detached mind of Poirot or the resigned world-weariness of Miss Marple. One step at a time, I made my way along that morbid path, up to the spot where the bright red Father Christmas suit was partly submerged in the snow.

She'd fallen between two pine trees and I wondered if she'd been seeking shelter as the blows rained down. With my heart beating in my ears, I pulled my gloves on tighter and turned her over.

"I see now," I said, out loud for some reason. "It is you after all."

Astrid's horrified gaze stared up at me, frozen forever in time. The events of the night before had marked her out not just as a potential killer but the unlucky victim. What she was doing dressed up as Father Christmas was another question.

There was more blood than on most bodies I'd seen. The snow underneath her had been flooded with the stuff and looked like a child's lurid ice drink. Whatever weapon had been used had cut right through the body. It was hard to say what had caused the damage and, for a moment, I wondered if an animal had gored her, as the wound was so large.

I wanted to cry for Astrid. I wanted to feel grief and anger for her family and the life that had been cut short, but all I could think about was the way she'd talked to her own daughter the night before and no emotion came.

I also didn't know what to do next. Normally I would have phoned the police or gone for help but, so far from civilisation and cut off by the snow, I wasn't sure what good it would do.

I heard someone stirring back in the village and called out to them. "Over here," I yelled then heard their footsteps coming closer. "Follow the prints through the chalets."

"I'm coming," a voice called back and, a minute later, Ramesh appeared in one of his outdoor funsies.

"Izzy, what have you done?" He sounded appropriately shocked. "That poor woman."

"I didn't kill her!" I was more than a little aggrieved that I had to explain this to him. "She was like this when I found her."

"Ohhh." He rolled his eyes and let out a laugh. "I am a silly! And at least it's not Katharine lying there. It would have been awful if you'd lost your client after she specifically paid you to-"

I decided that this was a good moment to cut him off. "Okay, thank you, Ramesh. Do you have your phone with you?"

"Yes, Izzy. Sorry, Izzy." He'd learnt not to mess around when I'm on a case.

I took the phone from him and attempted to dial with my gloves on, which was a stupid idea as there was about a foot of material between my fingers and his touchscreen. Removing them would have taken too long and so I used my nose to dial instead. Presumably this is the only way Highlanders can use modern phones in winter because it is cooooooooooold out there.

The call soon connected. "Police, I've found a body," but I didn't get the response I was expecting.

It was an electronic message, repeating, "We're transferring your call to your local police station," over and over again until someone answered.

A new, more human-sounding voice eventually came on the line. "This is Arnie!"

"Is that the police?"

"Aye, like I saed. Arnie!"

"I don't suppose you know Aggie?" I asked, getting sidetracked.

"Aye, she's ma auntie, Hiv ye seen her the morn'? If ye dae, can ye tell her that I wasnae too happy wi' ma Christmas pressie this year. Thon socks she gave me dinnae match."

"Arnie, are you a policeman?"

"Aye. 'Am a polis-man. And dinnae you go lettin' Andy or Archie tell ye any different."

I needed to get him back on track. "I've found a body. We're at the Santa's Glen Christmas village, off the Cairngorm Mountain road and I believe a woman has been murdered."

Ramesh was listening in intently and we both waited for Arnie to think things over.

"A body, ye say?" I heard him clap his hands together like we'd already made progress. "Okay, we should be up there wi' ye by

Saturday at the latest."

I was starting to panic. "That's two days' time. Didn't you hear me? There's bin a murrrder!" I found myself involuntarily putting on a Scottish accent when I said this for some reason.

"Are ye sure she's bin murrrdered?"

I took a deep breath. "I'm as sure as I can be. There's a huge gaping wound in her back and blood everywhere."

"So, if she's definitely deid, then what's the hurry? We'll mek it up there as soon as the snow clears. Thank ye for callin' Aviemore polis station. Be sure and have a good day!"

"Did he just hang up on you?" A strain of panic had entered Ramesh's voice. "No, Izzy. No, this isn't right. There's a killer on the loose and I could be next!"

He flopped down in a hollow in the snow to hyperventilate in peace.

"Just relax, Ramesh. No one will kill you."

He started breathing into an imaginary paper bag. "How can you know that Izzy?"

"Well, first, you're completely inconsequential to any of them."

He took this the wrong way. "Is that supposed to make me feel better?"

I ignored him and pressed on. "And second, you're the chef and no killer has time to be plotting murders and preparing food, so you'll be fine."

"And third?" he asked.

I shrugged before replying. "There is no third. I thought number two was strong enough."

Ramesh put his head in his hands. "Good things come in threes, Izzy! Everyone knows that. We're doomed!" He also said this in a Scottish accent for some reason, it was clearly catching.

I knelt down to talk to him. "Listen, Ramesh. People are going to be waking up soon and they're going to be hungry. Get back in the kitchen and make sure they have a nice fried breakfast to comfort them."

Looking up at me through his huge, brown eyes, like a cat who had just received some bad news, he nodded his head. "Okay, Izzy. I can do that." He paused. "Well, I think I can. I was up half the night learning to make individual cheese soufflés, so bacon and eggs shouldn't be too difficult."

I pulled him up to standing. "Good, let's go to work."

He scampered back off along the path and I stayed behind to examine the body. It was true what I'd told P.C. Arnie, there was a large open wound in the back of the Santa suit. Her head had blood on it too and I wondered whether a bash with a blunt object had finished her off. It gave me a chill to think of the savagery required to carry out such an attack and the fact that the perpetrator was presumably still with us.

I could see no murder weapon but that was hardly surprising. It could have been thrown out into the snow or taken away by the killer. I looked again at the tracks in the snow. Astrid's own prints had come from the woodshed and only got as far as the trees where she lay, but the bigger ones – which were almost double the size – looped back round the way I'd come. I had to conclude that she'd run over here to take cover from whoever was pursuing her. But then, what was she doing out before sunrise in the first place?

The body was surrounded by more presents and she had a sack just under her with the remaining gifts. The paper was still pretty dry, so this, and the fact that there was no snow on the body or covering the blood, suggested that she'd died a short time before I'd got up. If only I hadn't had that last half-hour lie-in, snuggling up to my big cuddly pillow, I might have saved her.

Thank goodness we had that extra half-hour lie-in, under that lovely warm duvet, or the killer might have got us too!

I took one last look at her face before turning the body back over. Her eyes were open and her mouth distended. It was a terrible otherworldly sight and it was hard to believe that a person could end up that way without having been cursed by some witch or evil spirit.

Presumably the cold would preserve the body to some extent, but forensic evidence would be deteriorating by the hour. I considered covering her over in snow but worried that would contaminate the scene even worse.

The first thing I had to do was follow the tracks to see where they'd come from so I headed towards the woodshed. Astrid's footprints had come from there, that was clear, but the only thing inside – except for firewood under a large tarpaulin – was the empty suitcase I'd seen her with the day before. Inside there was nothing but some squares of wrapping paper and a spare roll of sticky tape. I took the tarpaulin and went back to cover the body.

Simple enough so far then. Astrid stashed the presents in the woodshed and went to get them this morning for her Santa routine. What next?

Next, I had to see where the larger footprints had come from. They really were immense and led me to the central chalet. From there, whoever they belonged to could have stuck to the side of the building and, as the eves protruded far out in an Alpine style, reached any one of the other houses without making a dent in the snow.

So that was good; my first dead end of the case.

Chapter Ten

I looked around for Santa's Glen staff, but there was no one on site. I couldn't see any cars in the car park either and it seemed safe to conclude that they'd all gone home the night before. Back inside the main building, Ramesh was the only one there and he was not happy.

"Someone's been in my kitchen and they've messed it all up," he complained as, mop in hand, I found him dealing with a wet floor.

"Was it Goldilocks?" I'm so sorry for making this joke at such a truly inappropriate time, but I'm afraid I couldn't resist.

He gave me a stern look. "They left the oven on and the kitchen got all steamy. Some people have no respect for my work."

It was at that moment that Penelope and Rupert appeared and I went out to break the news.

"Murdered?" Rupert checked. "Like actually murdered?"

Lady Penelope examined me through suspicious eyes. "People just drop dead wherever you go, don't they, Izzy?"

It made me a little defensive and my voice got all squeaky. "It's not my fault. Until recently, no one ever died around me. I can't help it if there've been seven corpses this year."

"Eight!" Ramesh shouted from the kitchen, "You forgot about the one in the caravan."

"Seven… eight. That doesn't mean any of them were my fault." I decided to move things along. "I'll need you both to keep my secret." I barked my orders at the earl and lady like they were a common sir and dame. "I'm going to find Astrid's killer, but not without the help you promised me."

Penelope was wide eyed and up for the challenge. "Absolutely. The hunt is on." In her tightly fitted, tweed jodhpurs and matching jacket, she looked like a rather slinky Sherlock Holmes.

"Rupert, I need you to do something. Go to each of the other chalets and wake up your friends, but don't tell them what's happened yet. I want you to look for any sign that they've already been up this morning. Footprints, dirty shoes, anything like that. Oh, and tell me who has the biggest shoe size too. That may be important."

He nodded martially, clicked his heels together and headed out of the kitchen. I think I remember reading something about Earl Rupert being in the army after university so he was good at following instructions.

"Penelope, I need you to tell me every last secret you promised me."

Just then, Ramesh emerged from his station, a great smile on his face as he bowed once more to his favourite royal. He'd obviously overheard the conversation. "What about me, Izzy? You know I love helping out with your investigations." He straightened up and swapped the mop to two hands, like it was a lance that he would protect Lady Penelope with at all costs.

"You've got a very important job, Ra. You have to finish making breakfast. They'll all be here soon."

His smile disappeared but he went off to do his job all the same, muttering, "I better be getting paid for this."

I was finally free to talk to Penelope without interruption. "You weren't at university with the others were you?"

We settled down on the sofa. "No, Rupert's quite a bit younger than Katie and I'm younger again so I didn't start until they were long gone, but Rupert's heard everything that's gone on over the years and, naturally, he told me." She paused and then, as if I'd suggested otherwise, added, "We have no secrets from one another."

"Okay… good." I didn't want to sound like I was checking up on their relationship. "So tell me about Astrid."

I could see that this wasn't just about finding the killer for Penelope, it was a new game to play. To be honest, I thought it was a bit insensitive. A woman had died and it wasn't the moment to be-

You do realise that you and Ramesh did exactly the same thing when your boss was hacked up with a small, medieval-style letter opener?

SHHH! I'm pretending to have principles.

With that playful smile on her face, Penelope began. "Okay, but, before I do that, have you considered what the letters might mean now? Could it be that the murderer thought he was killing Katie? Perhaps they got the wrong person."

Oh, I hate it when witnesses try to help us by jumping to the same conclusions we have and making it seem like they're so much smarter than us.

"Thanks for that, but it had already crossed my mind." I probably sounded a bit smug. "We can come up with theories later, but what about-"

"Yes!" Full of excitement, her brown hair bobbed as she raised one hand in the air to stop me again. "Or maybe Astrid's husband is behind it? I've never liked Grantham, he's a terrible snob and a bit of a sleaze, I wouldn't put it past him."

"That's more like it," I said, happy that we were finally getting to the good stuff. "You promised to dish the dirt on the nest of vipers we came on holiday with. So let me hear it."

She lowered her voice a little before speaking. "If I'm honest, they're one as bad as the other. Astrid, Suzanne and even Katie when she was younger. The three of them lived together in their first year at Oxford; they were best friends. But that was only until they got to know Toffee, Grantham and Howard and things really changed."

"Do you mean because Astrid was in love with Howard but he chose Katharine?" It sounded like we were compiling stories for a society gossip column.

"Well, that's part of it." She looked impressed that I already knew this much. "But it was more than just who was with whom. They were hypercompetitive and it became a contest to them. Though they all had different goals in life, the three of them wanted to win. When Howard wasn't interested in Astrid she took the second prize – or at least it looked that way back then – Grantham came from a rich family and was on track to become a money person... you know..." She hesitated, looking for her words. "You know, one of those city men who shout a lot."

"A stockbroker?"

"That's the chap." I loved the posh phrases she used. She spoke with all the bubbly enthusiasm of a new Girl Guide. "Anyway, Astrid chose him as her consolation husband and was determined to become the richest woman on earth, no matter whom she had to trample on to get there."

"So she went for riches and Katie had her art career, so what about Suzanne?"

"Well, that's where it got interesting. You see, Suzanne had been studying business too and was the smartest of the lot, but she couldn't compete with Astrid when it came to the schmoozing and networking, so she changed degree entirely. She switched to history and started her first year again, all so that she could outshine her rival."

"Which means Suzanne is a likely suspect?" I was putting this together as I went along, not entirely sure it deserved saying out loud. "Maybe she killed Astrid to finally win their long-running battle."

Penelope's eyes glinted in the glow of the ceiling lights. "Well, hang on a second, because it was a three horse race remember. She might not seem it now, but Katie was the worst of the lot back then. You might have heard that Howard chose her over Astrid, but he didn't have much say in the matter."

She paused, making me wait for the next chunk of scandal. She was a supremely skilful storyteller and had me on tenterhooks. "Katie convinced her all-powerful father how wonderful her new young man was. Lord Gravely-Swans knew just about every high-ranking officer in the Metropolitan Police and helped to fast-track Howard to the top of the force."

There was a canvas in my mind right then and the first brush strokes were just landing down. Soon, it would be a grand landscape with immense layers of detail, but I was starting with the basic shapes and lines.

"Okay, but twenty years have gone by since then. Why would any of this be relevant today?"

She swished her hand through the air, as if she was plucking up the next thread of the story. "Because nothing ever changed. Until last year, the three of them were still at it. Astrid was the director of a massive Anglo-French pharmaceutical company and had a penthouse overlooking the Seine, but it wasn't enough for her. Suzanne is about to produce and present her first TV series but that didn't change anything. It was an unwinnable war they engaged in. The fact that Katie shut herself away from everyone after her parents died and decided not to fight anymore, just made the other two angrier."

I put the obvious theory to her once more. "So perhaps this is only the first stage. If Suzanne wrote the letters, she could go after Katie next?"

She struggled with her answer. "I think that-"

Bertie burst in then to interrupt. "It's clouding over, I'm certain it will snow again." For a second I couldn't understand where he'd come from as the front door hadn't opened, but then I realised he was still in the same clothes as last night and figured he must have passed out on the sofa upstairs.

Suzanne, Admiral Toffee and their two children appeared from outside a moment later. Little Aidan was once more overwhelmed by the festive scene and ran up to the larger of the two trees to see if any of the presents that had been deposited there had his name on.

His brother Kevin looked typically unenthused, as all good teenagers should. He crashed down on the sofa without acknowledging us and took out a portable games console from his backpack, to kill as many of whatever he had to kill as he could.

Urghhh! He left the sound on. I hate it when people leave the sound on their games. Tell him to turn it off, Izzy!

No way. I'm too polite. Let's just sit here and look put out.

Okay. Good plan B.

Katie and Howard arrived with Amelia who had clearly missed me as she giggled and guffawed as soon as her mum placed her on my lap.

"You need to make the announcement," I whispered to Penelope when no one was listening. "Wait till Grantham and Justine arrive and then get everyone's attention."

We didn't have to wait long. The dead woman's husband showed up with their daughter a few minutes later. He immediately complained about having to get up so early. "My favourite Christmas tradition is spending as much time as possible in bed. What was the big hurry in waking me up?"

I noted that he hadn't asked where his wife was, which seemed odd considering she was the only one missing.

"Has anyone seen Astrid?" he immediately asked, putting paid to that theory. "I thought she'd be here to greet you all. She had this big plan, you see-"

"Grantham, I need you to sit down." Penelope moved away to give him space and then hovered in front of the hearth as Howard got to work adding logs to the already impressive fire. "I'm afraid I have some terrible news."

The others came to crowd around and even baby Amelia fell silent, like she could tell that something serious was going on.

"Sally here found traces of blood outside in the snow. She followed them and discovered Astrid near the woodshed." Her voice was calm, with just the right amount of emotion in it for such an occasion. "I'm sorry to tell you that she's dead."

A staggered gasp burst across the room. It was a ricochet that travelled from one person to another as the news sank in. The two boys were the only ones who didn't react. Little Aidan was a little young to realise the implications and Kevin was too focussed on his game to have heard. Katie was standing back from everyone with the same panicked expression on her face that I'd witnessed when we first met.

Astrid's daughter ran over and launched herself into her father's lap to immediately burst into tears. He barely reacted at first, but glanced between the faces of his friends in search of understanding. If he was behind the murder, he was good at hiding his guilt. Silent tears came to his eyes and there was remorse and anger visible in his slightest movement.

He attempted to ask a question but only the first two words came out. "Was she…?"

"We believe she was murdered," Penelope replied so that he wouldn't have to say it. "And as far as we can tell, the staff went home last night. So, excluding the kids, that only leaves ten of us as potential culprits. Eight if we rule out Sally and Ramesh, who barely knew her."

"But she…" The new widower's sobs finally became audible. They tore through his body so that, for a few seconds it was difficult for him to even breathe. "I saw her first thing this morning. She had this goofy idea to dress up as Santa and deliver the presents while you were all asleep."

So at least we knew this much.

What if she'd used it an excuse, though? What if she was meeting someone and didn't want anyone to know?

"She felt bad about what happened last night," Grantham continued. "She wanted to make it up to everyone and, in her family, they always give presents on Christmas Eve, so…"

It had all got too much for him and he broke down entirely. His face turned Rudolph red, his nose started to run and his tears flooded as fast as Highland streams.

It was down to Suzanne to comfort him. I don't know who the obvious choice would have been, but it surprised me that she was the first to go over. Perhaps sensing that Justine was equally distraught, Baby Amelia reached out to her. Her tiny hand brushed the girl's hair and the teenager plucked the baby off me like a cuddly toy.

"I should look at the body," Howard said, immediately assuming his role as senior investigating officer. "What did the police say?"

"They weren't particularly helpful." I cleared my throat to answer. "They won't be able to get here until the snow is cleared. I've covered Astrid with a tarpaulin for the moment."

"Okay, good." He looked set to run outside but then paused to think things over. "I'll see if I can pull some strings. I've got some contacts in Edinburgh but I don't like my chances."

Bertie, who had sat in stunned silence until this moment, suddenly found a jolt of energy. "What about the reindeer?"

"What *about* the reindeer?" Penelope asked, struggling to disguise a note of cynicism.

"We could ride them out of here." The rotund lord's face took on a cautious smile.

"Have you ever ridden a reindeer through snow, Bertie?" his brother-in-law Howard responded.

"No, but we could at least try." The positivity had drained out of him and he dawdled off to the kitchen in his usual plodding manner. "I'll see what's keeping breakfast."

Howard had made it to the door and I was eager to go with him to see what evidence he could discover but, for the moment, I wanted to keep my identity under wraps. I was enjoying my anonymity and hoped it would prove useful as the investigation progressed.

Penelope found her voice again but was soon interrupted. "Until the police get here, I think we should stay where we-"

"One of you did this to her!" Grantham looked around at us, his gaze positively homicidal. "One of you murdered my wife!" He stood up, forcing Justine away from him. "Well, damn you all. You selfish, savage beasts. I'll see you hang for this."

"Steady on, Grantham," Admiral Toffee tried in his suitably authoritative voice.

"Keep your mouth shut, Toffee. You know you're the first one on my list." There was such aggression in Grantham's eyes right then that, if he wasn't a murderer, he clearly had the capacity to become one.

His daughter looked more frightened than any of us. She peered up desperately at her father as he stormed after Howard, back out into the snow.

Chapter Eleven

In the time we were talking, Ramesh had learnt to fry bacon and produced some delicious sandwiches. He really was on form and it made me want to take time off from my detective agency to watch YouTube videos and improve my cooking.

There was more than just bacon though. Ramesh brought out eggs with chives, a homemade tomato chutney and the cheese soufflés were particularly impressive.

"It's all in the wrist," he told me, as he proudly served the plates around the dinner table, where the remaining guests had convened for breakfast. I had no idea what he was talking about.

"Does anyone have any idea what happened?" Penelope was really good at maintaining focus and, as the highest ranking aristocrat present, possessed a level of respect in the group which I could never have had.

Eyes dropped down to plates. No one seemed willing to hazard a guess and it looked like I might have to help things along if we were to get to the truth.

Feeling like a pauper popping up at court to say my piece, I cleared my throat and began. "I know I'm just the nanny and I've got no right to intrude, but don't you think it would be best for everyone if we work out what happened before the police get here?" I figured that appealing to their vanity might work best. "You're all important people, imagine what will happen when the press finds out about this. Think what it will mean for your jobs and your families."

Rupert had returned as I was talking and came up to the table. "Think what it will mean for the Gravely-Swans and the Windsors!"

I thought this remark was rather flippant but I could see that it had the right effect. His friends began to mumble between themselves and I heard a few squeaks of, "...the Queen's second cousin," "... someone should think of Her Majesty" and, from Bertie, obviously, "Is there any ketchup to go with these bacon sandwiches?"

Kevin had snapped out of his gaming trance and was comforting his girlfriend by the fireplace as Ramesh delivered them some food. It was good to see that the teenager was providing the literal shoulder to cry on that Justine needed. Even if she hadn't got on with her mother, I doubt she wanted her dead.

Except that, pretty much the last words she said to Astrid were "I wish you were dead!" right after her mother humiliated her in front of everyone. Can we really rule out the possibility that she's the killer?

When Howard rejoined us, he was oddly quiet. He passed no comment on the state of the body and didn't make eye contact with anyone there.

"So?" Toffee attempted.

The chief superintendent was reluctant to give anything away. "So, she's dead. No luck on the phone to my contacts in Edinburgh either. And as the police won't be here anytime soon, I think it's best if I start taking your statements, one by one."

"Why should we trust you?" Suzanne's voice had lost its mumsiness and the comment was delivered with a spiteful undertone.

Howard did not seem intimidated. "Because I'm the only one here who has experience solving crimes."

The history professor was clearly not afraid of conflict and her features sharpened. "But who's to say you're not the killer? We'd have to be fools to let you investigate. You could use the opportunity to cover your guilt."

"But I'm *not* the killer!" Howard's voice rose with great indignance.

"Calm down." All eyes turned to Penelope, who evidently had experience dealing with unruly toffs. "If you don't trust Howard, maybe you'll make do with me. Of everyone here, I had the least to do with Astrid so perhaps I should be the one to ask the questions."

"What good would that do?" Toffee replied through a mouthful of soufflé. "It's not like we're going to own up to killing her."

"That could be a confession in itself." Katie finally broke her nervous silence. A spark of viciousness came out with her words. "Your little dalliance with Astrid was an open secret. Did you murder her to cover it up?"

We all stopped eating and the room froze. Suzanne's mouth dropped open in horror, a shameful look crossed Toffee's face and Penelope couldn't help glancing over at me in excitement as another secret fell into our lap.

"There was nothing between us." Admiral Winters spoke in calm, certain tones. "You've let your imagination run away with you and it wouldn't be the first time."

It was Howard who jumped in to reply. "What's that supposed to mean?" The Scotsman did not sound impressed. His cheery tone was long gone and the dark intensity I'd seen in him when we'd first met had returned.

"You know exactly what he means." Suzanne gave her friend a withering look. "Katie's been a total nut all year. Every time we see you she's distant, depressed or downright paranoid. After what happened with her parents she-"

"And whose fault is that, Suzanne?" It wasn't just Katie's voice that was aflame with anger, her whole body was like a weapon pointed straight at her rival.

The history professor didn't look frightened and continued in her usual confident tone. "All I'm saying is that-"

"That's enough!" Katie screamed, triggering a fragile hush. "I think I've got every right to be a little upset. First the letters and now this. How do we know the killer didn't mistake Astrid for me?"

That question again. Was it really possible? Two short women in a Father Christmas costume may look a little similar, but was that enough to stab the wrong one to death? I kept my counsel and continued listening.

Standing up from the table, Penelope was in charge once more. "This is getting us nowhere so I'm sticking to my plan." She looked into the faces of the other guests with immense confidence. "I'm going to choose an assistant and, together, we'll find out exactly what happened. By interviewing each of you alone, we'll be able to eliminate possible suspects and get to the truth. Does anyone have a problem with that?"

The atmosphere in the room still felt like it could crack to pieces. No one around that table spoke and even little Aidan, who was quietly munching his bacon sandwich, appeared to have realised the importance of what was going on. It was one of those moments when no one wanted to incriminate themselves and so no one said a word.

"Very good." Penelope smiled her youthful smile. "I think I'll pick…" She looked around the table once more. Bertie licked the grease from his fingers and sat up straight in the hope it might be him.

Katie was desolate, Suzanne oddly calm, and I felt nervous though I was fairly sure I knew who Penelope was going to choose. "…Sally."

"But she's just the nanny," the admiral was the first to react. "Why would you trust her over one of us?"

Penelope didn't waste a heartbeat before replying. "Because she's neutral, like me. Plus she was the one who found the body and I've always trusted my own nanny better than any other person on earth." She looked across at her husband who did not seem too worried by this confession. "Sorry, Rupee."

He shrugged acceptingly. "Perhaps I can be your first witness to make up for it?"

"Of course, my dearest darling." Penelope made her move across the room and it was clear that she expected me to follow her.

I deposited Amelia with her father and the three of us walked from the lounge, through a set of double doors which Penelope slammed behind us with a dramatic bang.

Chapter Twelve

We had arrived in an even more impressive, formal dining room. Whoever had designed it had taken things to a whole new level of Christmassiness and I had to wonder what Santa's Glen was used for the other eleven months a year.

The ceiling was painted gold, the floor red, there was a water feature in the corner of the room with what looked like ice water and snowflakes cascading down it. Each chair around the long, bedecked dining table had a different winter scene carved into the back and the fireplace, which took up a whole wall, was somehow already lit.

"My goodness," Lady Penelope said as soon as Rupert had closed the door behind us. "I thought I was going to mess that up. I didn't know what I was doing."

"You were brilliant," I told her, aware that our work was only beginning. "You played it just right. But we'd better keep going." I turned to her husband. "What did you find out when you were gone?"

He took a chair at the table, composed himself and looked straight at me. "I'm afraid that every single chalet had large, wet footprints running into them. Presumably the killer wanted to make it harder for us to work out where they'd been."

"Or he was looking for Astrid before he killed her."

"Yes, but wait." His eyes gleamed in anticipation. "Only one of the buildings I went into had a great big pair of boots stashed inside the front door. There are a pair of black size fourteens in Katie's chalet."

"Did you look at everyone's shoes?" Penelope was quick to ask. "Who has the biggest feet?"

"Yes, I did." With a confident grin he delivered his comprehensive reply. "The men take size eight to ten. The ladies fours and fives, Kevin has five and a half, Justine fours and little Aidan takes a child's size eleven, bless his little feet."

"So they're all far from size fourteen."

The earl beamed across at his lady. Seeing them together in person made me realise how well-suited (sort of a) Princess Penelope and Earl Rupert were to one another. They had the same vim and spark about them. They looked at each other lovingly and I could tell that

Rupert had enjoyed his spy work.

"Okay, that's good." I added up what the discovery might mean in my head. "As careless as it would be for him to leave them there, the fact that the boots were in Howard's house puts him in the frame. And that's not the only thing we've got on him. When Katharine hired me, she said that she thought the letters she'd received were from her husband. She was convinced that he was the one who wanted to harm her."

They looked at each other again, but this time there was no joy in it.

It was Rupert who eventually spoke. "That may be nothing I'm afraid." He folded his arms across his chest. "My sister has been deeply depressed since my niece was born. Howard has discussed getting her help but she won't listen. In fact, she's made the same accusations to me. She said he's trying to control her and won't let her do what she wants."

"But what if she's telling the truth?" I was thinking out loud. "What if Howard really had sent the letters as a way to scare Katharine and make her look mad? The first one came a month ago. Perhaps he's been plotting this all along."

Penelope spoke up to set my theory straight. "That doesn't make any sense. Why would he go to such lengths to make Katie look mad and then murder Astrid? Unless-"

"Unless that blighter was trying to make it look like Katie was involved." Those two were so sweet they finished each other's posh sentences!

I may have let out a little "Ahhh, you guys are too cute," which caused them both to blush. They were the Kylie and Jason, Brad and Jennifer or Tom and Nicole of the royal family.

You do realise all those couples broke up at least fifteen years ago?

Well, shame on me for not paying more attention to Ramesh when he starts blathering on about celebrity gossip. I figured that was your job.

Rupert hadn't finished debriefing us on his secret mission. "I went looking for Jing Jing and his elves but there's no one here. We didn't have any activities scheduled until twelve this afternoon so I suppose they went home last night and got cut off by the snow. At least we can rule them out as suspects."

"Good." I was glad that the chubby old Father Christmas wouldn't turn out to be a homicidal maniac.

The Earl of... actually, I don't know where he was an Earl of, but Rupert had another thought. "I think we can cross Grantham off the list too, unless he's a secret method actor. You see, I was snooping about in his chalet when he came storming back inside like the world was about to end. He went up to his bedroom without seeing me and positively exploded in tears. Poor chap, I thought I might send Justine up to check on him if she's up to it. It's a pretty rum lot he's been handed."

"Did you spot anything else of interest?" Penelope got in before me.

Her husband considered the question. "Well, I have to say. Astrid had the most incredible collection of hats. I've never seen one person with so many. And bringing them all on holiday too; it's baffling!"

"Anything useful?" Penelope knew how to deliver such questions almost as well as I did and I'd been a professional detective now for months!

He looked guilty under the force of his wife's gaze. "Um, no."

"What about you two?" I figured it was overdue that I ask this. "Why should I dismiss the possibility that one of you was involved? You were the first up this morning."

Rupert looked worried but, with all her peppy Girl-Guide energy, Penelope was happy to answer. "Well, for one thing. We didn't know Astrid nearly as well as the others. I'm not saying we haven't spent time with her family at dos and functions, but I don't think we've ever been to her house. We lived in concentric circles, but you'd be surprised how rarely we interacted."

"Okay, that's a good start," I had to concede. "Anything else?"

"Well, yes. We were still asleep." Rupert's quiet confidence and gentlemanly manner reminded me of my stepdad's. It made me like him a whole lot more. "We only woke up when we heard the chef running past our house screaming, 'We're doomed. We're all doomed!'"

Their story checked out for now. In my experience, murders are committed out of love, lust, hate or personal gain and I couldn't see how any of these things could link them to shrill, bossy Astrid.

"Okay." I paused to consider yet another thread to the strange tapestry in front of us. "You're free to go Rupert. Thank you for your help." He nodded back at me with his eyes closed.

"Please send in the next witness on your way out." Penelope sounded like a doctor.

I wasn't ready to deal with our suspects just yet. "Wait. Let's do some poking about before we interview anyone else."

"Perfect!" She flicked her eyes about conspiratorially, like a little girl playing detective. "The game is afoot."

Chapter Thirteen

When we got back to the lounge, only Justine and her father were missing. No one said much and, except for Bertie who was helping himself to a third ration of breakfast, most stared down despondently at their half-finished sandwiches. I could tell that, in our absence, the reality of death had set in.

"You should all stay here until we get back," I announced and then remembered it was Penelope's job. "That's what you said, wasn't it, your ladyship?"

Penelope nodded self-assuredly, once more eyeing our suspects as we came to a stop in the centre of the room. "That's right. No one move a muscle until you have my say so."

"Oh… umm, Sally. Would you mind?" Howard was holding baby Amelia out in front of him like she was a ticking bomb. "She's been changed and I'd look after her myself, it's just that…" He motioned to his wife who was laid out on one of the sofas, staring at the spitting fire.

I didn't see what choice I had, so I picked up my ward and, grabbing the baby carrier which was hanging beside the door, strapped her to my chest before wrapping the two of us up against the cold.

"What should we do first?" Penelope asked once we were outside.

Amelia gawped at the snow to suggest that the correct answer was *play in it,* but there were more pressing concerns.

"We'll go to Katharine's chalet," I answered. "The last letter was found there and the boots too."

We began the trudge across the square and Penelope chatted as we walked. "It was Katie who hired you, so doesn't that mean we can rule her out along with Grantham?"

"Woah. Not so fast, rookie." I was enjoying the crunch of snow again as we added our footprints to the trails that criss-crossed the yard. "Why do you say that?"

"Because she wouldn't have paid you to come here if she was planning to kill someone."

"It's a nice theory. But I'm not sure it's quite so simple." I'd read too many Christie novels to rule anything out so early in the investigation. I was still trying to get a picture of the victim so turned the conversation to her. "What was Astrid like? I saw her mini meltdown last night, but was that typical of her?"

"Well, she was always pretty dreadful to her family. I think she was one of those people who shouted constantly to make sure that no one had time to point out her own flaws."

"A bully," I said simply. "It's called being a bully."

Penelope smiled. "I suppose you're right. I always wondered why she bothered though. She spent her whole life telling everyone else how to live, but what did she get out of it?"

I tried to put myself in her place. "It can't have been easy running a massive company and dealing with a family. She'd probably got used to ordering people around and having her own way."

"Right, sure, but it didn't make her any happier. She was forever arguing with her husband and made everyone around her feel miserable. She should have learnt to relax a little and maybe she wouldn't have ended up face down in the snow."

Wait! How did she know that!?

My heart started racing, my brain listed potential evidence and I blurted my response out like a bad actress in a straight-to-video thriller.

"But how did you know that Astrid fell face down?"

Penelope was not impressed by my question. "Because Rupert sneaked a peek and told me about it."

Well that was disappointing.

"Oops, sorry." I'm not going to lie; I was blushing like an idiot. I moved the conversation on and tried to pretend that nothing had happened. "So what do you think of Astrid's daughter? Could she be involved?"

We'd got to the front door of the far chalet and Penelope pulled it open. "Justine seems like any normal fifteen-year-old, to be honest. She's constantly bored and terribly self-important. You should have seen her at my wedding. Thousands of people lining the streets to get a glimpse of my dress and there she was scrolling away on her phone as I walked down the aisle past her. A real little brat, but no sign of homicidal tendencies as far as I can tell."

There was a sort of air-lock entrance to each chalet, with two sets of doors, so we undid our coats there before the blazing central heating could cook us.

I had a confession to make. "I was one of the people lining the streets on your wedding day, you know? I'm not really a royalist, to be honest. But it was a beautiful day."

Penelope adopted a more public smile than I'd seen from her that weekend, like she was about to thank me for my kind words but instead went with, "Did you cry?"

My face once more took on a healthy crimson hue. "Urmmm, I might have, but only because my boyfriend was going away and the emotion got too much for me. I'm not one of those soppy girls who cries at the slightest thing."

Ahem... What about 'It's a Wonderful Life'?

I said "the slightest thing" not the most devastating Christmas movie ever made!

Penelope smirked at me. "I'm sure you're not, Sally Starmer. And neither am I."

In front of us, as we came in, was a pair of huge black boots with shiny silver buckles. They looked like they belonged to Father Christmas which isn't surprising really.

"They're the same as the old man was wearing in the grotto yesterday," she pointed out.

"Yes, but about six sizes bigger. Who wears a size fourteen? Bigfoot?"

Not your best joke, Iz.

Lady Penelope didn't agree and nearly bent over from laughing so much. "Bigfoot! Oh, yes. That's a good one." I wondered if she was being sarcastic but then she bellowed out another laugh. "Ha! Very clever!" I'm not entirely sure she'd ever heard a joke before.

"Someone must have taken a spare pair from the workshop after we wrote our Christmas lists. There was a changing room for the actors as we left, I suppose that whoever took them must have stashed them on one of the sleighs. But why bother?"

"Isn't it obvious?" she asked and I was once again a little peeved that such questions sounded so much cooler coming from her mouth. "To make it look like the killer had much bigger feet than they really had. Which would suggest it was one of the women after all."

"Yeah, or a man with small feet."

She laughed again. "Oh, yes. That's another good one. A man with small feet, hilarious." It wasn't supposed to be a joke, apparently she'd never heard of men with small feet either.

It was interesting to see how the different families had immediately stamped their identity on each chalet. It hadn't occurred to me before, but Katharine and Howard's had something almost artificially neat about it. It reminded me of their house on Clapham Common.

I remembered our arrival at Santa's Glen the day before when I'd looked after Amelia as her mother took time to, "Straighten things up." We were staying in a perfectly clean and tidy luxury chalet, but that wasn't good enough for her. She'd gone around the house making sure everything was up to her standards and then, piece by piece, removed the perfectly folded clothes from her suitcase and refolded them into the drawers in her bedroom. I'd offered to do the same for the baby clothes, but she gave me one of those dizzy looks of hers and said it would be quicker if she looked after it.

Perhaps this incredible neatness was the reason that we didn't find anything of interest in the house. I was hoping to discover chopped up magazines and stationary supplies to incriminate Howard in the letter writing enterprise but there wasn't even a scrap of paper so we moved on to the Winters family Christmas residence.

Suzanne and Toffee's chalet was the opposite of Katie's. Piles of shoes littered the space in front of the Christmas tree, as if they'd been left there for Santa Claus to fill. Half-way into the room, the family's cases had been disembowelled and discarded. Jumpers and trousers stretched out across the floor, like they were making a break for freedom. Books, bags and children's toys were piled up around the living area. One thing that had been unpacked was Kevin's games console, which had pride of place on the coffee table in front of the sixty-inch television.

"How curious that people can be so messy." For all her grace and charm, there was something incredibly naïve about Penelope that only served to make her more appealing. "I'm not sure I've come across anything quite like it before."

"Is that because everyone you know has servants who put things away for them?"

She smarted at my question. "No… not everyone. Some people sure. Families like mine are job creators. If it weren't for us, our staff would be out of work." She said this as if she wasn't entirely sure it was true. "Anyway, that's not the point. I didn't have any servants when I was at university or living alone in London. I simply kept things in the right place. This is…" She looked around the room, her eyes landing on the dining area where countless dirty drinking glasses had been abandoned, despite the fact that the family had barely spent any time in the house. "…different."

We continued our search upstairs.

"I was hoping it would be easier than this," Penelope told me with a huff as we reached the landing. "I mean, it's lovely to be working out puzzles and nosing about, but where's the evidence?"

"You'd be surprised. Sometimes the clue that gives the game away is something I completely ignore the first time round." I opened the door to the boys' bedroom to find an even messier spectacle than we'd seen downstairs. "Though I very much doubt we'll find it in here."

There was chaos everywhere. The beds were now home to a host of toys, trading cards, computer gaming magazines and a rather serious selection of history books, which their mother must have chosen. Strewn across the floor, there were discarded clothes and shoes, an inordinate number of balled up socks and several dirty plates.

Penelope held her nose and walked into the room, but instantly regretted it. "Oh, yuck it smells like boy!"

I laughed at her then. "Perhaps we should start with the parents' room instead."

We crossed the hall to the master bedroom which looked like it had been modelled on the one from 'Home Alone'. The wallpaper was red, the bedding green and everything was patterned with holly and berries. It would have been nice, in a dated, 1990s way, if it hadn't been for yet more junk scattered everywhere.

Suzanne had brought a library's worth of history texts with her. There was everything from Machiavelli to modern warfare. Toffee had piles of papers from his naval career too but none of it seemed to hold any connection to their deceased friend.

"So were Astrid and Toffee really having an affair, do you think?"

Penelope cleared her throat delicately. "It's the first I've heard about it, but I can see why Katie might have thought that. Astrid was a terrible flirt with him." She looked out of the window at the snow which reflected the light of the sun back to us. "We went to Howard and Katie's once for a dinner party and I swear that Astrid took every chance she could to touch and tease Toffee. She was sitting right on top of him at one point."

Still strapped to my chest, Amelia was happy to remain a silent witness.

"When was that?"

"Oh, a few months ago now. Suzanne is an absolute brain and, I think she's rather pretty in her mousy, academic way, but she couldn't compete with Astrid on looks. It was another battle they engaged in – only fitting for a professor of war studies, I suppose – but one which Astrid knew she could win."

I flipped the question around. "What about Toffee then? Do you think he'd have gone off with his wife's rival?"

She didn't need to think about her answer. "He's a man, so I'm going to say yes. In my experience, most of them would. My Daddy is a notorious letch, Rupert's father wasn't much better. There are plenty of good men around, and my husband is one of them, but they're not always easy to spot."

I was surprised by the anger in her voice. Presumably her father's past behaviour had left its mark on her. I was going to ask more about the admiral when we heard a loud bang out in the square, followed by the sound of snow falling from the rooftops.

"Come out here, Toffee!" I recognised Grantham's voice.

We took one look at each other and sprinted downstairs. We'd almost got our coats back on when he shouted again. "I'm not messing around, Toff. Get out here now, or I'm coming in after you."

Chapter Fourteen

By the time we made it outside, everyone was there except Toffee.

"Don't be a fool, Grantham," Howard shouted, his policeman's instincts kicking in again as he emerged from the group of onlookers with his empty hands out in front of him.

"I'm not interested in you, Howard." Grantham cracked open the rifle and reloaded it with an extra cartridge from his belt. "I want to talk to the man who was tupping my wife."

"How can you be sure about this?" Suzanne shouted across to him. "If you knew something, why didn't you tell me?"

"Everyone calm down," Penelope tried. "We don't know anything yet and flying off the handle isn't going to help."

Grantham fired once more without aiming, knocking a few of the icicles off the side of our chalet as he did so. "You hear that, Toffee? The next one's for you unless you get out here right now."

I walked around the edge of the houses, to give Amelia to her mother, then ushered the kids inside. Justine refused to go which meant that Kevin stayed behind too.

"Daddy, what are you doing?" she screamed, in tears once more. "Listen to Uncle Howard and put the gun down."

He wouldn't look at her. He kept his eyes on the house where his rival was still sheltering. "I can't do that darling. I want answers."

Justine wasn't giving up. Despite only wearing jeans and a fluffy, white Christmas jumper, she waded out into the snow and past Howard who was wavering in no man's land.

"As if this is even fair on me." She was using a patented teenage argument on him, but I couldn't see it garnering results. "My mother's dead and my father's about to get himself arrested for murder. Good plan, Dad."

I foolishly decided that I was the one who could resolve this situation.

Hey, what are you doing? My brain asked and I didn't know how to answer. I'd drawn alongside Justine but didn't stop there. *Unless that snowsuit's bulletproof and you've forgotten to tell me, please step away from the madman with the gun.*

I see what you're saying, brain, and I agree of course. I mean, I'm no daredevil. I used to be scared of tennis because the sound of the racket hitting the balls made me jump. But, I don't think I can turn back now.

"What are you doing?" Grantham asked, sounding just as confused as I was.

"I'm sorry, Mr Spear." My voice had gone all squeaky. "But I can't let you shoot anyone."

The neat little man seemed pretty irked right then. "I'm not going to let some hired help tell me what to do. Out of the way or I'll shoot you too."

He makes a good point. Why don't you go inside and have a cup of hot chocolate? Do you remember how much you like hot chocolate, Izzy? So much nicer than a bullet in the face.

As I stood negotiating with him, Suzanne finally convinced Justine to retreat back to safety with the other kids.

"I'd like to, Grantham. Can I call you Grantham?" I didn't want to overstep.

"No you can't, but you can get out of my way." He had the pompous, throaty voice of every middle-aged Mercedes driver that my mother had been in a minor traffic accident with (which is a worryingly common occurrence, now that I think about it.)

"I can't do that, Mr Spear. I'm the only person here you haven't known for half your life. I've got no connection to these people, no allegiances or grudges, so I thought it might be a good idea if I was the one to talk to you."

What about Ramesh? He doesn't know Ramesh. I'm sure Ramesh would love to be out here in our place.

Gripping the gun tighter, he wasn't even looking at me so I kept talking. "I know you're suffering, but this isn't right. What good would it do Justine for you to end up in prison?" I thought that, just maybe I was getting through to him so I kept walking closer. "If you put the gun down and come inside, no one will mention this to the police and you'll be free to get on with your life."

You're endangering your reputation as a terrible coward, Izzy. Would you please step away from that crazy person!?

That was when Grantham's anger turned to sorrow. His face grew red and tiny crystalline gems fell from his eyes. "I can't just get on with my life, Sally. There's nothing to live for without my Astrid."

"I understand that you feel that way, but why don't you give Penelope and me a little longer to work out why she died? One day could make all the difference. What do you say?"

"I say, no." His shout travelled around the square and back to us. "Either Toffee comes out of that house to answer my questions or I'll go in shooting."

I was only two metres away now. Practically in touching distance. "I don't think that's true. I don't think you want to hurt anybody. And do you know why?"

"No, but I'm sure you'd like to tell me." Particles of saliva shot from his mouth with every word.

"Because you know now how it feels to lose somebody. Astrid's been stolen from you. You wouldn't want to do the same to Aidan and Kevin and Suzanne."

His tears continued to fall but he said no more. He glanced at the faces of his friends who were spaced out around the buildings. A quiet sob emerged from him as he considered what to do next.

I tried one last time. "You're not going to shoot anyone. You're going to give me the gun and come inside. Isn't that right?"

His head fell limp and I really believed that I'd got through to him. "No... No, I'm not." His body jerked back into life, he switched the gun between his hands and I realised what he was about to do.

Of course, I had no idea what *I* was about to do and still don't fully understand what happened. Time certainly didn't slow down like it does at exciting moments in the movies. And there was no drawn-out moan of fear as I jumped across to him, feeling incredibly glad that I'd given baby Amelia back to her mum.

You see, I'm no Will Smith. When I realised Grantham Spear was about to turn the gun on himself, I didn't land a roundhouse kick to his weapon arm to send the rifle flying harmlessly away from the crazed man. No, 'Izzy Palmer; action star,' is not a phrase I'm likely to hear in my lifetime. When I realised what he was about to do, I took one step forward, slipped on the snow and fell on top of him.

He looked terrified as he watched me flailing through the air. Forget the fact he was planning to shoot himself in the head with a hunting rifle. The sight of a ridiculously tall nanny, falling towards him like timber, caused Grantham to cry out in fear. He was a pretty solid sort of bloke, but no match for me and I knocked him flat.

Applause instantly went up from the crowd and I heard late-to-the-party Ramesh say, "That was incredible! Why wasn't anyone filming?"

Penelope took a deep, reverential breath. "Sally Starmer; action star."

Howard was too busy to offer any compliments. He trudged over to me, threw the discarded rifle towards the trees and came to help us up.

"You should have let me die." Grantham was a sniffly mess by this stage. "I can't live without my Astrid. You should have let me die."

Toffee peered outside to see if the coast was clear, Katie was looking at Howard like he might just be the man she married after all and, though this moment of insanity had acted as a form of melancholy catharsis for all those who witnessed it, we were still no closer to finding out why Astrid had been murdered.

With Rupert's help, we took Grantham back to his house and wrapped him up in a blanket in front of the fire. He lay prone there, whimpering to himself and occasionally muttering his wife's name. It was a tragic sight and I couldn't help but feel sorry for him. I was rather keen to stop anyone else being murdered though, so I gave him five minutes then started in on the questions.

"I'm sorry, Grantham. I'm sorry for what happened to Astrid and what you felt you had to do just now. But do you have any evidence to prove that Admiral Winters was responsible for your wife's death?"

His eyes flicked up to look at me. "I know he was sleeping with her. Isn't that enough?"

Izzy, the guy's a faker. What better way to throw us off the trail than to make it look like he's so incensed about the death of his wife that he tries to kill the man he holds responsible?

Do you really think so? That's not what I took from this at all.

I was trying to go gently but there are some questions in life that it's impossible to sugarcoat. How do you know that your recently deceased wife was sleeping with your best friend? is one of them.

Luckily, he told me the answer without any prompting. "I'd known about it for months. Astrid might have been a great organiser, but she wasn't the best at remembering where she'd left her mobile. I came across it one day down the back of the sofa with a message from him on the screen."

"It had Toffee's name on?"

He paused and pulled the blanket up over his shoulders. It was like talking to a sick kid in a school nurse's office. "Well, no. He was saved in her phone as 'Sweet Boy'. Sweet Boy: Toffee? It didn't take much to work it out. The message said he couldn't wait to unwrap my wife at the first chance he got. And besides, whenever we went to their house, Astrid was all over him. It made me sick, but every time I asked her about it, she laughed and said it was all in my mind."

Kneeling down on the floor so that I could look him in the eyes, I thought about how to phrase my next question. "But if she treated you like that, why are you so cut up about her? Why did you almost murder a man?"

His reply came back to me like a bullet train. "Maybe you'll be in my position one day. Maybe you'll love someone and they'll die and you'll do whatever you can to get revenge."

Well that's a cheerful thought! Merry Christmas, Izzy.

"I'm sorry, but if they'd been cheating on me and treating me like dirt, I wouldn't give a damn about them." I struggled to hide my feelings on the matter. "What kind of a person acts like that?"

He slowed down and really stared at me. "The only woman I've ever loved." He let out one long stab of sound. It was a cry and a laugh mixed together; a raw burst of pure emotion. "I always knew I wasn't good enough for her, but when Howard turned her down to jump into bed with the Gravely-bloody-Swans, I took my chance."

He peered up at the Christmas tree as if that joyous symbol might stand in for the woman he'd loved and lost. "She used to say I made her laugh. She thought we'd be this world-beating power couple but I knew I'd never amount to anything. The only money I've made is because I knew the right people in the right places to give me a leg up. Astrid worked her way up from nothing and made it to the top. She was ten times the person I was." His full-on pity party was really kicking off. "I'm worthless, a complete joke. Even ludicrous Lord Bertie has achieved more in his life than I have. But do you know the one good thing about me?"

He looked as if he really wanted to explain and I didn't feel I could disappoint. "I'm sure there are lots of good things. But, go ahead."

His face convulsed as tears squeezed from his eyes, like blood throbbing from a wound. "Her. She was the best and the worst of me; the only thing worth mentioning. And now she's gone."

I was feeling pretty terrible for the guy right then. If he was acting, he should have been up for an Oscar. Even Ramesh couldn't put on a performance like that, and he's been the lead in his amateur dramatic society's musical for the last four years running – The Croydon Advertiser even described his appearance as Stanley in a musical reimagining of 'A Streetcar Named Desire' as "…better than you'd expect from such a cheap and poorly conceived production."

I had another thought. "Where did you get the gun from anyway?"

Grantham was dribbling onto the cushion that his head was on and had to clear his mouth before speaking. "Toffee, Rupee and I all brought them. We were supposed to spend the days after Christmas hunting deer. You didn't think we came all this way for the ice sculptures and dancing elves, did you?"

"Alright, but even if Toffee and Astrid were sleeping together, that didn't mean he killed her. Why did you go after him with a gun?"

A smile cut through the tragic look he wore. "I had to do something. I couldn't just sit here crying until the police turned up."

"So you've got no evidence whatsoever on Toffee?"

He shrugged and then a look of supreme distress occupied his face. I had no doubt that his head was filled with a thousand images of his wife right then. A thousand happy moments from their past bombarded his brain; falling in love, their wedding, the birth of their daughter and everything before, after and in between. He remembered all of this and the knowledge of his loss came back to him.

Grantham pulled the blanket tighter around himself and cried.

Chapter Fifteen

Chief Superintendent Howard arrived and I left him to comfort poor Grantham. On my way out, I noticed a few signs of Astrid's previous existence. Her high heels were on the doormat, a distinctive purple coat she'd worn hung by the door and her handbag was just beside it. I was tempted to dig out her mobile in search of Sweet Boy, but, as far as Howard knew, I wasn't a detective and I doubt such things fall under a nanny's jurisdiction.

As I walked back across the snowy village square, I tried to form a clear picture of the increasingly mystifying quest I'd embarked on. It felt cruel to blame the victim but I had to conclude that, whoever had plunged the knife in, it was Astrid who'd upset them in the first place. Even her husband knew she was rotten, but loved her all the same. Controlling, money-hungry and a love-cheat to boot, she wasn't exactly my cup of tea.

Go easy, Izzy. Don't forget what mum always says; two wrongs don't make murdering someone right.

She's literally never said that.

I thought about the body lying among the pine trees and it occurred to me that there may not have been a knife to plunge in the first place. I'd seen knife wounds before and they tended to be more discreet than the gaping hole in Astrid's back. It made me wonder what had been used as a murder weapon. Sadly, such questions would have to wait, I had a bigger problem to deal with right then.

"I think it's best if we stay here together," Penelope was saying as I opened the door to the main chalet.

Toffee had his coat on and looked set to run away, but it was his wife who'd hatched the plan.

"I'm not going to stay here and wait for that lunatic to shoot my husband." Suzanne spoke with her usual fiery determination. "We'll go back to our accommodation and lock ourselves inside. I think that's safer for everyone."

"I've made mince pies," Ramesh shouted with far too much excitement and pride for someone who was supposed to be a professional chef. "It's my very first time and I can't believe how well they turned out." He saw that all eyes were on him and that pretty much every last pair was disapproving, so he cleared his throat and clarified. "I mean… I've never made this recipe before. It's a really hard one."

"I'll have a pie or three." Bertie jumped up to abduct several cakes from the silver tray that Ramesh was carrying.

I have to say, if I hadn't been mid-investigation and about to lose access to the two main suspects I was eager to talk to, I'd have been scoffing down those delicious yuletide treats by the handful.

"I told you, I think we should all stay together." Penelope no longer sounded so sure of herself and glanced at me for backup.

Admiral Toffee, who, until this point, had offered very little leadership, finally spoke up for himself. "You're not the police, Penny." There was disdain in his voice and perhaps a note of fear. "So go back to doing whatever silly little girlies like you normally get up to and leave us be."

I could see that the words had got under her skin. "What's that supposed to mean?" Her voice hit a reproachful high note.

"I mean, Princess Penelope, that you should get another manicure and return to your castle." Toffee's anger magnified. "But don't go thinking you're anything more than a pretty girl in a nice outfit, just because your ancient ancestors happened to marry their cousin and make it to the head of their tribe."

Penelope was standing beside the table where someone had landed upon the good/terrible idea to open some wine. Her eyes flicked towards the bottle and I knew I had to intervene before things got violent again.

What is wrong with these people? Can't they kill one another off with a touch of civility?

"How about if Ramesh and I come with you to the house to have a chat?" I suggested and the hostilities were put on pause. "We don't know you, so we've got no reason to treat you any differently from anyone else."

"Why would I-" the admiral began but his wife spoke over him.

"Yes, that makes sense. I think it would be better if we left personal disagreements out of this." Her voice resolute, she was clearly a fast thinker. "I'm sorry that we lost our temper, Penelope. I'm sure that

112

Toffee didn't mean a word of it." Suzanne tugged her unrepentant husband towards the door to stop him from saying anything worse.

Before I joined them, I thought it was best if I did something about the guns scattered about the place so I told Rupert to collect Howard and Toffee's rifles and put them somewhere safe. Unexpectedly, Ramesh had an order of his own to issue.

"Keep an eye on the Christmas Pudding," he shouted at Lord Bertrand Gravely-Swans, whose face and waistcoat were covered in sugary crumbs. "I shouldn't be too long."

"Yes, chef." He lurched up from the table like he'd been reprimanded by his commanding officer. In doing so, he knocked the remaining mince pies onto the floor. "And I'll make sure that mess gets cleaned up too."

In typically debonair fashion, Ramesh sailed from the toasty warm lounge, wound a red cashmere scarf around his neck and donned his silver bomber jacket with the flashing red and green LEDs on. I gave Penelope a sympathetic look before I followed the three of them out of the door.

In the village square, there were six buildings in total, with only the chalet on the right-hand side of the crescent unoccupied. Presumably it was reserved for Bertie but the only person I'd seen going inside was Kevin the night before, when he'd wanted to get away from quarrelling parents.

"What was that about?" I asked Ramesh as we set off along the well-trodden path to the chalet three doors down.

"What?"

"The way you spoke to Bertie? Why did you order him around like that?"

He waved my question away. "Oh, him. He's been hanging around the kitchen all morning begging spare raisins and bits of last night's cake, so I put him to work in exchange for some tasty treats. I wouldn't have minded except that I have to go to the bathroom every time I need to watch a YouTube video." My friend sighed dramatically. "He must think I have a terribly weak bladder."

Inside the Winters' house, Kevin was shooting demons on the massive TV screen whilst Justine slept with her head on his lap and Aidan egged his brother on to an ever higher body count.

No one had tidied up. The place looked like it had recently been liberated from an invading army. Toy cars and bouncy balls, marbles, Lego bricks and action figures studded every inch of carpet and the two parents picked their way across it, clearly used to such precise navigation.

"Is there somewhere quieter we can talk?" I asked as a monster's head noisily exploded. I was on my seventh corpse-

Eighth!

Oh, yeah; the caravan. Sorry!

I was on my eighth corpse already and I still found the blood and guts on display on the television screen stomach-churning.

Suzanne nodded and so I followed her upstairs with Toffee and Ramesh hot on my heels. I could tell that she thought she was in charge now and I knew that, if I ended up with her in the room whilst I was talking to her husband, she'd smother the investigation and hide anything useful I might be able to discover.

When we got up to the bedrooms, I found a solution. "Ra, perhaps you could have a chat with Suzanne while I talk to Toffee."

He nodded with a steely look on his face. This wasn't his first time helping me and I liked to think that, over the course of our various investigations, a little of my focus and efficiency had rubbed off on him.

I led the admiral into their bedroom and left Ramesh to take the famous historian into the boys' smelly hovel.

"Thanks for agreeing to this," I said, as I closed the door behind us and he took a seat on the red wooden chest in the bay window.

"I don't see that I had much choice." He was even grumpier than his teenage son.

The bed was unmade and there were pyjamas, underwear and various books laid out upon it. There was Winston Churchill's 'Triumph and Tragedy', a biography of Oliver Cromwell and a well-thumbed copy of Machiavelli's 'The Prince'.

"Not mine," Toffee explained as I moved them out of my way to sit facing him. His voice was full of snark and anger. "I'd say I'm more into fiction, but, either way, the only book I've read since I was at school is 'The Da Vinci Code'."

Seriously? 'The Da Vinci Code'?

114

You snob, I quite enjoyed it.

Focus, Izzy!

Then stop interrupting.

I got comfortable on the bed and laid down my opening gambit. "I don't think you were having an affair with Astrid Spear." I said it as much to see his reaction as anything else, but, as I spoke the words, I realised they were true.

"Thank goodness someone believes me." He sighed then and all the tension that had been building up inside him, ever since Katie had tossed the accusation of his infidelity like a hand grenade, drained away. "I'd never betray Suzanne like that."

His voice was soft, sincere. It was not the tone of a man who felt he needed to defend his actions. He was trying to prove to me how much he still loved his wife. "It may sound cheesy, but I fell in love with her the moment we met. To this day, every time I see her I feel exactly the same way." He paused as if to savour that rush of admiration for the millionth time. "How did you know it wasn't true?"

I had to think before responding. "Because everything I've heard about Astrid suggests that she wouldn't have bothered with you."

He laughed. "Thanks very much."

"Perhaps she would have done it to get one over on Suzanne, but you weren't her endgame. Astrid's world was all about money and status and, I don't want to sound rude but…" I didn't know whether I should say this, considering that the outfit I was wearing had cost about seven pounds. "You may be an admiral, who's married to a minor celebrity, but you don't have much money, do you?"

Another laugh, another cautious look. "What gave it away?"

I could have listed the evidence which, in comparison to the rest of the immaculate bunch told me all I needed to know – Kevin's games consoles being two generations behind the newest trend, the number of patches sewn onto Aidan's trousers and the fact that his wife had worn the same smart blue dress two days in a row – but I didn't think he needed to hear it.

He spoke again anyway before I had to reply. "Bertie is paying for this whole trip. He's a bit of a sucker in most ways, old Bertie, but good for a bob or two when we can't afford to keep up with his luxury lifestyle. That's why I got so angry at Penelope back there. I've been around her sort my whole life and none of them understand what it's like for people on less than half a mil a year."

I tried to put myself in his place, but it wasn't easy. "You can't be doing that badly. Suzanne gets plenty of work and the navy must pay a decent wage."

Toffee's dark, chiselled features crumpled a little as he considered his predicament. He wasn't wearing his uniform but he still looked every part the man of authority. "For a normal family, sure. We pull in a few hundred thousand each year, but that's not enough. Suzanne has invested all our money in this new show she's producing. She promised me she'd get funding for it but nothing came through and it's too late to back out now. We can barely pay the boys' school fees." He closed his eyes and shook his head like he blamed himself.

"I'm sorry. I can imagine how hard that must be for you all." I tried to look as sympathetic as I sounded. To be honest, I was too busy feeling relieved that he still hadn't thought, *hmmm, why is this nanny so good at assessing people's income whilst knowing so little about them?* and worked out who I was.

"The funny thing is, we wouldn't even be in this mess if it weren't for our so-called friends. Rupert convinced Suzanne that she simply had to send the boys to the best school in the county, with a thirty grand a year fee." His anger was mounting with each new complaint on the lengthy list in his head. "When we were buying a house, we couldn't possibly live far away from the others so, before we even had kids, we were up to our bloody scalps in debt and, I can tell you, having two sons these days does not come cheap."

He let out a despondent cry. "I shouldn't take it out on the boys. It's hard enough at home with us arguing over money all the time. Kevin puts his bloody headphones on and hides away from the world and Suzanne says Aidan is too young to be bothered by it but I can see how much he suffers, poor kid."

I kept wanting to say something to make him feel better but, by the time I'd thought of it, he'd moved the conversation on again.

"You know, the worst part of it all is that what I told you is true; I adore my wife. Most people who've been married as long as we have can't stand one another. I might say that the boys have it bad, but imagine being Justine with crazy Astrid and paranoid Grantham always watching over her. Theirs was not a happy home, I can tell you."

I shuffled on the mattress a little and I suppose he read it as disapproval because he suddenly backtracked.

"I'm not saying it's better that she's dead or anything. I promise I'm not." His gaze was intense and I could tell he needed me to believe him. "I just think the wretched woman should have divorced the guy years ago and they'd all have been better off."

His rant over, I hoped he'd feel better and I finally had something to contribute to the conversation. "So why did Katie think you were having an affair?"

He picked up a cuddly snowman from the windowsill. "I have to admit, Astrid did flirt with me. I never took it seriously though. She was a nasty piece of work that woman and got a kick out of seeing me squirm."

"What about Suzanne? What did she think about it? Your friends had noticed what was going on so I imagine she had too."

He looked back up at the ceiling and gave a barely perceptible shake of the head. "Of course she had, Grantham too. But that was all part of the fun for Astrid. She was killing three birds with one stone." He fell silent, his strong hands closing tighter on the fluffy white toy.

"Did you talk to Suzanne about it? Have you denied that anything happened since Katie made her accusation?"

His eyes turned back in my direction but they were hazy and unfocussed. "I couldn't. I tried to, I honestly did, but I've never been good with words. Never had the courage to confront risk either."

It was my turn to laugh. "But you've been in the navy for decades and led troops of sailors. Surely you've been in dangerous situations and done valiant deeds?"

His mouth opened a little, like he was waiting for an answer to slide out. When it did, his voice was cold and uncertain. "That's different. At work, I've always felt as if I was acting the heroic leader and it came easily. There are rules and structures to fall back on in the navy but in family life…"

Perhaps it was stupid of me, but I genuinely felt sorry for him. He was a man with a perfectly good life and a family he loved, who simply couldn't find the right balance to be happy anymore.

Yeah, you're stupid! Stop falling for his sensitive but strong act. He was clearly tupping Astrid and did away with her when she threatened to tell his wife.

Thanks for your input. Also, why do people keep saying "tupping"?

I cued up my next question. "I'm sorry to ask you this, but who do you think killed Astrid?"

Any life that was left in his face disappeared. "Whoever she did the most damage to, I guess. I'm not going to say she was evil. She never killed anyone of course, but she lived her life without a care for who she hurt. Find which one of us truly resented her and you'll have your culprit." He thought for a moment, then smiled hesitantly, as if his words had been an immense effort to deliver. "Yes, that's it. Find the person who truly despised her."

Chapter Sixteen

I left Admiral Winters looking out of the window at the dying light. It was barely lunchtime but the sky had clouded over and we would not see the sun again that day.

"So what did you find out from Suzanne?" I asked Ramesh once I'd extracted him from the boys' room.

He looked both ways to check there was no one listening. "She told me that my Christmas cake was the best she's ever eaten." His silly grin spread across his silly face. It curled up the ends of his Freddie Mercury moustache which he'd been promising to shave off for weeks. "How good is that? My very first Christmas cake and it's the best she's ever had."

"About the case, Ra!" I pursed my lips together and wrinkled my nose. "What did you find out about the dead woman in the snow?"

"Why would I have asked her about that?" He sounded like the very idea was ridiculous. "You told me to have a chat with her!"

I let out a weary groan. "So you didn't discover anything that could be useful?"

"Nope." He sounded quite proud.

"You don't even have an inkling of what Suzanne might know or what I should ask her?"

He bowed his head gallantly. "That's right. We mainly talked about my 'Downton Abbey' erotic fan fiction. I have to say, she sounded very interested in what the Dowager Countess got up to in my last story."

I took a deep breath. It had already been a long day. "Great. So you weren't any help whatsoever."

He took my hands in his. "On the contrary, good lady. On the contrary." Wiggling his eyebrows at me, he attempted a wise expression but ended up looking like a hammy stage magician. "I've lulled her into a false sense of security so that you can go in there and extract all the facts you need."

"Really, Ramesh," I began. "Sometimes I think-

"No, Sally Starmer." He held one hand up to stop me. "You don't have to thank me. But I'd better be getting on with lunch, so I must run." With a full bow this time, Ramesh retreated downstairs.

I knocked on the door to the children's room. It was red with golden stars all over and had a large Father Christmas head painted on the centre. It reminded me once more how much nine-year-old Izzy would have loved this place. It was the ideal, cosy Christmas holiday destination (except for the crazed killer).

"Come in, Sally," Suzanne replied and I pushed on Santa's nose.

I was about to start in on my questions when a feeling of tiredness came over me. "Do you know what?" I asked her. "I really fancy a hot chocolate. Shall we see what's in the kitchen?"

She smiled in reply. "Not just a pretty face, are you, Sally?"

Pretty? Us? Oh you do jest. But please continue cos we like it!

The kitchen in her family's chalet was the only tidy room in the house. I had to assume this was because no one had actually set foot in it. Like all the facilities in the holiday village, the cupboards were well stocked. There were all sorts of pre-packaged goodies with fancy labels and the fridge had enough food in it for a month, barely any of which would be used. Suzanne sat on a stool beside the breakfast bar, which had its own miniature Christmas tree, and I fished out a tin of hot chocolate and a packet of marshmallows.

"Boys!" she yelled as soon as I'd got the milk warmed up on the stove. "You'd better get in here now if you want hot chocolate as I can't promise I'll be sober enough to make any for the rest of the holiday." I may have looked a little concerned then but she quickly explained, "I'm not actually an alcoholic, it's just an on-running joke we have in the family."

Aidan and Kevin zoomed in to claim their prize and I dished out lashings of the delicious brown nectar for them. "Hey, look at this," I said as I grabbed two wooden skewers from the drawer, and speared a couple of giant marshmallows. The boys observed the process, reserving judgement on whether it was actually of any interest to them.

"You take the marshmallow. You take the skewer," I explained, in a vaguely Dracula-ish accent for some reason, then spun to the counter beside the fridge where an inevitably red appliance awaited. "You turn the toaster on full power, and you wait for the gooey deliciousness to begin."

The three of us were transfixed by the slowly morphing chunk of pink sugary mess which I held over the toaster. When it was clear that the marshmallows would slide off into the flaming jaws of death, I plopped the first one into Aidan's mug.

"Brilliant," he cooed and I noticed his mother watching her sons with pride as he scampered back to the lounge.

"Thanks, Sally," his big brother said when his drink was served up. He blew his floppy fringe from off his face. "That's pretty cool."

I took advantage of the moment to pump him for information. "I don't suppose you know anything about what happened to Astrid, do you Kevin?"

He looked nervous, poor thing, but then his mother encouraged him to answer. "You're not in any trouble darling, but you should share with us anything you know."

He did it! He's the killer! It has to be him. He spends all day long murdering creatures in his video games, what's to stop him knocking someone off in real life?

What absolute nonsense. So you're saying that every kid who plays on their computer is a killer in training?

Yes, I am!

I performed a slow clap in my head to celebrate this next-level reasoning.

Kevin still looked uncertain as he delivered his response. "I know that she wasn't very nice to Justine." His voice faltered for a moment but then he found what he wanted to say. "And Mum said that she was having an affair with someone."

Suzanne was flustered by this and quickly corrected him. "Yes, but that's all sorted out now. I think I got it wrong."

Kevin looked up at me through his large brown, Disney-style eyes. "You should talk to Justine about it. She'd know more than me." He paused once more and a shy smile crossed his face at the very mention of his girlfriend, who was still asleep in the lounge. "I'm sorry I don't know anything more."

"That's alright." I winked at him for some reason. "Enjoy the melty marshmallows!"

The sixteen-year-old gave a little laugh and wandered out, but not before his mother could plant a quick kiss on the top of his head. He managed to look both embarrassed and appreciative at the same time.

"You're really good with kids," she told me. "Did you always know you wanted to be a nanny?"

I thought about the best way to lie in reply. "Urmmm, yeah. Since I was about twelve and I read a bunch of books about… nannying."

Good plan. Always mix an element of truth in with the lie!

She looked puzzled. "About nannying? I don't think I've come across any kids' books like that."

Quick, Izzy! MARY POPPINS!

"I mean, since I read Mary Poppins."

Thanks, brain. That was fast thinking.

She still didn't look convinced. "You read Mary Poppins when you were twelve?"

Damn it, brain!

I scrambled for an answer. "Well… yeah. But they're much darker than you'd imagine from the film. There's some pretty scary stuff in there actually." I made an awkward laugh and changed the subject. "Anyway, enough about me. What about you? Do you really not think that Astrid and your husband were having an affair?"

The silence that followed was excruciating. Whatever Ramesh might theoretically have done to relax her had immediately been reversed. She was like a cat with her hackles up and she narrowed her eyes to reassess me.

"I admit that I wasn't comfortable with how she acted around Toffee, but then you have to understand that the two of us have always been very competitive." Something about the way she phrased this made me wonder whether I wasn't the only one mixing truth and lies.

"You didn't answer my question." I'd started out tough on her and there was no going back now. "Katie suggested that your husband was having an affair with Astrid because of the way your deceased friend used to flirt with him. And Grantham was so convinced that Toffee and Astrid were an item that he would have shot him if I hadn't fallen… I mean, stepped in to defuse the situation. So, tell me, do you think that your husband was having an affair?"

She extracted her fingers from the handle of her mug and plucked up a marshmallow from the counter which she proceeded to decapitate with a snap of her jaws. "The thought had crossed my mind. Toffee has to travel a lot for his job and I noticed once that he and Astrid were both away at the same time, but it was nothing. I checked with his secretary and he was at a function several thousand miles away from where Astrid had flown for business. I felt stupid for even considering such a thing." Her voice had dropped lower as she was speaking but rose once more when she followed up with, "My husband loves me very much."

I could see from her answer that my suspicions had been correct. Even if the affair never happened, the very idea of it would have been enough for her to seek revenge. "Tell me about the rivalry between you and Astrid. How did it come about in the first place?"

I put the ingredients away and took a sip of my drink. It was pure, sweet and delicious.

There are wine competitions and beer festivals, why on earth doesn't hot chocolate get the love it deserves? It's chocolate... that you can drink!

Suzanne's feline attitude was still engaged. She watched me the whole time and didn't speak again until I'd sat down on the stool in front of her.

"We were at university together. Katie, Astrid and I were inseparable – best of friends in fact. But in the second term of our first year, we started hanging out with three boys from another dorm. One wanted to go into the police, one claimed he was going to be a millionaire and the other came from a long line of high-ranking navy officers." She smiled then and pulled the warm mug into her for comfort. "It sounds like a joke, doesn't it? A policeman, an admiral and a stockbroker."

Or a murder mystery plot.

I said nothing and she continued. "It was clear from the beginning that these were *our* boys. Something about the way we interacted from the first night we met meant we were fused together." She blew on her drink and her eyes shone like she was attempting to outdo the fairy lights on the tree. "Astrid was the most outgoing of the lot of us and told the big Scottish policeman that he would be hers. Well, that wasn't Howard's style at all and, for all his brawn and macho looks, he was terrified. So Astrid moved on to the next best thing."

"Grantham."

She rolled her eyes, unimpressed with my skills of deduction. "No, of course not. Grantham has only ever been a hanger-on, a bandwagon jumper at very best. When Howard wasn't interested, Astrid went after Toffee. If she couldn't have a policeman, then a sailor would have to do, but this time she was clever about it. She didn't let on to the rest of us. She pretended she was still hung up on Howard – which is the story Katie believes to this day. Astrid knew I'd started seeing Toffee myself and so she didn't say a word but, the whole second year of uni, she was plotting to get him. Or rather, she was plotting to turn him against me."

She paused and glanced down at the little tree as its lights pulsated in frenetic waves. "What she didn't reckon on though was that my sailor boy loved me. He loved me from the very first moment and wouldn't hear a word against me. So no matter what Astrid did – no matter how much money she planned to make, or how sexy she was – she couldn't compete with the mousy bookworm who was less popular, less pretty and less duplicitous than her."

I remembered something that Penelope had told me. "Is that why you changed degree? To put some distance between you?"

Suzanne brushed a hand down her thick blue sweater dress like she was trying to get rid of an invisible stain. "Far from it. I loved our little competition. I loved every last tactic and technique she came up with. If anything, the rivalry between us pushed me towards studying the history of war. There's nothing quite so revealing than trying to wrap your head around the concept of murder on a massive scale. In our own ways, Astrid and I both studied to become warriors – it's what we excelled at."

Her voice had become oddly distant. There was a clinical manner to her which I hadn't witnessed before.

My skin prickled as I formed my next question. "Why are you telling me this?"

She leaned over the counter, like she wanted to tell me a secret. "Because I want you to know that I was fully capable of killing Astrid Spear, but the right moment never presented itself." Her motherly sweetness had disappeared and she gripped onto me with a cold stare. "If I'd found out she'd even touched the man who belonged to me, I would have cut the life out of her."

My whole body tensed up. For all the time I'd spent with murderers over the last year, no one had ever told me outright that they were capable of killing. But Suzanne had more than just an academic interest in death. She hadn't spent the last twenty years studying wars and battlefields to understand the past, but the lengths that people will go to in order to achieve their goals.

"So that's how far you'd go to fulfil your ambitions is it?" I asked, my thoughts becoming manifest. "That's what you would have done to get even with the woman that you were at war with?"

Her smile was pure hunger then. It was positively bloodthirsty. "Exactly. Only I didn't have to, as someone got there first."

A chill ran through me and I must have shivered because she started to laugh and, as I rolled my shoulders to push the feeling away, she leaned back in her seat. "Oh, Sally, you're just too easy to wind up. But I had you going there, didn't I?"

Chapter Seventeen

I ran outside and collapsed into a virgin patch of snow to cool down. Lying on my back looking up at the darkening sky, I was still shaking from the way she'd spoken to me.

Had I just found the killer? Though she'd claimed to be joking, I'd looked her dead in the eye as she'd confessed what she was capable of. Had Suzanne Winters despatched her long-time rival?

I'd seen people deny such things plenty of times. Cold-blooded killers had told me as plain as day that they could never hurt another human being and, at first, I'd been sucked in, but I was seriously struggling to understand how Suzanne could have described her savage nature and not meant it.

It could be her. Plenty of killers have boasted about their kills. Maybe she fell for little Sally Starmer's innocent act and thought she could get away with it.

Even as the cold seeped through my snowsuit, my whole body was ablaze. My heart beat so loudly I thought it was thundering out of the village sound system and my nerves were jittering along in time with the music. It was the perfect time to get a call from Mum.

My phone buzzed in my pocket and I unzipped two different layers to get to it.

"Darling?" The video call was framed by rows of lightbulbs on the dressing room mirror behind her. "Is everything okay? You appear to be lying down on the floor."

"Fine thanks, Mum. Just tickety-boo really. What about you?"

She was wearing the contents of a fruit bowl on her head and a brightly coloured dress like Carmen Miranda. "We're having a lovely time. The moonlight buffet is exquisite and your fathers have spent their whole time trying out the different swimming pools on board. It's just heavenly really."

"Hi Izzy!" Mum's hairdresser Fernando stuck his head into the shot. "We're getting ready for the next show. Your mum's been going down a storm. You should see the flowers that are thrown after every performance. It's hard to know where they even come from on a-"

"There's no time, Fernando, darling." My mother was momentarily distracted by his interruption. "Izzy must be calling us about the murder."

This made me sit up. "You called me! Wait, how do you know about the murder?" It was a stupid question. I really should have guessed.

She looked at me with a reproachful shake of the head. "Ramesh has been live texting us all day. Isn't it wonderful news about his Christmas cake?"

"Hello, Izzy!" Dad rolled into shot on a wheelie chair to look at me. "I think that the policeman chap, Howard is it? I think that he must be to blame. Remember that this whole business started with those letters to Katie."

"Who I never trusted in the first place," Mum was quick to add. "Gregory, you're not holding the phone straight."

There was some mumbling from behind the camera and my stepdad adjusted his grip.

I figured I'd canvas the lot of them whilst I had them on the phone. "What do you think, Greg? Any idea who the culprit is?"

He turned the camera around then paused for a moment before delivering his verdict. "My advice, Izzy; don't cross any of them off your suspect list too soon. It sounds like a real viper's nest there to me."

That phrase again!

It was Fernando's turn next. He didn't look at the camera as he combed a loose lock of my mother's hair back into place. "That's right. Can you actually rule out Penelope and Rupert just because they seem friendly, would gain nothing from the death and there's no evidence against them? Perhaps Astrid made fun of Penelope for only coming second in the Celebrity Hairstyle of the Year Award 2019."

"Wait, is that a real thing?" I asked, but the conversation had already moved on.

"What about the husband of the dead woman?" Mum helped out. "So what if he threw a wobbly? That could just be a cover for his terrible crime."

My father let out a mournful sigh. "It's not an easy task, is it, Izzy?"

"No, Dad. It's not. But maybe if you've got a bit of time-"

"Sorry, my angel." My mother had already turned to inspect Fernando's handiwork in the mirror. "Time is one thing we don't have a lot of. Perhaps we'll find a moment between shows, but I really must be getting on."

128

"Quite," Greg said in his usual slow, careful way and turned the camera to look at me once more. "Your father and I have discovered there's a Jacuzzi on board that we haven't tried yet. This ship is gigantic."

I tried to smile, though it probably looked like I was having a muscle spasm. "Well... Thanks for calling."

Mum obviously noticed my disappointment. "Don't be glum, sweetie. We have every confidence in you. You'll have this case cracked open in no time."

"Thanks. And good luck with your performance!"

"Merry Christmas, Izzy!" They shouted as one and then Greg and Dad spent about fifteen seconds trying to hang up and failing.

"The damn button keeps disappearing," my stepfather complained.

"Give it here." Fernando yanked the phone off them and the line went dead.

Well, that could have been more useful.

Yep. And all I can think about now is who beat Penelope to the Celebrity Hairstyle of the Year Award 2019.

As tempting as it was to lie back down (and possibly make a snow angel) I forced myself up to standing. The snow wasn't quite so light and powdery now. It was turning to ice already and I had to think about poor Astrid, face down just twenty metres from where I stood.

The skin on my lips beginning to chap, I staggered back across the square. What could I honestly say I'd learnt so far? That Suzanne was capable of murder but hadn't got round to it? That no one particularly liked Astrid except the husband who she was cheating on? Normally, my family's wild theories helped me see through all the evidence to get to the truth but it turned out long-distance assistance isn't the same as in-person help.

On the bright side, it felt good to be back in the warmth of the main chalet. I stopped in the entrance to enjoy that gorgeous scene. For a moment, I could stand there and pretend that everything was just fine. Penelope and Rupert were sitting by the fire having a cuddle, the smell of Ramesh's next meal was wafting over to me and the lights, strung around the bannisters in a candy stripe pattern twinkled prettily.

It was a perfect scene in the kind of house I dreamed of owning but in amongst all those beautiful people was a killer. Bertie was sitting at the newly laid table helping himself to the last mince pie, Howard and Katie were bringing food in from the kitchen and Grantham, his eyes red and his face still twisted in a look of tortured agony, was propping up the wall in the corner of the room.

It was time for lunch.

Once Penelope had rounded up the missing members of our party, some words needed to be said.

"Listen, Grantham." Toffee was unable to look him in the eyes. "You're one of my oldest friends and I promise I would never have betrayed you..." He paused to find the right expression. "...the way you think that I did."

Having taken his place at the table, Grantham scoffed in reply.

"I don't know what to say to make you believe me." The admiral finally looked at his friend dead on. "But you know how much I love Suzanne. You know that I have been a good friend to you and that I've always tried to support you through hard times. So, I'm asking for you to trust me now."

Everyone at that table was watching for Grantham's reaction. He glanced down at his empty plate, as if counting the silver stars around its rim, but said nothing.

The silence clung there uncomfortably and I could feel the tension in the air as we all willed the widower to respond.

"Who's for haggis?" Ramesh's high-pitched question broke the mood in two and he would probably have stopped and realised how bad his timing was, but was apparently past caring. "Come on, everyone. Eat up or it will get cold!"

Howard's eyes had grown to the size of the plate of sheep's stomachs that had been placed in front of him. "It's just like my grandma used to make."

No one else seemed quite so excited about the promise of Scotland's national dish.

"Aren't you supposed to eat it with a dram of whisky?" Bertie asked. "Perhaps it would make the whole thing seem a bit more... palatable."

Howard's positivity would not be shaken. "Don't knock it until you've tried it, man." He was already up on his feet helping himself to neeps and tatties. "It's absolutely delicious. You wait and see."

I retained an open mind as I grabbed plates and dished up the balls of assorted animal parts for my fellow guests. Amelia was asleep upstairs so I was free to sit down with the others. Not that this was a comfortable experience. Few people could look at one another after the morning we'd just been through and the only person who seemed willing to make conversation was little Aidan, who was chattering away happily about all the gifts he hoped to get the following day.

Part of me wondered whether he was doing this for our sake as much as his own. He was seven years old, not a tiny infant. He must have cottoned on by now that Astrid had been murdered. I just hoped he was dealing with it well.

Justine and Kevin sat next to one another and, whenever he sensed she was feeling low, he'd rub her shoulder supportively or give her hand a squeeze. I was pleased to see how mature he could be for her sake. I guess kids are more resilient than we give them credit for.

The scraping of cutlery on the pretty porcelain plates was too much and Howard finally spoke up. "I know this isn't the holiday any of us imagined and obviously I couldn't feel worse about what happened to Astrid but I am extremely thankful to have you all here."

He looked around the table, perhaps expecting disagreement and, as none came, he continued. "When I was a kid, I never had a big Christmas celebration. I lived with my grandma and my parents were hardly ever around which is why I knew, from the time I was Aidan's age, that I'd do whatever it took to have a family of my own."

He looked across to his wife who had been quiet ever since I'd returned. "Well, this year is my first Christmas as a father and, whatever else happens, I can't wait to spend tomorrow with little Amelia and all of you." His smile right then was filled with sadness and his eyes locked onto Katie's. "I love you darling and I always will."

She was crying before he'd finished the sentence. They weren't sentimental tears but full on sobs. The longer she cried, the louder she got and, before long, she lurched up from her chair and ran from the room.

"What was that?" Suzanne said angrily to Howard. "Our oldest friend has been murdered and you're banging on about family and Christmas? How did you expect her to react?"

"I'm sorry, I…" Howard looked traumatised and I again had to wonder how his wife could have been so convinced that that this soft, sensitive chap was the one who'd been threatening her. If there was a reservoir of darkness beneath his sunny exterior I was yet to discover it.

"We'll go," Penelope said, surprising me by grabbing my arm to pull me towards the dining room as she walked past.

"Oh good, Sherlock and Watson are on the case." Suzanne's deep brown eyes shot daggers at us over the heads of her loved ones. "I'll sleep sweetly in my bed tonight knowing that our guardians are here to protect us."

"Don't start, Suzie," Rupert said, as his wife opened the door to leave. "You don't want more enemies than you already have."

The professor was quick to anger and snapped straight back. "What's that supposed to mean?"

I didn't hear the answer because the door closed behind us and I was back in the cosy dining room with its log fire still blazing. Katie had curled up in an armchair and was staring into space, her eyes glassy and still.

Penelope knelt down in front of her. "How many people have to tell you before you listen, my darling Katie?" She spoke tenderly and I believe she really cared about the poor woman. "You need help. You haven't been the same since Amelia was born."

Katie didn't reply so Penelope put one hand on the side of her face and continued. "No one's saying you're a bad mother or a bad person but you're clearly depressed. I know that Christmas Eve may not be the day to deal with such things, but there's no reason to feel ashamed. It's entirely natural. Especially after everything you've been through."

"I don't want to talk about it." Katie slumped deeper in her chair.

I'd been hanging back from them both, unsure what part I should play, but finally decided that, as Penelope wanted me there, I would try to help. I sat cross-legged on the floor and said the only thing I could think of to make her feel better.

"I had a friend at university who suffered from depression. In my second year there, Amanda and I did everything together but some days she simply couldn't function. I'd knock on her door and she wouldn't answer. I knew she was in there but she couldn't engage with the world until the cloud had passed and she was back to her bubbly self."

I hadn't thought about Amanda for a long time and the memories pricked at me. "I begged her to get help but she said she didn't have the energy to do anything about it. So I know how hard it must be for you to take the next steps but you have to try to focus on the positives. You have your incredible daughter and Howard, who I honestly do think adores you."

Penelope took her sister-in-law's hand and then reached out for mine. "And you have people who will support you all the way through it. Depression is nothing to be embarrassed about. It's just an illness like tendonitis or tonsillitis or any other -itis that I can't think of right now." She laughed and some tiny fragment of light must have got through to Katie.

She opened her mouth and for a very long moment, it seemed like her words wouldn't come. "I wish I could do something about it." Her voice died away but then surged back to life stronger than before. "For Amelia's sake more than anyone... but I swear I don't have it in me."

She breathed in and back out again like it was the most difficult thing she'd ever achieved. "My daughter is so good, so pure and sweet, but when I'm with her I feel like I'm the last thing she needs. Every time she laughs it makes me wonder how much happier she could be with a better mother."

"There is no better mother for her." Moving closer, Penelope spoke to her sister-in-law with firm conviction. I realised that it was rather stupid that I was there but neither of Katie's brothers had come in to support her.

"We'll help you," I said and I took her hand to complete the circle. "I mean it. I don't know you well, but if there's anything I can do to make it easier, you can count on me." Penelope squeezed my hand and I felt strong for a second. I just hoped we could do the same for Katie. "I'll take you to the doctor and I'll say, 'Doctor, this woman is suffering from a clear case of post-natal depression,' and he'll say, 'Well, that's bloody dreadful. She'll need to do this, this and this and, over time she'll start to feel a hell of a lot better.'"

I'd put a Dracula-ish voice on for the doctor for some reason and a smile cracked on the poor woman's face.

"I can't just say yes. I can't. It's not that simple. I wake up in the morning and wish I was still asleep. I see my beautiful baby and she coos and sings for me and all I feel is empty inside." This time her slowly exhaled breath became a frustrated moan and she looked at Penelope. "But I will. I'll do it for her. I'll do whatever you tell me if it means I get to smile with Amelia each time she's happy."

Penelope was the one crying now and, okay, I admit, she totally set me off. After another thirty seconds of 'It's a Wonderful Life' level tears, it was Katie who had to comfort us.

"Don't cry, little ones," she said, though she couldn't have been more than ten years older than either of us. She leaned forward in her chair and rested her head against Penelope's then pulled me in to do the same. It was a weird pyramid of sorrow and relief and we might have stayed there forever if Katie hadn't started laughing.

"Aren't we ridiculous? It's supposed to be Christmas. Ho ho ho and joy to mankind and all that stuff." We pulled back to look at her and, somehow our roles had switched. She was the sensible grown up now and we were two silly kids crying our eyes out. "Let's get back in that room and show them that we Gravely-Swans and Starmer-Palmers are made of stronger stuff than this."

We were smiling like loons by now but there was something I needed to do first. "Penelope, you go back in. Katie and I will join you in a minute."

She wiped her eyes on her checked sleeve and nodded before doing as I'd requested. Katie and I stood up too and waited until we were alone.

"Katie," I began and then hesitated as I didn't want to be too blunt, "do you still believe that Howard was responsible for the letters?"

She walked a few steps to warm herself by the fire. "I thought you might ask that." The positivity she'd found moments earlier seemed to hide away again. "I don't know what I believe anymore. Howard promises me it wasn't him and I know I haven't been myself, so... perhaps I was wrong."

"That's okay." I waited for a moment to show that I didn't blame her. "But, can I ask what made you think he'd be capable of something like that? I haven't seen him be anything but kind and supportive to you. But you can tell me if I've got it wrong."

She put her hands out in front of her to enjoy the warmth. "I thought he was trying to control me. He was always asking me questions and checking where I was and... Then, when the letter turned up, it just seemed to make sense. All these little coincidences piled up and I really believed that he was having me followed. I saw the same type of people wherever I went – men with long black coats and black umbrellas. I know it probably sounds stupid to you…" She didn't finish that thought.

I remembered what my friend Amanda told me had helped most when she was having an episode. She said that having someone to talk to who understands where you're coming from can make the cloud seem lighter, so that's who I tried to be.

"It doesn't sound stupid. You've been through a lot. Maybe you were right about Howard, but I hope for Amelia's sake that you weren't. I hope it was just a series of unfortunate coincidences and we'll find out who sent you those messages and who killed Astrid."

"Do you mean that you think it could be different people?" she asked, turning her mind to the mystery at hand.

I let her words sink in before replying. "I think that might make sense but…" It was my turn to leave things unsaid.

"Well, either way, I hope you're right and it's got nothing to do with Howard." A half smile shaped her face and, in a whisper, she told me, "I'm glad you're here, Izzy. Whatever else happens, you've done your job and made me feel safer."

"Come on," I said and held my hand out to her. "Let's get some of that haggis,"

We walked back into the lounge together and people tried not to stare as we returned to the table and Katie gave her husband a kiss on the cheek.

Chapter Eighteen

"We're not going to sit here and play charades like everything is okay!"

We'd finished lunch and everyone was sitting on the sofas, wondering what came next. To be honest, things were following the typical pattern of my Christmas whenever we spent time with Mum's side of the family. Big breakfast, big lunch and then a big argument to follow it up.

And while my Uncle Bradley and Cousin Axel like to argue about Brexit and their divided love of Manchester City and Manchester United, we were arguing about charades.

"What else are we going to do?" Howard said, staring at Toffee like he was being entirely unreasonable. "We're trapped here until someone comes to dig us out, or the snow melts. Astrid's been murdered, one of us is the killer and it's down to the nanny to investigate. So tell me, Toffee, what's wrong with charades?"

It was the first time I'd seen Howard really worked up and, when his question had faded out, silence reigned once more. I was sitting in one of the huge, comfy armchairs – like Father Christmas's throne – but Amelia had woken from her nap and there was a smell emanating from her that was far from the cinnamon and cloves I normally associate with this festive time of year.

"Urmmm… Howard?" I looked over at him, my head twitching in his infant daughter's direction. "Nappy changing time."

He seemed happy to escape the conversation. "Sorry, Sally, I should have thought." Shaking his head like he was a very silly daddy indeed, he stood up and walked straight past me, without taking Amelia from my knees. He returned a minute later with a changing bag. "There you go."

Until then, her parents had done the duty each time but the dark reality had dawned on me that changing smelly nappies must be part of a nanny's job.

This is terrible! You never saw that in Mary Poppins!

It can't be that bad.

I bet it is! I bet it's the worst thing in human history. So, just tell them who you are and get out of it. Sally Starmer might have to change nappies but Izzy Palmer doesn't.

Ignoring my brain's very tempting idea, I shook my head like I was a very silly nanny indeed. "No trouble. I'll just go and do that."

Not knowing what else to do, I headed towards the kitchen for some moral support.

"Umm? Sally?" Penelope looked horrified. "Where are you going?"

I searched for an explanation. "It's an old nannying trick actually. Kitchens have all the most important facilities of a bathroom but plenty more open space."

Lady Penelope shot me a look which said, *but that's where we make food!* So I pretended I hadn't noticed and pushed through the swingy door to Ramesh's hideout.

"No time to talk, Sal!" He was racing about the place, closing drawers and opening ovens. Steam filled the air and he appeared to be doing the job of a whole kitchen crew. It's funny that he's never efficient like that when helping me with my cases. "I've got the main meal cooking for this evening, the veg all peeled and washed and dessert is on its way."

Until this moment, he hadn't taken the time to look at me but, when he did, he came to a total standstill. "Baaaaaaaaaaaaaaby!" He threw a slotted spoon into the sink and ran over to pinch Amelia's cheeks and rub her little red head. "Can I have it?" He looked up at me pleadingly.

"I think you mean, 'Can I hold her?' Right?"

"That's the one." By this point, he only had eyes for Amelia and he whisked her across the room to sit down by the kitchen's own blazing fire. "Ooh, someone's a smelly girl."

"That's why I came in here. I don't suppose you know how to operate one of these things?" I pulled out a nappy from the bag.

There was a sparkling silver table in the middle of the room that would be perfect for what we needed. I got the changing mat out, put it in place and Ramesh revealed another hidden skill.

"It's really not that difficult. I have to change my nieces and nephews whenever I visit my family." He paused to reflect on this. "Though, now that I think about it, this may be one of the reasons I don't go home very often."

I extracted a wet wipe to clean Amelia and Ramesh prepared for the operation.

"Right, you remove the dirty nappy," he said, as he tossed the offending article in the stainless steel bin. "Take the wet wipe, clean up the mess, slip the fresh nappy under the little baby dumpling…" He got distracted at this point and made cutesy faces at Amelia, who laughed angelically in reply. "You pull the tabs over, push them closed and bish bash bosh, the baby's as good as new."

Isn't it weird that so few murder mysteries take a break in the middle to explain how to change nappies?

He picked up the adorable creature and cradled her in his arms. Amelia reached out to grab his moustache like it was one of the toys hanging above her crib.

"That wasn't too difficult, after all." I sounded surprised and he looked at me with a puckered brow.

"What did you expect, Izzy? An extra set of teeth down there? Poison pins?"

I changed the subject. "She's just the best baby ever, isn't she?"

"Yes she is." He made another funny face. "She absolutely is. I could eat her up!" His soppy expression disappeared and he handed her back to me. "But now I'm busy and you have a murder to solve."

I wasn't paying any attention because I was looking at the hearth again. "Ramesh? Who started the fire? Everywhere I've gone today, there've been bright burning fires ablaze. They can't have lit themselves."

"Oh some woman," he said disinterestedly and went back to his cooking.

"What woman?"

"I don't know, Sally, Izzy, whatever your name is. There was some old woman in here this morning. She told me to add wood to it whenever it dies down. I got big Bertie to look after the others."

"You mean there's someone here we don't know? A worker from the resort or something?"

He was doing an impressive job of chopping up a carrot into tiny slivers with very neat, repetitive cuts, like a well-programmed robot. "Something like that." He picked up a second carrot and waved it at me angrily. "Really, Sal, I have to get on, take your little ball of cuteness away with you and stop coming in here unless you're planning to help."

I was going to hand Amelia back to her parents but they were no longer in the lounge. So, I told the others I was popping outside, took the baby carrier again and strapped my cheery companion to my chest.

It had just gone three o'clock but the sun was already obscured by the mountaintops. The many thousand fairy lights, wound around fences, trees, buildings and signs would pick up the slack though. As I strolled through the snow with my very own borrowed child to keep me company – her blissful coos the perfect soundtrack – it really was like walking in a winter wonderland.

First we headed to the North Pole to look for help, but Santa's workshop, the elves' factory and the grotto itself were quiet and dark.

"Now what?" I asked Amelia.

In reply, she said, "What about that little lodge building we passed when we drove in here yesterday? Maybe someone lives there."

Well, okay, she didn't actually say that. In fact, it was me doing a silly voice, but she certainly didn't object to the idea so we set off towards the park entrance.

Through the village square and past the houses we went. There was no sign of life in the car park, or any cars for that matter, and we soon arrived at the outer fence of the resort. We heard the growling rev of an engine before we saw anyone and then a snowmobile sped out from behind the trees. Pulling to a stop in front of us, like some scary biker in a movie, I saw an old lady I recognised.

"Aggie?" I asked, face to face once more with our chauffeur from the day before.

"Nae, Maggie!" The woman explained. "Aggie's ma sister!" She looked at me suspiciously for a moment. "I dinnae suppose ye had anything to dae wi' thon dead body I just found up by the woodshed? It's a terrible thing to go killing people, ye know?"

I didn't take her accusation too personally. "It wasn't me. I'm the one trying to work out who killed her."

"Fair enough." She appeared to accept the explanation at face value.

"I'd feel a lot better if night wasn't about to set in though. There are kids back in the village and I'd rather not be trapped here with a murderer."

"Aye, I cannae say I blame ye." She was incredibly calm about the whole thing, as she pulled a pipe from her pocket and began to chew on the end. It crossed my mind that, if worst came to worst and the killer turned violent again, we could hide with this fierce, bright-eyed old lady and she'd protect us.

"The police said it will take days to get up here." I hoped this might spur her into action.

"Aye, but who did ye talk to?" She squinted one eye as if to work out this conundrum. "Was it Arnie? He's nae the brightest bulb in the Hogg family."

"Yeah. That's right, Arnie."

She huffed out a sound which filled the air between us with fog. "Well, he mebbe ma son, but he doesnae know his elbow from a Christmas tree. Ye shoulda asked for Artie, he's the smart one."

"Do ye think…" I found myself copying her accent so I cleared my throat and started over. "Do you think that it's worth ringing him now?"

She looked down the mountain road towards the loch and, hidden somewhere beyond that, the little town we'd passed on our journey. "Well… I'm nae sure that's such a clever idea. It's Christmas Eve, lass. Artie'll be home wi' the wee ones. Ye'd only get Andy if ye rung now and, Andy's dumber than Arnie."

The hope I'd had of being rescued was fading, until good old Maggie took pity on me. "I tell ye what. I'll race down the station and gie the lazy beggars a clip round the ears. Alfie has one o' them snowplough thingummyjigs. That should do the job in no time."

"Aye, that'd be greeet!" I yelled with joy. I'm pretty sure my voice had gone full Mel Gibson in Braveheart by this point. My only saving grace was that I didn't put my arm in the air and scream *Freeeeeeeeeeeeeedom!*

She looked sideways at me but said nothing as she revved the engine to shoot off down the snowy mountainside. Amelia and I watched her go. The blinding lights on the 'Santa's Glen Christmas Village' sign picked her out until she was little more than a speck and we turned to head back home.

"There you go," I told my favourite little bub. "Everything will be sorted before you know it." I knew whose benefit I was saying this for and it wasn't Amelia's.

Chapter Nineteen

"I don't even like charades," Toffee was saying back in the main chalet. This was just the sort of argument my extended family has. It had been going on all afternoon, neither side had a clear advantage and the games that would follow it would only make things worse.

"Let's play something different then." Howard's positivity had returned.

"What about Trivial Pursuit?" Suzanne suggested and I saw that hunger in her eyes again. "Us Winters would wipe the floor with the rest of you, especially in history, culture, geography and arts. In fact anything but sport and we'll be fine."

"That's fighting talk." Howard was clearly warming to the idea.

Suzanne wanted to prove her point and turned to her sons. "Kevin, who said, 'Any man who tries to be good all the time is bound to come to ruin.'" The teenager looked fed up and pulled his still red-eyed girlfriend closer to him on the sofa. "I don't care."

"Aidan?" As much as he wanted to please his mother, little Aidan simply didn't know the answer so she gave him a clue. "It's from 'The Prince'?"

"Was it…" Her younger son struggled to think up the answer. "Saint Exupéry?"

His big brother was happy to set him straight. "That was 'The Little Prince' dummy. Machiavelli wrote 'The Prince'. It's a political treatise which justifies immoral means for achieving one's goals – not a kids' book."

"You see what I mean?" their mother replied, looking at her sons adoringly before turning to Howard again with a snarl. "We'll destroy the lot of you."

"We don't have Trivial Pursuit, I'm afraid," Bertie informed us from over by the games cupboard. "There's Hungry Hungry Hippos though? I'm rather good at Hungry Hungry Hippos."

"I bet you are," Toffee scoffed.

I watched Bertie's reaction but he didn't seem too concerned and laughed off the insult. "Ha, good one, Toffee. You always were a bit of a wag." He gripped his tummy then and shook it like a body-positive

Father Christmas.

"We could have a multi-player game of 'Zombie Death Squad IV'." Kevin had a mix of hope and antagonism on his face.

"It's Christmas," Howard replied. "We're not here to kill zombies."

"You don't have to kill zombies. ZDSIV is great because you get to be the zombies. You have to eat as many brains as possible before the world explodes. It's hilarious."

Howard was looking increasingly desperate. "Please, can't we all just play charades? Everyone loves charades."

"I don't," Suzanne crossed one leg over her knee and looked as bored as her teenage son. "I hate charades, I thought everyone did."

"For goodness sake, all I wanted to do was play a game." I could see that Howard was getting dangerously close to storming out of the chalet and locking himself away for the rest of Christmas – which is just what my cousin Axel does each year.

I thought I'd better intervene. "Hey, Howard. The Christmas lights have turned on outside, shall we go for a walk through the crystal trail with Amelia?"

He said nothing in reply but nodded. A beleaguered expression languished on his face.

I didn't want to sound like I was trying to steal him from his wife, so I quickly followed the question up with, "Katie, what about you?"

"You go on without me," she said rather sleepily. "I think I'll stay by the fire."

"Anyone else?" Howard was still agitated and presumably not expecting much in reply.

A chorus of "Nooooo," and "Too cold!" struck up.

Amelia gurgled a goodbye to her mother and it was her dad's turn to carry her. We got ready to once more embrace the sub-zero temperatures outside.

Izzy, you do realise that you're about to go out into the cold, lonely woods with a man who could be a killer?

Nah, not Howard. I'm telling you one hundred per cent that it's not him.

Where's your evidence?

Urmmm… he has funny hair and sings Christmas carols? And besides, Baby Amelia will be there to keep me safe.

"Thanks for saving me," Howard said once we'd left the village behind and started on the trail through the forest. "I'm just trying to make the best of a bad situation but no one seems to care about that except for me."

It wasn't an entirely selfless act. I had a whole bunch of questions for Chief Superintendent Howard and it would have been difficult to get him on his own otherwise.

"I don't know what's wrong with them all. I love Christmas." I tried to find the exact words to explain what the season meant to me. "I mean, I **LOVE** Christmas. Which is probably why I was so sad that, first my boyfriend, then my parents chose to spend it without me this year."

"Ah well, we're two of a kind then."

As we got to the first chain of cut-glass decorations hanging from the trees, Amelia's little head wobbled excitedly on her shoulders. Bright lights shone on the crystals so that fragments of rainbow danced about on the snow. It was like a magical Christmas disco.

"While we're out here, do you mind if I ask you a few questions?"

"Go ahead, Sergeant," he joked and then had second thoughts. "Well, so long as Amelia promises not to share my secrets with anyone."

His smile instantly returned and I reflected that I'd never met a police officer who was anything like him.

I prepared my first question. "I need to ask you about your wife. I know she's been suffering from depression but I don't think it started with the pregnancy, did it? I'm pretty sure she was having problems before that already."

He looked at me sternly and I could tell his professional persona had slipped back into gear. "To be honest, I'm not sure I want to answer that. What you and Penelope are doing could be risky and I think you'd be better off leaving it to the police."

He sounded so resolute that I didn't know what to say to change his mind, but I couldn't give up. "Please, Howard. We've come a long way already. You must know what it feels like to get so close to the truth. If only for my own understanding, please tell me what you can."

He squashed his lips up at the side of his face and I knew that he'd give in.

"Ahh, well, as long as you promise not to do anything stupid." He paused again before answering my original question. "I think you're probably right. Ever since her parents died last year, Katie's nae been herself."

He hid his sadness then by pointing up at the next set of decorations for Amelia to marvel at. When he spoke again, his voice had fallen quieter. "You should probably know that it took us a long time to have kids. We'd practically given up when this one came along." He stroked the woollen hat on his daughter's head and pulled her up a little higher in his arms. "So all those troubles wore Katie down and I guess she'd invested a lot of hope in the idea that, once she was a mother, everything would be better." He let out a sigh. "Isn't this all a bit too gloomy for a crystal forest trail?"

"Sorry," I said, then looked at Amelia and apologised again. "Sorry, baby. I'm just trying to understand what's been going on here. Can I ask you another question, Howard?"

He nodded so I continued.

"Do you think you were acting any differently this year? It's no secret that Katharine thought you were the one who'd written the death threats. Do you know why she would have come to that conclusion?"

He hugged Amelia a little more tightly. "I suppose I haven't been at my best to be honest. Katie may be the one who's depressed, but I've been suffering too."

In an attempt to disguise just how serious a conversation we were having, he took a big jump through the snow to cheer his daughter up. "Work hasn't been easy; I never imagined that leaving this wee bairn at home each day would make me feel so torn. And I guess I've been doing what I can to make sure that Katie is okay but I ended up making a mess of it. I always check how she's feeling and ask what I can do to make her feel better but I should have pushed harder for her to see a doctor. In the end I think I did more harm than good."

I paused to look at the next sculpture and find the right words. "I can't imagine it's been easy for either of you, but Katharine said she thought you were trying to control her." I let out a breath which turned into a puff of fog. "She promised Penelope that she'll get help and I think she really means it."

"I know, she told me." The look on his face was stern once more.

"I pray that she goes through with it, for all our sakes."

This was just a crescendo. I had bigger worries to address, bigger questions to ask and I'd been slowly building up to them. "Howard, how exactly did Katie's parents die?"

He was walking in slow motion through the snow and Amelia thought it was hilarious. Her laugh was as joyful as any Christmas song I knew.

Seriously? Even 'Rockin' Around the Christmas Tree'?

He shot a question right back at me. "How could that have anything to do with Astrid's death?"

"It's something that Suzanne said. Please, Howard. I need to know."

"She…" he began, before correcting himself. "There was a car accident. Katie and her family were coming back from a party and people had been drinking. They went straight into the back of another car. Her parents were killed and Katie was in hospital for weeks."

"Who was driving?" I asked a little too quickly and I knew he wouldn't answer.

"Listen, Sally. I know you're only trying to help but I think I'd rather talk about something else."

I smiled to show there were no hard feelings and searched for a more neutral topic. I should have just told him who I really was and got to the truth. Sally Starmer could only take me so far.

We'd come to the highlight of the crystal trail. A giant polar bear on skates was pirouetting on an icy rink. The snow had almost covered it, but the bear's tireless turning had cleared a window through for us to see, which made it feel even more special.

"Do you like it, baby bear?" he asked, holding his daughter up so that their eyes were level.

I let them have their moment together before starting in on my next thread. "I was going to ask you what your instincts tell you about the murder. As a police officer yourself, I mean."

He brightened up. "Oh, so this is a professional enquiry. Sergeant to Chief Super?"

"That's right." He'd made me smile. "Do you have a hunch for who it could be?"

"Huh, you know, it's strange. I haven't put too much thought into it." We walked on again as he reflected on this. "I guess that says a lot about what kind of policeman I've become. I spend more time attending meetings these days than working through evidence. Pretty sad really."

"What about if I take you through everything that Penelope and I have discovered and you give me your expert opinion?"

Both Amelia and her father seemed happy with this arrangement. "Sure, go for it. I'll do what I can."

I took a deep breath and prepared myself as we crossed an ornamental bridge over a tiny stream. The frozen water beneath shone almost as brightly as the crystals which adorned the path.

"Okay, so we know that Astrid wasn't popular. As far as I can tell, she remained friends with Suzanne and Katharine to continue their rivalry, rather than out of any affection they once shared."

He pulled his neck in and looked impressed. "Wow, you're good at this. And I'm not going to lie and say you're way off because you really are not." He sighed then and looked wearier than he had all holiday. "I prefer it when it's just my wife and her family to be honest. Whenever the friends come along, it gets too dramatic and someone always ends up having an argument."

This surprised me a little. "But you and the other husbands get on well, right?"

He raised his eyebrows contemplatively. "Well we play golf together. Does that count?" He laughed then and added, "No, we do. We get on fine."

"Right, so Katharine said that, despite everything, they're sort of like your family now so I guess that kind of explains it too. I mean, who doesn't have a love-hate relationship with their relatives?" I thought about my Uncle Bradley and allowed myself a shudder. "Astrid was making a lot of money, Suzanne is a celebrated academic and Katharine is a successful contemporary artist."

"Plus she's got a hunky Scottish husband." He looked a bit embarrassed as he said this, which made me laugh more than the joke itself.

I tried to get back on track. "Jump forward many years-"

"Hey, not so many!"

"Jump forward *many* years and you all go on holiday together, Astrid has a big argument with her daughter, some nasty words are exchanged and then, the next morning, she tries to make it up to you all with a cheery Santa routine that backfires when someone decides to jump out on her and stab her to death with… with an unknown weapon that still hasn't been discovered."

"Good recap, Sergeant. But what evidence have you got for me?" He lifted Amelia up to perch on his shoulders like she was Tiny Tim.

"Astrid was having an affair. Her husband knew about it and thought it was his old buddy Admiral Winters."

He looked almost amused by this. "Toffee? Not a chance. He's only ever had eyes for Suzanne and, I'm sorry but Astrid's flirty routine wasn't the most convincing attempt at seduction I've ever seen. It got Toffee hot under the collar but only because he was embarrassed."

"So who was she having the affair with then? That only leaves you and Bertie."

He actually laughed at me this time. "No, it doesn't. It leaves half the men in London, including every handsome young intern at her company, all the swaggering colleagues who drive Mercedes and no doubt a bunch of guys from the Paris office too. There's nothing to say that Grantham has ever heard the name of his wife's lover."

Ha, he's got you there!

"True," I reluctantly admitted. "But the fact she was having an affair could still be important. It speaks to her character at least. We know she wasn't the most loyal person around so maybe there wasn't one single factor which led to her murder but a whole bunch of them."

"I'm with you there. Has anyone told you about the way Astrid treated her family for example?"

I shook my head as I wanted to hear his spin on the topic.

"Well, last night was nothing. She was a true mum-zilla to Justine. It wasn't just that she controlled the poor lassie's schooling, she mapped out every element of her life. The last time I was at their house, I saw a massive poster on their fridge laying out Justine's timetable in fifteen-minute blocks, seven days a week. The only time the girl got to relax was when her mother drank too much wine and forgot to check what time it was. Astrid wasn't much better with Grantham either. She constantly criticised him. I hated seeing it."

A picture was forming in my head, the canvas I'd been sketching out was slowly adding layers and detail. "Okay, so maybe someone saw the way she treated her family and thought they'd do them both a favour?"

He made a noise which told me to think again. "Bit of a jump isn't it? Where's your proof?"

I stopped in front of a wall of crystals which were blowing gently in the wind, reflecting tiny points of light as we watched. "Can I call it a hunch for the moment and get back to you with the evidence?"

"You do know that's not how the police work?" One side of his mouth turned up slightly. "But I'll let you off this time."

I regrouped my thoughts. "Astrid's story is tied up with Suzanne and Katharine's – that much is sure. Penelope knows more than me but even she's struggled to make sense of all the history and competition that runs between them. I know that Katharine opted out of all that, I'm guessing that was after her parents died. Am I right?"

"Good guess."

"Okay, so what about Suzanne? She's got some pretty crazy opinions. She's an incredibly driven professor of war-studies and, from what I can tell from their reading material, has brought her sons up with a similar worldview. Plus she told me, in her own words, that she considers herself a warrior and a potential killer."

He reached out to shake the crystal waterfall for Amelia to watch the rippling patterns. "Nice work, Sergeant. I like your thought process there. Suzanne is a very charming nutter if ever there was one. But there's one thing you haven't considered. If Suzanne is a warrior, she's not exactly going to give up the battle and retire now, is she? She's in this fight to the end and killing Astrid robbed her of her greatest adversary."

I kicked my boot into the snow in frustration, happy to play up to the idea that I was a real amateur.

But that's what you are, you're an-

Don't start! At least three people have already paid me to investigate murders, which makes me a professional. It's not like I only solve crimes on a Sunday afternoon.

Fine. You say potato…

That's right. I say potato and no one on earth says puh-tár-toe!

Howard hadn't finished ripping my theory apart. "You said it yourself, Astrid and Suzanne were still friends because they love

150

battling one another. I can't see Suzanne throwing that away."

"Toffee?"

"He's a desk jockey, just like me. He's held far more pens than guns and didn't give a damn about Astrid. Why would he have bothered?"

"Bertie?"

"Was Astrid made of apple pie?"

"So then it's Grantham!" I admit that I shouted this at him. My powers of deduction were not at their peak right then. Poirot would have made a big old Gallic tut and called me *imbécile*. Miss Marple would have compared me to some tryhard from her village and even Howard didn't seem impressed.

"Haven't we already ruled him out once?"

We started walking down the final stretch of the trail. A projector hidden in the trees was shooting stars across the white blanket which covered the path.

"Go on then, who do you think did it?" I asked, hoping he'd put me out of my misery.

He stopped and looked a little preoccupied. With her head just above his, I saw the similarity between baby and father's expression right then. It was rather wonderful and I had another brief, broody urge to find out what my own child would look like.

"I think..." He seemed reluctant to deliver his verdict. "I think I'm on holiday."

"Oh, go on, Howard," I begged. "Please tell me!"

"I'm not trying to be difficult. I just don't know for sure who killed her. Okay, the girls like to play tough sometimes and Suzanne can come across as a right headcase, but I really can't say that one of them in particular is an obvious killer."

My face crumpled up in frustration and he softened his voice and told me, "If I were you I'd look more carefully at the one clue that tells us most about the murderer."

He started walking back to the village and I pumped my legs through the snow to catch up with him. "And that would be?"

He laughed again. "The letters, Sally. The death threats sent to my wife."

"But there's nothing to say that the killer sent them? They could be the ultimate red herring."

We were back in the square by now and the flashing lights, which were strung between lamp posts, shone back off the snow. "So there's a killer and a poisoned letter writer here with us? Does that sound realistic?"

"No, but since when do murder investigations have to be realistic?"

Holding Amelia firmly in one arm, he put his free hand on my shoulder. "Trust me on this. Focus on the letters; that's your path to the killer."

He squeezed my shoulder a little tighter then walked off towards the main chalet. I let him go this time and stayed outside to breathe in that beautifully fresh air and clear my head for thirty seconds before I had to plunge back into all the uncertainty and doubt of my stuttering search for the killer. I was trying to stay confident for once and not let my own insecurities hold me back.

I've solved six different murders, I told myself.

Seven including the one in the caravan.

Damn it! I've solved seven different murders and this one will be number eight. I know I can do this.

Yeah you can! You go, girl! Shoot for the moon!

In the centre of the square was a wishing well with a rather irritating light on the top that swung round in circles like a lighthouse. I turned my eyes so as not to be blinded and followed the path the beam took around the square. It reflected off the snow and the eves of the houses and then, right on the last chalet, before the light disappeared off into the forest, it showed me something I would never have noticed otherwise.

Just at the corner of the building, the ice running down from the gutter was partially snapped off. This didn't mean anything in itself, but, as I went in for a closer look, I could see that another icicle had been removed from half-way along the side of the chalet. More importantly though, there were a trail of footprints which I was pretty sure were made by a pair of size-fourteen boots.

Chapter Twenty

When we got back inside the lounge, a game had started after all.

"Charades!?" Howard sounded almost homicidal with rage on realising they'd started without him. Only joking, he was mildly cheesed off. "That's not fair, you said you hated it."

"Oh, just sit down and play, Howard. Amelia's more grown up than you sometimes, aren't you darling?" Suzanne made a pouty face at the little critter.

I noticed that Katie did not look too happy at the attention her old friend was giving her child. She pulled Amelia off her husband's lap as Ramesh stood up to take his turn in the game.

"Why aren't you in the kitchen?" I asked him.

"Why aren't you in the nursery?" he responded before starting on the next charade. "Okay, I bet none of you get this one."

He began to mime a… film! With… three words!

Bertie really got into the game and shouted out whatever came into his mind. "Very camp chef? Convincing Freddy Mercury impersonator? 'Gone with the Wind'?"

"'Gone with the Wind'?" Ramesh replied, giving up on the big monster he was doing an impression of. "How did you get 'Gone with the Wind' from that?"

"Anyway, it's three words, not four," Toffee said calmly. "Keep going, Ramesh. Do a different word if you like."

Ramesh held three fingers in the air.

"Third word," Aidan said proudly.

Ramesh held two fingers in the air.

"Second word," we all shouted but he shook his head.

"Two?" Kevin tried and Ramesh pointed at his nose and the boy at the same time.

"'Jurassic Park Two'!" Suzanne squealed before anyone else could.

Ramesh and Bertie clapped their hands and Katie looked put out. "How did you get that?"

"He did a dinosaur and then the number two. It wasn't so difficult."

"Doesn't count!" Howard shouted. "There's no such film as 'Jurassic Park Two'. The Sequel to Jurassic Park is called 'The Lost

World: Jurassic Park'."

Suzanne curled her lip. "Of course it counts! That's another point to Team Winters."

The Scotsman shook his head. "No, no. The problem we've got here is that nobody has set any rules. You can't play charades without clearly defined rules. I'll get a pencil and we'll discuss how to go forward from here."

No one seemed particularly enthusiastic about the idea, Suzanne least of all. "And that is why I hate charades. I'm out."

"Me too." Kevin pulled out his computer game.

"So what do we do now?" Justine asked.

"Sally's right," Ramesh conceded. "I should get back to the kitchen." He disappeared through the swingy door again and didn't come out until dinner time.

"We could watch TV," Aidan suggested, somewhat optimistically, but another idea soon took precedence.

"We could open some presents." This was the first thing that I'd heard Grantham say since he'd returned to the house having attempted to shoot his best friend.

"Great idea!" Howard clapped his hands and a huge smile ripped across his face. "My grandma used to let me open one present on Christmas Eve."

Happy with the alternative plan, Aidan zoomed off the sofa to hand out gifts. "This one is for you, Justine." He was such a nice boy and I was sure that he'd started with her first to make her feel better about the situation.

She smiled as she took it from him and I noticed that her boyfriend went all red too. On unwrapping the slim, rectangular box, she discovered a silver chain with a tiny heart on it.

"Oh, Kevin!" she enthused. "I can't believe it. It's so pretty."

I watched for his mother's reaction and was interested to see Suzanne squirming in her seat as the teens went in for a full smacker on the lips. Though she'd tried to make out that she was fine with her little boy having a girlfriend, this made me wonder just how much her previously laidback attitude had been a reaction to Astrid's uptight approach.

"Aidan, if you have a bit of poke about, you'll find one from us." Katie sounded more relaxed than she had earlier and watched the child curiously to see if he'd like what she'd bought him – and, yes, the glow in the dark robots went down well.

The little boy was soon back to work handing out another batch of presents. "Here's one for Uncle Bertie, one for Mum and Dad and one for you Katie."

The adults got busy tearing the paper off.

"Who are these from?" Toffee asked as he examined the neat red paper with the perfectly tied green fabric bow.

"They're from us," Grantham replied but the last word stuck in his mouth a little and his voice wavered. "Astrid brought them here this morning."

It was Suzanne who leaned in to comfort him once more and kept her arm round him as everyone made appreciative noises for the gifts they'd received.

"They're great." Toffee was holding a *his and hers* dressing gown set with their names on. Even in the dim light of the Christmas tree, I could see how expensive they were.

On Bertie's lap was a box of candied fruits from Marks and Spencer.

"Lovely," he commented, though I could tell it stung a little to open the most generic present imaginable. Astrid clearly hadn't made much effort with his gift.

Katie was the last to unwrap hers and found a silk pashmina scarf in rich colours which swirled together like a tornado. "Oh, Grantham, I don't know what to say." She looked quite moved by the gesture and got up from her sofa to go across to him. "It's so perfectly me."

"I didn't have much to do with choosing them, I'm afraid," he replied, as Katie put her arms around him and patted his back appreciatively. The crumpled up little man looked even more sorrowful as she pulled away. "Astrid was always in charge of that sort of thing."

"Well, she had brilliant taste." Kneeling down beside him, Katie smiled. "But then we already knew that."

Grantham looked shyly down at the floor as the compliment sank in. Suzanne eyed Katie with her usual aggressive detachment and I could tell she didn't like to be upstaged.

"Yes. Thanks very much, old chum." Bertie was clearly hiding his disappointment, but then, with friends like his, it was something he was good at.

"Shall we leave the rest till tomorrow, maybe?" Penelope suggested. "Only I haven't had time to wrap ours yet and I'm feeling a bit guilty."

"Fair enough," Howard agreed. "Now come on, I want my turn at charades."

An alarm that was probably set for about four hours earlier but had never gone off, finally started ringing in my head.

"I'll be right back." I needn't have worried. No one was watching as I slipped outside. Howard was drawing up the rules on a piece of paper and Suzanne was having a team talk with her sons and husband.

I ran across to Grantham and Astrid's house and searched in her bag for her phone. It wasn't there but I found it a minute later tucked into her coat pocket. There was only five per cent of the battery left and I didn't know the pin number but I was hoping that wouldn't be a problem.

I was back in the main chalet in no time and only Penelope noticed me as I came back through the door. I wondered if she'd figured out the same thing as me as she nodded supportively and gave me a look which said, *I'm here if you need anything.*

As Suzanne, Howard and even Rupert were busy shouting guesses at Kevin's charade, no one thought much of me coming to have a quiet word with Justine.

She nodded and stood up to follow me to the kitchen. "I need your help," I told her once the noise of the game was muffled by the swinging door. Ramesh was artfully tackling some sort of pastry that he'd made and didn't pay us any mind. "I think that I can get to the bottom of who killed your mother, but I need something from you."

She looked at the phone I was holding and pulled it away from me. "Pin number, right?" She said, her pretty features stretching out in a smile. "Mum used to change it sometimes but it never took me long to find out what it was." She tapped the screen four times and the phone bloomed into life.

The whole process had been wrapped up pretty quickly and I felt guilty that I hadn't started the conversation by asking my next question.

"How are you doing with… everything?"

Her smile disappeared and her eyes jumped about the shiny silver kitchen. "Crappy of course. I miss my mum. I hate what someone did to her and, every time I think about it, I feel so guilty."

More guilt again. I made a mental note to come back to a theme that kept re-emerging, before trying to comfort Justine. "Nothing that happened is your fault. You know that."

She tucked a lock of wavy hair behind one ear. "My very last words to Mum were 'I wish you were dead,' it's kind of hard not to feel guilty." She sat down on the metal table in the middle of the room and I realised that I had a duty to hear her out.

The battery, Izzy! The phone is about to die and we'll never get the answers we need.

A fifteen-year-old girl is grieving. Priorities, brain, priorities!

"I can't begin to imagine how hard that must be for you." I wished I could have thought of something more personal but this was the best I came up with.

"Thanks, Sally. Everyone's been so nice." It was right then that her tears came. "You know, the worst thing of all is that I can't forget how much I hated her last night. I remember the way she embarrassed me and how angry I was and I…"

I put my arm around the poor girl. Talk about a double whammy. Not only had her mother been murdered, she'd have to deal with all the negative emotions of their last day together for the rest of her life.

Yeah, poor thing. She must be heartbroken. Now look at the phone!

Oh, calm down, would you? Someone's bound to have a charger.

I tried again to reassure her. "If it makes you feel any better, I like to think of mothers as our very best enemies. We love to hate them and hate to hate them, but we always love them."

She dried her eyes with the back of her sleeve. "That makes a lot of sense actually."

"Honestly, Justine. Don't feel bad because your relationship with Astrid was complicated." I perched next to her on the edge of the table.

She looked up at me and let out a sad, wet laugh. "But… do you want to know something horrible?"

"Always."

"The thing is… I can't believe I'm even telling you this. You see, the fact that someone killed her, kind of makes me feel… better." Once the words were out, she rushed to explain what she meant. "Not that she's dead – I don't mean that at all – but it's almost a relief that someone hated her more than I did."

There was a warmth and gentleness to her that I hadn't witnessed before and I felt bad that she was having to work her way through a whole truckload of conflicting emotions.

"I'm not going to lie to you, Justine, that does sound pretty weird, but it's also completely natural. When I was your age, I despised my mother. I was nearly six foot tall, just about the least popular girl in south London and she always made me sign up for afterschool activities because she thought it would help me make friends. So I did ballet and tap dancing and I was in a drama group. Can you imagine me doing ballet?"

This information had pricked Ramesh's ears and he came over to listen.

"Haaaaaaaaaaaaaaaaaaaaa!" this was Ramesh, not Justine. "I can't tell you how much money I would pay to see you in a tutu. Please tell me that your mum has photos."

I ignored him entirely. "It was possibly the most embarrassing moment in my life and, I've got to be honest, there've been some pretty bad ones."

Ramesh was on hand to lend weight to my account. "Yeah, remember that time you couldn't stop speaking in a Welsh accent around your boyfriend's family? Or when that boy you fancied thought you were a bloke?"

"Is that true?" Justine asked, sounding both shocked and amazed. "Did that stuff really happen?"

Ramesh hadn't finished. "Or when you got up in front of everyone at a party and sang Robbie William's "Angels" to try to cheer up the most popular girl in your school?"

I let his words wash over me and focussed on Justine. "Well, there may be some truth in what my idiot friend is saying. But none of it was as bad as being an abnormally tall teenage girl at her very first ballet recital, alongside a bunch of five-year-olds."

"Haaaaaaaaaaaaa! Please tell me there's a video!?" Ramesh had nearly fainted from excitement. "You know what, I'm going to get on the phone to your mum right now. Every second that passes is a second that I'm not watching your first ballet recital."

I pulled little Justine in closer to me. "So don't feel bad about what went on between you and your mum. You only have to scratch the surface a little bit to see how much you loved her. I know she could be tough, but that doesn't mean she wasn't a good person. I bet she only wanted what was best for you."

Ramesh had run off to ring my mum but I stayed there with Justine until she felt a bit better. "Hey, I don't suppose you know who wanted her dead, do you?"

She thought for a second then shrugged. "Nope, sorry. Not a clue. She got on everyone's nerves wherever we went. It would be hard to pick just one person." She sniffed then and I could tell she was both happy and sad to say this. Sad because it had led to her mother's death but happy because she was proud of the strong, terrifying woman who had raised her.

Phhhhhhhhhhhhhhooooooooooooooooooone!

Alright, I'm going!

I jumped down off the table and it was Justine's turn to say something smart. "I reckon you'll find what you're looking for on there. Mum was worse than me; she never went five minutes without using her phone."

"Come on, let's see what the others are up to." I threaded my arm through hers and we returned to the lounge.

Chapter Twenty-One

"Has this game *still* not finished?" Justine asked with a touch more optimism in her voice, as she went to give her dad a hug.

"It never finishes," Suzanne replied. "It goes on forever until one of us dies."

"Quiet, Suzanne," her husband said, jerking his head in Grantham's direction. "Don't be so insensitive."

She looked sheepish then but it was Penelope's turn at charades so everyone turned to watch the royal beauty strut her stuff. I kind of wanted to join in too but, there was only three per cent of Astrid's phone battery left and I was trying to be quick. I knew exactly what I needed to do. I went to WhatsApp to check out a theory, then pulled up her phonebook to ring a number.

To begin with, the sound of another mobile buzzing on the coffee table was drowned out by the game. Rupert was shouting out James Bond films – though the answer was clearly 'Love Actually' – and nobody noticed the vibrating device until Howard guessed the charade and a lull descended.

"Whose is that?" Grantham asked, peering first at the table and then around the room.

"Who could be ringing me now?" Bertie jumped up from his armchair to fetch the mobile and Grantham stared between the leaping lord and me over by the Christmas tree.

"Sally, that's not yours is it?" His expression hardened. "What are you doing with my wife's phone?"

Idiot! You should have removed the distinctive glittery cover from Astrid's mobile before carrying it out into the lounge for everyone to see.

Unless, of course, this was exactly what I wanted!

Was it?

Urmmm… nope.

"But, why…?" Grantham continued, not quite finishing his sentences. "And if you…?" He looked at Bertie and then at the box of candied fruit that his wife had given him for Christmas. He saw the mince pie, hot chocolate and pudding stains down the jolly man's waistcoat. Grantham put all these ingredients together and, like a highly unstable chemical compound, he exploded.

"I'm going to kill you Bertie, you fat…" That was one sentence he did manage to finish but I'll leave it to your imagination as to the particular noun he employed.

It took Bertie a moment to realise he'd been found out and Grantham was quick on his feet. He ran to the Christmas tree and grabbed whatever he could from it. Glass baubles and ornaments went sailing through the air to bounce off Bertie's bulging stomach. One crashed loudly against his head, but Grantham soon realised they weren't designed to inflict much lasting damage and changed his plan.

"Now, Grantham, old chap, don't do something you'll regret," the Lord of Winhampchestershire (or wherever) said.

"You'll live to regret what you did, old chap. Though maybe not for long." Grantham had seized a large, wooden nutcracker figurine and rather athletically jumped over the sofa to confront his new enemy. "You slept with the woman I loved. You tried to steal her from me, didn't you, Sweet Boy?"

Seeing the rage in the betrayed man's eyes, Bertie looked for a weapon of his own but the only thing to hand was a large, dancing Father Christmas who started singing 'Rocking Reindeer' as he dodged the first blow.

"Oh, come on, Granty." Bertie's voice was even plummier than usual, which did not help his case. "It was nothing serious between me and the old girl. Just a bit of fun really."

Grantham's surprisingly measured response, as he swung the nutcracker through the air was, "I'll kill you! You…" Again, it's probably best if you choose your own insult to finish that sentence.

"Dad, don't!" Justine was in the position of having to tell her father not to kill someone for the second time that day.

"Hit him, Grantham!" Kevin has no such qualms about violence and had taken out his phone to film the sorry scene. "Bloody hit him!"

It was Bertie who made the first contact. The dancing Santa smashed down on Grantham's back and the head went splintering off through the air with a "Ho ho ho!" for good measure. It was a decent blow but left Bertie to defend himself with little more than the wiggling legs of the figure. Standing back up, Grantham took his time. Lord Gravely-Swans dashed away to put some space between them but, with all the anger and determination running through his foe, it wouldn't be enough.

"To think I considered you a friend," Grantham's voice was hollow as he jumped up onto the table to hunt his prey.

"Oh, please. Your friend?" Bertie's attitude had transformed. "I'm not your friend. I'm only any use when you want something from me. 'Bertie, invest in my business.' 'Bertie, pay for my son's dental work.'" It was odd to see the previously placid man so worked up.

He couldn't spit the words out fast enough. "Oh yes, you all love Bertie when you need to milk me for something. But where are you when *I* need a favour? Where are you when I'm feeling lonely?"

This was all Grantham needed to hear. From the top of the table, he sent the nutcracker flying as a distraction and then jumped over to Bertie to deliver a well-timed fist to the face.

"That's enough." Toffee dashed in to break them up. "You're behaving like kids."

He held the widower back as Howard arrived to pull the battered lord to safety. "Come on, Grantham. We're going for a walk to cool you down."

I watched the remaining witnesses to see what impact these new revelations would have on the group. Justine was crying again, her boyfriend standing rather nobly in front of her. Katie had retreated into herself and was curled up in an armchair, unable to watch, and Suzanne was the only one who looked unconcerned by what had happened. If anything she seemed to have enjoyed the spectacle and, with the bloodlust in her eyes, I noticed what a different figure she cut from the first time I'd seen her.

Toffee pulled Bertie up to the mezzanine level and the newly sworn foes stared furiously at one another as Grantham was escorted out. Penelope shot upstairs with Rupert to give the leaping lord a talking to and I figured I'd be nosy and tag along.

"What were you bloody thinking?" Rupert asked his brother.

"Astrid?" this was all that Penelope could get out and so, in obvious disbelief, she said it again. "I mean, Astrid?"

Bertie crashed down onto the sofa and lay there like a pharaoh, looking up at us disdainfully. "I'm not saying anything with him here," he grunted in the admiral's direction.

"What have *I* done?" Toffee's voice had become a lionish growl.

"You're just as bad as Grantham. You use me and I'm sick of it. So push off back to your mouthy wife and nasty children."

"Hey, steady on," Rupert seemed equally surprised by the change in his brother's attitude. Not wanting another fight, Toffee took his cue to head back downstairs.

Bertie was a sad sight. He had his shirt tails untucked and several buttons on his waistcoat were missing. His eye was beginning to swell up too from where Grantham had struck him. The only bright side was that the nutcracker hadn't made contact.

His sister-in-law sat on the coffee table to reason with him. "What's this all about, Bertie? What have you got yourself into?"

He'd never been the most charming person but, by this stage, any decorum he'd once possessed was absent. "Don't you two start! I'd rather talk to a brick wall than have you judging me all the time. I'm sorry I'm not like you, Peter Perfect with your Princess Barbie wife, but we can't all be saints."

Penelope couldn't react to his rude comment because she was still processing the recent revelations. "But... Astrid?"

"Yes and so what? At least she took an interest in me. At least she entertained the idea that I was worth talking to. Even my own family treat me like I'm worthless." He cast his disappointed gaze over the two of them. "She gave me more time than either of you ever do and Katie's not much better."

This outburst appeared to have sapped all the energy from him and he lay back with his feet on the arm of the sofa and his head on a cushion.

"We don't want to judge you, old man, but..." It was Rupert's turn to be confused. "Astrid? Astrid Spear?"

"She was a very beautiful woman!" He got all defensive.

"No one's debating that, Bertie," Penelope replied. "It was the words that came out of her mouth that I disagreed with. Not the way she looked."

The aggression in Bertie's voice died down a little but he continued to feel sorry for himself. "Rupee, get me a bag of peas or something. The wallop Grantham gave me is starting to sting."

Rupert looked at his brother and gave a shrug before heading back downstairs in search of something cold. It was my chance to quiz Bertie. "Is there anything else you've been keeping from us?"

He shifted in his seat to reply. "Me? Never. I don't know anything about anything."

"So you don't know who killed your girlfriend." I'd chosen the word carefully and I could see it had the desired effect on him.

"That's right, she was my girlfriend." He sounded practically shy. "We cared about one another and she wasn't nearly as bad as everyone's making out. But, I'm sorry to say, I don't know what happened to her."

It suddenly made sense to me that Astrid had shown so little interest in taking Toffee as her lover. Why bother with a mere admiral when there was a lord going spare?

Penelope was up next with a question for her brother-in-law. "Astrid never told you that she feared for her life?"

"No." Bertie sounded surer of himself than before.

"What about someone she didn't trust then?"

"There was no one," he began and then an almost physical change came over him as something clicked in his brain. "Except Suzanne and Katie of course. They were like vipers those three. Sniping and biting at one another the whole time and Astrid was tired of it."

It was interesting that Bertie was the only person who had presented the three women's rivalry from Astrid's side. In some ways, they were quite alike. They were both pariahs in the group, though one was a lord and the other had built herself up from nothing. It was fitting that they'd ended up together.

He had more still to tell us. "You know, I think she came on this holiday in order to call a truce. She sounded so excited when she'd asked me to pass on the money so that Suzanne and the boys could come."

This was news to me. "You mean that she was the one who paid for their holiday?"

He reflected on this for a moment. "That's right. She knew that they'd never have accepted if they found out it was from her, so I was the go-between." His round face turned all smiley then. "You should have heard her telling me about the presents she'd bought and the plans she had. She was as giddy as a little girl."

Staring downstairs, as if waiting for Astrid to pop back in, Bertie retained a peaceful look. "I don't believe our little Katie would have been capable of hurting her, but I'm not so sure about Suzanne."

"Do you have any reason-" I began.

Bertie swung his legs down to the floor. "You wanted a name, didn't you? You wanted to know who I think could be the killer. Well, there you are; Suzanne Winters. That's my best bet. Now go forth and prove me wrong."

He stood up and it would have been a killer closing line if he hadn't been sitting on a fluffy, red Christmas G-string. There was only one person in our party that I could imagine having left it there.

"Bertie, why did you sleep here last night?"

He crossed his arms and looked even more put out than before. "I had one drink too many and crashed out on the sofa. So what?"

"I don't suppose you had a visit from Mrs Christmas this morning, did you?" I picked up the underwear but immediately thought better of it and dropped them again.

"Oh…" He laughed. "Whoops!"

Chapter Twenty-Two

I needed a break from everybody. I needed five minutes on my own to catch my breath and set my head straight. Well, what I really needed was my mum and dads to comfort me and make everything better, but I was thirty years old now and there's supposed to come a point when you grow out of that sort of thing.

With every murder I'd investigated, I'd become more sure of myself, but there was always a little voice at the back of my head saying, this time, you're going to mess up. This time, people will see what a hack you really are.

I was tired of doubting myself, tired of always expecting failure, but on this case, more than any other, it felt like the truth was too far out of reach. The suspects were a bunch of over-privileged aristocrats. They all hated one another, two of them were having an affair, one of them thought she'd make a great murderer and I still couldn't land upon any concrete explanation for why Astrid Spear had been killed.

There were a hundred different half-reasons for why someone might have wanted her dead but no knockout blow. I could pick a name from a hat, lazily conclude that it was down to her adultery or the rivalry with her old university friends, but that wasn't enough to build a case.

What had changed in the twenty-year friendship of a small group of friends that meant Astrid had to die? And what about the death threats written to entirely the wrong person? Either I had to look for someone who hated the two women equally or the letter was a red herring. Perhaps the killer got confused and murdered skinny Astrid instead of heavy-set Katie, but, if that was true, I should probably have been looking for a culprit with very poor eyesight.

So, I'm sorry that I was once again feeling less than steady on my feet, but I'd actually started to believe that I was getting good at this. I'd found the confidence that I'd been lacking my whole life, only to have it ripped out from under me by this absurdly unyielding investigation.

My boyfriend was a million miles away, my family had picked Christmas of all times to swan off on a cruise and my best friend was busy becoming Gordon Ramsay. As I crouched beside my chalet in the freezing cold, with the last traces of daylight now gone from the sky, I needed someone to support me; I needed someone to help me get my thoughts in order.

"Izzy?" Penelope whispered, as she tiptoed across the square to find me. "Are you alright?"

That was all it took. Just that question and I felt a thousand times better. I didn't cry or complain how lonely I was, I just answered her plainly.

"Yes, I am." I said this rather too proudly, like a superhero delivering a cheesy line.

Penelope continued to look worried. "It's just, you're out here in the snow, it's about minus ten degrees and you left your ski suit inside."

I rose to standing. "Thanks for asking, Penelope. I honestly appreciate it and, you're right, if I stay out here any longer my fingers will fall off, but I think I know what we need to do next."

"That's good." Her smile warmed me up a little. "So... are you going to tell me what that is?"

"Yes." I was still sounding far too heroic as I wrote up my list of suspects on an imaginary flip pad in my head. "Yes, I am."

Next I did the Evidence list, then the Hypotheses and I began to see a thread running through the three columns. Being away from home and the people who normally helped me on my cases meant that I'd lost my usual rhythm. I'd forgotten to do the basics but it wasn't too late. Either the police would turn up to save us from our lovely cosy prison, or I'd find the killer first. It was true, I knew exactly what we needed to do.

I'm guessing a good fifteen seconds had gone by as I'd stood there with my hands on my hips feeling epic but saying nothing. Penelope looked puzzled and it finally clicked that she was waiting for an explanation.

"Oh, sorry, Penelope. I get a bit carried away with my thoughts sometimes. I was in another world for a minute."

"That's okay." She was incredibly sympathetic. In fact, if I had any female friends – beyond the one excessively impersonal detective inspector who sometimes helps me with my cases – I'd want them to be just like Penelope. "I had a great aunt who was a bit like that."

"Oh really, what happened to her?"

She looked uncomfortable for a second. "Daddy took her out behind the kennels one day and shot her."

"Oh my goodness, really?"

Her face remained straight. "No, Izzy. Obviously not. She died aged ninety-four in a retirement home."

That sounds dreadful! Give me a swift shotgun shell behind the kennels over a long, slow drift into senility any day!

It's lucky you don't get to decide then.

Penelope helped me get back on track. "Are you going to tell me the plan then?"

It was harder to put into words than I'd imagined. "Perhaps 'plan' is too strong a word for it. A notion maybe? Or perhaps a concept? Yes, that's it."

"Izzy, stop being a wimp and tell me what you're thinking." It was this kind of bluntness I needed from her if my patented Izzy Palmer *concept* was going to work.

"I have a feeling – ooh, actually that might be better than concept." She glared at me so I raced to explain. "I have a feeling that I might, just possibly-"

"Izzy!"

I practically jumped into the snow to get away from her. "You're making me more nervous!"

She put her hands out to calm me down then spoke in her poshest TV voice. "I'm sorry, please explain what your idea is and I will do my best to facilitate its realisation."

"That's it! My 'idea'!" I pointed at her and my nose at the same time, like we were playing charades. "Okay, so my 'idea' is that I'm almost entirely sure who killed Astrid, except that I can't definitively narrow it down beyond my final two suspects."

This revelation seemed to make up for my previous hesitance. "Oh, how exciting. Let me guess. Is it Katie and Bertie?"

"Nope." I paused to consider on her choices. "Though I do find it interesting that you picked your in-laws as the potential killers."

"So who then? Actually, hold that thought. Your lips are turning blue, let's finish this conversation inside."

"Good idea." My teeth were chattering so much that I'm not sure this was entirely comprehensible.

We ducked around the edge of the building and into her chalet. Inside, the fire had died down but it was still perfectly snug and I ran to warm my hands by the glowing embers. The Christmassy room looked even prettier in the low light and, from some unseen music box or children's toy, a simple version of 'Silent Night' was playing.

Penelope crashed down on a beanbag beside me. "So, who do you think *done it*?"

As the warmth from the fire ran through me, I allowed myself one last shiver and began my explanation. "Well, I've spoken to practically every person here about what they think could have happened and, though others have lied to cover their backs, when I talked to Toffee and Suzanne earlier, they were the only people who showed true anger towards Astrid."

She bit her lip and thought for a moment. "Yes, I think you're probably right. We've seen how distraught Grantham's been today. I don't think he could have faked that. And besides, Rupert heard him crying when he didn't even realise anyone could hear him. There's acting and there's plain overkill."

"Exactly," I replied. "And we saw his attempt to murder first Toffee and then Bertie. He wasn't particularly good at it and, based on the size of the hole in Astrid's back, whoever killed her was a total psycho."

"Can you really rule out Bertie then?"

I looked at her judgingly once more. "You really don't like your in-laws, do you?"

Izzy, focus!

"Izzy, focus!"

Ha! Great minds think alike.

Spurred on by her pushiness, I went back to my explanation. "Okay, so yes. I think I can rule out Bertie. You saw the way he was when Grantham found out that he'd been sleeping with Astrid. He had no shame whatsoever so it's not like he was desperate to hide the affair. Plus there's the fact that he's the richest person here…"

She looked a little smug and embarrassed at the same time. "Well, not quite the richest. I am set to inherit half of Hampshire, you know."

I didn't think this required a reply. "Lord Bertrand Gravely-Swans is extremely rich and so it's unlikely he'd kill for money. Short of being so in love with Astrid that he decided, 'if I can't have her, no one will,' we haven't discovered any other reason why he'd be the killer."

Penelope let this sink in for a moment. "Which still leaves Katie and Howard. Don't you think that Katie could be involved? She really hasn't been herself recently. Perhaps her paranoia got the better of her."

I'd already gone through such possibilities in my head. "No, I can't see it. Katie opted out of the competition that Astrid and Suzie still enjoyed, she didn't care enough about them to want anyone dead. And besides, not even I'm so cruel as to pin a murder on a new mother who's lost her parents and is battling through a deep depression."

Penelope finished the summary for me. "And it couldn't have been Howard because – well, because he's Howard. Perhaps underneath his giant teddy bear façade there's a killer lurking, but that wouldn't explain why he'd want to get rid of Astrid."

I smiled, thinking about the chirpy Scotsman's infectious enthusiasm for all things Christmassy. "I know, such a sweetheart, right?"

She had one more point to clear up. "And I can solemnly attest that it wasn't Rupert as we are still very much in the honeymoon phase and, at the time that Astrid was being hacked up, he was in bed giving me-"

"Yes, thank you, Penelope, but I think I can imagine what you were doing."

"Oh, my goodness." Her face lit up like the star at the top of the Christmas tree. "Who would have thought that the great Izzy Palmer could get upset at the mention of a little nookie? I'd never have imagined that a woman who makes her living poking around dead bodies could be such a prude."

I huffed out my answer, wishing by now that I'd made a hot drink before starting in on this conversation. "I'm not a prude, I just think murder investigations are interesting enough without everyone taking their clothes off."

"Prude!" she teased me again. "Anyway, I was going to say he was giving me a massage." She paused and the glow from the fireplace danced mischievously in her eyes. "And then we had sex."

"Urghhhhhhhhhhh, can we please get back to work?" I rapidly replied before she could go into any detail. Okay, I admit, I might be a bit of a prude after all.

It was her turn to apologise. "I'm so sorry. Though, can I just say how much fun all this is? I totally get now why you wanted to become a-"

"Penelope, focus!"

I wonder if her inner monologue was thinking the same thing.

She looked suitably repentant so I continued. "And all that goes to prove my original point that Suzanne and Toffee are the obvious suspects. Remember how angry he got at you this morning when you wanted to ask him some questions."

"He called me 'a pretty girl in a nice outfit' which I would normally take as a compliment but I could tell that's not what he meant."

"Exactly, it struck me as odd at the time that he displayed such aggression towards you, but perhaps it was a cover to avoid answering questions. And then Suzanne interrupted him and seemed completely fine about the chef and the nanny barging into their chalet to interview them."

Penelope made an impressed face, like I'd said something really clever. "You know you're right. I didn't think of it at the time, but I've never once had a problem with Toffee and he suddenly went crazy at me."

"I'm certain that Suzanne was afraid of what we'd all think, which is why she hushed him up. It made them look guilty as hell, though."

"Excellent. So what's the plan? How are we going to get the truth out of them?" She was clearly looking forward to one last interrogation together.

"Well I want you to be in charge again when we speak to Suzanne. I'm going to give you a list of things we need to find out, but I won't get involved until it's necessary. And, first I've got a question for you."

She looked a little nervous then, like she was scared this whole thing was a trap and I was about to deliver the damning evidence that would prove my favourite Girl Scout cheerleader princess was actually the killer all along. She needn't have worried.

"I need you to tell me everything you know about the accident that led to your in-laws' deaths. I need to know the truth before we go in there."

"Okay." The startled look hadn't left her but she sighed and began the story. "Katie took it very badly. You see, they'd all been to a party and she was the one driving them home. Bertie was in the seat behind her and their parents were on the passenger side of the car. Another group of guests were in the vehicle in front and the idiot driving had drunk far too much. A stag jumped out in front of them and he screeched to a halt."

Penelope paused, I could tell she didn't like reliving this part of the story. "Katie tried to swerve but she was too close. The whole left-hand side of her car was crushed. Her parents were killed instantly."

I gave her a moment to breathe. "What happened afterwards?"

"Katie had a ruptured spleen and a broken vertebra. It was touch and go to begin with but she made it through. Bertie walked away with nothing more than a torn shirt and a black eye of course."

She came to a stop again, as if trying to remember the missing pieces of the story. "I have to say though that Suzanne was wonderful. She was there for Katie as soon as she was allowed visitors and practically nursed her back to health all on her own."

"What happened after Katie was discharged?"

She glanced back at the smouldering log in the fireplace. "It was strange. As soon as she was home, she said that she didn't want any visitors. Rupert and I still went to see her and so I guess what she really meant was that she didn't want Suzanne there anymore. I don't know what went on between them at the hospital but they'd been friends for years and, suddenly, Katie couldn't stand hearing the woman's name. She got pregnant soon after and she was so radiantly happy that I think it helped her to move on from whatever had happened."

We both fell into silent thought for a moment.

"Do you think it means anything?" she eventually asked and I stood back from the fire because my whole body was starting to burn.

"I guess we're about to find out."

Chapter Twenty-Three

We marched back to the main building where a brutal game of Pictionary was under way.

Penelope had tied her hair up in a ponytail and was ready for war. "Okay, enough games, enough mince pies and enough messing about." Her words instantly froze the scene but Bertie still found a quippy response.

"There's no such thing as enough mince pies, Penny."

To be fair, my brain was thinking exactly the same thing.

Ha! Great stomachs think alike!

"Shut it, Bertie. Or I'll tell everyone what you really got up to on your holiday to Bangkok last year." Penelope was fierce and I loved it. "Sally and I know more about each and every one of you than we did this morning. We believe that one of the people in this room right now was responsible for Astrid's death and, in the next hour, we're going to get to the bottom of who that was."

She looked around at our audience. The only people missing were Justine and her dad, though, presumably sensing another lecture was coming on, Kevin wisely took this moment to slip out while he could.

"I didn't kill anyone, Auntie Penelope," a little voice spoke up and my partner in solving crime had to struggle really hard to keep her steely expression as seven-year-old Aidan looked up at her innocently.

"We know you didn't, sweetheart."

Happy with this verdict, he shrugged and grabbed his brother's games console from its bag.

Penelope tried to regain her intensity. "So, listen up, this is what's going to happen. We're going back into the dining room and, if one of us calls your name, you'll join us for your interview. We'll ask you the questions and you'll tell us what we need to know. The police will be here before long so you might as well get it over with."

I think it's fair to say people were impressed with her performance. Suzanne lost the aggressive smile she'd had while playing the game, Toffee suddenly looked worried and Bertie started clapping.

"Good stuff, Penny. That's what I like to see."

She turned, spun on her heel and I scuttled along after her into the dining room.

"Was that what you were hoping for?" she asked as soon as we were alone. Well, alone isn't quite the right word as Ramesh was already in there laying the table for the big Christmas Eve dinner.

"Don't mind me," he said, as he dumped down a load of jangling cutlery. "You won't even notice I'm here."

I pretended that he wasn't and answered Penelope's question. "Yes, it was perfect. I never manage to sound so tough and authoritative. You're a natural."

"Hardly," she replied rolling her shoulders like she was gearing up for a fight. "Daddy paid for assertiveness training so that I could destroy my enemies in the workplace."

Rich people are weird.

"Okay, great!" I tried to sound like I meant it and then grabbed three chairs to position in front of the fire. "Are you ready?"

"Definitely. Send in the first moron." She sat down in the chair with her back to the flames and her face merciless, before breaking into a smile. "That was my bad cop voice, did you like it?"

I left the room, running through my list of evidence once more as I did so. There were very few physical clues on it, no bloodstained dagger or bottle of poison, but plenty of scandal.

The letters to Katie
The wounds in Astrid's body and the missing murder weapon
Astrid's affair with Bertie and her early-morning visit
The size-fourteen boots
The Oxford girls' long running rivalry
Suzanne's Machiavellian instincts
The circumstances surrounding the previous Lord and Lady Gravely-Swans' untimely death

By the time I'd collected our first suspect, I felt surer of myself than I had in… well… a good half hour at least.

"Toffee, tell us what you did last night." Penelope's first question was delivered with just the right amount of fire.

I'd turned the main lights down in the room and placed our chairs so that our interviewees would only see our silhouettes against the fire. I hoped this would strike fear into them even if nothing else did.

The admiral had got changed at some point and was now wearing a rather natty Christmas jumper with a snowy village on. "Well, much like the rest of you, we had some drinks after dinner and then an early night. We were tired from the trip and, with it getting dark so early up here, it felt like we'd been travelling for days."

"Did Suzanne go to bed at the same time as you?" I asked.

"No, she sat up reading while I dozed off."

Ask him what she was reading!

Why?

Just do it.

"What was she reading?"

"A truly gripping sixteenth century political text, if you must know. Italian in fact. She's read it any number of times."

It was Penelope's turn for a question. "And what time did you get up this morning?"

Toffee didn't look particularly scared by our tactics and it didn't help that Ramesh returned to the room at that moment with "Plates!" as if he was actively trying to destroy all the tension we'd worked so hard to build.

Ignoring the interruption, Toffee glared at Penelope before answering. "I woke up when your bloody husband ran into our house at the crack of dawn shouting the place down."

"So Suzanne was there with you?" Penelope poked her words at him in the hope of a reaction.

"Yes, that's generally what happens when we go to bed together; we wake back up together too."

This wasn't going as planned. I'd assumed that Toffee would be an easy touch compared to Suzanne.

I decided to raise the stakes. "Do you think your wife was capable of killing her friend?"

That at least got him to pull at his shirt collar a little.

"Yes, I do."

Penelope sucked in a breath excitedly. It probably didn't help her hard-as-nails demeanour, but that was a minor issue compared to the fact that Ramesh was whistling Mariah Carey's 'All I Want for Christmas is You' as he distributed plates around the table. I turned to glare at him and I think he got the message.

The admiral continued. "I've worked with a lot of tough men over the years but none of them were as ferocious as my Suzanne. That's why I fell in love with her. She's intelligent and charming, but it's more than that. She's a viper."

How many times is that now? Was there a memo we never got that obliged everyone to identify the women in this case as vipers?

"And you loved that about her?" I asked, the surprise plain in my voice.

"Absolutely." There wasn't a hint of irony in the way he said this. "You have to understand that Suzanne has dedicated her life to studying mass murder. That might not be the term that most historians use but that's what war is. It's genocide, massacre, destruction on an unparalleled scale. If she wasn't able to put herself into the mind of the kings and generals who have sanctioned such events, she wouldn't be nearly so good at her job."

"You're talking academically, aren't you?" I think Penelope was getting nervous.

Toffee peered up at the golden ceiling. "No, not at all. Suzanne is very different from anyone else I've met. I'm sure that she could take a knife and cut the beating heart from another person's body. Luckily for all of us, she has absolutely no need to do such a thing."

He was a gesturer and acted out each word with his hands. "We may not be the richest people in the world but we muddle through. We have a nice house, a nice life and two boys who she has devoted the last sixteen years to raising in just the way that she believes is best. We want for nothing."

Penelope folded her arms rather primly. "So you're saying that she could have killed Astrid but she didn't kill Astrid."

"That's exactly it." Toffee allowed himself a self-satisfied smile.

It was time to go all in. "Is that why you did it? To win favour with the woman you love, who, let's be honest, has never shown the same intensity of feeling in return." My allegation struck him just as I wanted.

He straightened his back and uncrossed his legs. I'd woken him up at the very least and didn't wait for his reply. "You're obsessed with your wife, aren't you? You could have chosen sexy, ambitious Astrid or rich, pretty Katie but you went for the mousey intellectual. You knew from the very first time you saw her that you would do anything for her. So what happens twenty years later when she doesn't look at you the way she used to? What happens when that love has become one-sided?"

"I don't know what you're talking about." His response was unconvincing.

Penelope could see that it was her turn to sit back and listen as I continued. "Don't try to deny it. I've been watching you since we got here. You hold her hand, you touch her face but Suzanne sits there like she hasn't noticed. At what point did you decide that killing Astrid was the only way to impress her? Did you plan it in advance or did the snowstorm trapping us here give you the idea?"

"This is insane, I didn't kill her." The channel of anger that I'd first witnessed that morning was beginning to show.

"I'm not criticising you. I have to say, it's admirable. You were worried that your marriage wouldn't survive so you did something about it. The boys are getting older, you're settling into middle-age – bogged down in the same old career just as Suzanne is hitting her stride. You were scared that, with her TV programme about to take off and all sorts of opportunities set to open up for her, she wouldn't have any need for a man like you. So you woke up early this morning, fashioned yourself a weapon and, like some pathetic supporting character from an Elizabethan tragedy, you slayed your true love's enemy. That's right, isn't it, Toffee?"

He was enraged by now. "No, of course not. You're talking absolute rot. There are many things I would do for Suzanne but murder isn't one of them." He ran his fingers through his hair in one desperate motion.

"Oh yeah? So then who did it? Who else could have possibly wanted your old friend dead?"

I had pushed him as far as he would go and he stood up from his chair to scream at me. He raised one hand, about to launch his attack but the words never came. Instead he paused, calmed down and, in little more than a whisper, told us, "I have no idea who killed her, but it wasn't me."

I glanced at Penelope who had kept the neutral expression on her face throughout. I nodded and she understood what she had to do. "Thank you, Toffee. That was very informative. You can leave now."

I got up to escort him to the door. "You can send Suzanne in when she's ready. We greatly appreciate your time."

Chapter Twenty-Four

"What was any of that about?" Penelope asked me in the fifteen second break we had between interviews.

"Everything and nothing," I told her. "But most importantly, Suzanne will have seen what her husband's just gone through and be quaking in her fur-lined slippers."

As I finished speaking, there was a hesitant knock at the door. I pointed to Penelope, to remind her that she was in charge, then ran to sit back down.

"Come in?" The lead detective announced and Suzanne Winters stuck her head round the door. "Hi, Suzanne, why don't you take a seat?"

My plan was running smoothly. We'd set the whole thing up like a job interview and what could be scarier than that?

Urmmm… Terrorism? An environmental apocalypse? 'Spice World: The Movie'?

Suzanne sat down in the chair her husband had just vacated and waited for the first question.

"I was wondering if you could tell me about your new TV programme," my partner asked and I was proud of her for even thinking of this.

Suzanne looked surprised and tossed her long fringe from her eyes before responding. "Um, okay, sure. It's called 'Great Rulers' and it takes us through some of history's most successful leaders from Cleopatra to Winston Churchill."

It was a fairly standard answer, but Penelope was all over it. "That doesn't sound particularly original. What would you say makes your show different from all the others that are already on TV?"

One side of Suzanne's mouth curled upwards. "Let's just say that I consider these figures from a different perspective."

"You mean you look at the savagery required to lead, is that what you're saying?"

"Yes, that's right." Suzanne did not appear impressed by Penelope's insight, but I certainly was.

"I believe that's what you've become known for, isn't it? The warts-and-all approach to history. You tell people about the vicious reality of the events we are already familiar with."

Suzanne didn't reply to this but kept her eyes trained on Penelope as she continued in the same calm tone.

"Would you call yourself a violent person?"

A vein of arrogance emerged in Suzanne's voice. "Define violent?"

"Would you say you were capable of hurting another human being?" There was a brutal efficiency to Penelope's questions.

"I think that we are all capable of killing another person, we just need to be in the right situation to unlock those animal instincts."

Penelope leaned forward and raised one finger in the air. "I'd just like to point out that 'killing' was your word, not mine." Suzanne remained silent and I think that Penelope held back a smile. "What time did you go to bed last night?"

"Shortly after we all left here. Why?"

"We're trying to get a clear picture of everything that went on before the murder. Did you get up in the night?"

"No."

"Did you read a book before bedtime?"

Suzanne nodded her head in a single sharp movement. "Yes. Why?"

"What was it?" Penelope was getting better with each question. She kept a curated ambivalence in her tone and, no matter how Suzanne might respond, there was nothing she could do to break through it.

"I brought a new biography of Oliver Cromwell with me."

I'd prepared Penelope with a list of questions that needed asking, but she adapted them neatly to the unfolding conversation. "That's not what I asked." She paused, her stare as hard as the Highland rocks that shaped the mountains around us. "What book did you read last night?"

Suzanne peered past us at the fire. "It was 'The Prince' by Machiavelli. Have you read it? It's awfully good."

"No, I haven't, but I hear you're rather fond of it."

"Oh, you really should check it out. Machiavelli is a sadly maligned genius."

There was one more point I would have made here which Penelope never got to, but then I guess she didn't understand just how important Suzanne's bedtime reading was to the case.

Instead, she moved on to the next topic. "And what about this morning? What did you do first thing?"

Suzanne paused. She looked like she was about to spit her answer back at us but thought better of it. "The same as everyone else here. I woke up to discover that my oldest friend in the world had been murdered."

"And was your husband lying next to you when Rupert called to wake you up?"

She hesitated once again and, for all her brains and artistry, she was incredibly easy to read. "He... Yes, Toffee was there. Ask your husband if you don't believe me."

"What did you think of Toffee the first time you met?" I'd told Penelope to get as personal as she could with Suzanne and she was playing it just right.

Our suspect smiled. "I thought he was charming and a little pathetic."

"Really, in what way?"

"Well, he followed me round like a puppy. It was sweet but... well, pathetic. I wasn't really interested in having a boyfriend at that stage. I was only eighteen and I cared more about my studies than I did about boys and getting married."

"But he wore you down eventually?"

Suzanne breathed in and then spoke very fast like she wanted to get this over with. "I suppose you could say that."

"And what would you say?"

"I'd say that I came to realise the benefits of having a man who was totally devoted to me." There was no romance in Suzanne's words. They were the cold, detached assertions of a rationalist academic.

"Did you want to have children or did he?"

Another smile, another glance away. "Oh, that was one of the conditions to our arrangement. I always knew that I'd have two sons, spaced several years apart. Toffee agreed without much of a fight."

"And did Toffee get a say in the way you raised them?"

She let out a full laugh this time. "No, not really." Her head turned and her gaze snapped onto me. "Sally, don't you have anything to ask me? Sat there like a scarecrow. What's wrong with you?"

I said nothing and it was getting under her skin, just as I'd hoped.

I'd planned the next question myself but I couldn't help trembling a little when Penelope cued it up. "Do you love your husband?"

"Define love!" A wild abandon was creeping its way into Suzanne's already flustered tone.

"Have you ever had an affair?"

I almost gasped when she asked this, but perhaps it was a step too far because our suspect pulled back and became guarded once more.

"You're not my therapist. I don't have to answer that. In fact I'm beginning to wonder what I'm even doing here."

Lady Penelope Gravely-Swans, former IT-girl, tabloid darling and the woman The Sun newspaper once called 'Britain's favourite bit-of-totty toff', was far smarter than the general public knew.

"You're here because if we don't work out who the killer is by the time the police arrive this evening, they're going to drag through every last detail of our lives to discover why our friend is lying dead in the snow. And who knows what they'll find in your sordid little world. It certainly won't help you sell your TV show if you're being investigated for the murder of the woman you've spent the last two decades at war with."

Suzanne let out a shout of pure fury. "Ask your damn questions then."

It was the perfect moment for me to break my silence. "Did you send the letters threatening to kill Katharine Taggart?"

It was a classic bit of bad cop – bad cop and our victim screamed her answer like it hurt to get the words out. "No, I didn't!"

I swear that the flames behind us swayed a little from the force of the breath she'd expelled. The words pinged off the metallic paint on the ceiling and reverberated through the room. When they died down altogether, I allowed the silence to wrap around us like a blanket against the cold.

I waited just long enough, then started over in a softer tone. "When Katharine's parents died, you did what you could to comfort her, didn't you?"

Suzanne had found some composure but her hands were shaking in the dim light. "Yes."

"Just like you tried to comfort Grantham and Justine this morning when they learnt that Astrid had been murdered."

"That's right." She put one hand to her fringe as if to check that it hadn't been messed up in the previous exchange of words.

184

"Why?"

"I'm sorry?"

I didn't let up between questions but kept pushing her. "Why does a woman who takes great pride in the amorality of her worldview, choose to go so far out of her way to comfort others?"

"I'm a historian, not a psychopath."

I drew my eyebrows together in confusion. "Yes, but it is a little strange, isn't it? I mean, you've had a fierce rivalry with Katie and Astrid ever since you met and, rather than leaving it to their families to look after them, you jumped in to help."

She didn't reply this time, just shook her head and peered down at the floor.

"I heard that you were incredibly attentive when Katharine was in hospital. You were there every day, isn't that right? You must have taken a lot of time off work for that. What drove you to do such a thing?"

"Katie is my friend, it's what anyone would have done."

Penelope smiled over at me and I returned the look. It was just an act of course. There was no in-joke known only to us. We were playing Suzanne like a game of charades, pulling her like a cracker. We were-

Alright, you're getting cheesy. Move it along.

"Is it though? I once had a boyfriend who broke both legs falling off a ladder. I visited him twice in the hospital, once to give him flowers and once to give him grapes. He seemed to think that was enough attention. Well, he never complained anyway."

"Your point is?"

"My point is that you weren't just visiting Katie out of the goodness of your heart. You wanted something from her."

"You're talking nonsense." Her fingers were balled up now, the tips of her nails digging into the palms of her hands as she endured the interrogation.

"Oh, okay. I take it all back." I wore my most apologetic expression then and raised my hand to my chest in insincere sympathy. "But, if I'm talking nonsense, why did Katie refuse to see you after she was let out of the hospital?"

She scoffed and turned her eyes to look at the change-colour lights pulsating on the Christmas tree. "She didn't refuse to see me. She… she just… In fact, it was me. I was busy at work and couldn't spare the time once she was on the mend."

"You're lying!" Penelope shouted, but I had more to say.

"You went to see Katie in the hospital because you knew it was the perfect moment to take advantage of her. You saw the state that she was in – her parents dead, her body broken – and you decided to make the move you'd been planning for the last twenty years."

"No." Suzanne was back to monosyllabic answers.

"You cared for her day and night when Howard was too exhausted. You stayed in that hospital room with her until she was well enough to listen to you. And while everyone told you what a kind and selfless thing you were doing, you whispered poison into Katie's ear. Isn't that right, Suzanne?"

"I didn't. No, that's not what happened." This was all I needed to hear to know I was on the right track.

"I'm sure you were very subtle about it so that, at first, even Katie didn't realise what you were doing but, word by word and little by little, you sewed a narrative for her. You showed her that the accident she'd been in was a true tragedy – such a terrible shame – but one that could surely have been avoided if it hadn't been for her driving." I paused to let my accusation settle in. "You selflessly helped her to see just how difficult it would be to live with the knowledge that she'd killed her own parents. Am I close?"

In a single heartbeat, the fear drained from Suzanne's face and she gave up her pretence. "Oh you're clever, Sally. I've underestimated you until now, but I must say I'm very impressed." She let out a laugh to rival Cruella de Vil. "I'm not sure I was quite as crude as you're suggesting but I did what I had to do to get Katharine out of the game."

"But that wasn't enough for you, was it? You wanted her to surrender entirely. You tried to drive her out of her mind with guilt and shame for her parents' death and it almost worked. Perhaps if Amelia hadn't turned up when she did, Katie would have been focused on the past more than her future and crumbled just as you desired."

"Oh, she crumbled." Suzanne's voice was ripped through with schadenfreude. "She's a total raving mess or haven't you seen?"

"And what about Astrid? You couldn't compete financially, she was far more successful than you ever could be. So what other options did you have?"

Penelope released another faint gasp but let me continue.

"You plotted against her, bided your time. You knew that she was having an affair and I think that you overheard her plans to meet with Bertie this morning and decided that the moment had come. It really wasn't so difficult to slip out of bed, do the deed and get back home without anyone seeing you."

"That's not what happened."

"You killed her didn't you? You stabbed her through the back in more ways than one. You called her 'your oldest friend' and yet you murdered her in cold blood for the sake of an adolescent rivalry."

"You're wrong." She still wouldn't break. "Those weren't the rules of the game. If I'd cheated, it wouldn't have been a victory worth celebrating."

"Didn't Machiavelli say that it's 'safer to be feared than loved'? That the end justifies the means?"

She smiled smugly and I should have known not to get drawn into a war of quotations with a historian. "Yes, but he also believed that you should 'Never attempt to win by force what can be won by deception.'"

My body felt like we were locked in a wrestling match. Every inch of me ached, but I wouldn't give in. "I have to say, I feel rather sorry for you. Clinging to such a petty ambition when the rest of the world has moved on."

Suzanne's breathing was heavy, her nerves twitched. "What are you talking about?"

"You can't see it, but the others gave up long ago. You say there were rules to the game, but you were the one who drew them up and no one else really gave a damn."

For all the guile she'd handled us with up to now, I could see that this cut her deeply. "That's not true. No matter how it happened, I'm the last one standing."

"You really don't get it, do you, Suzanne?" I pushed my chair back, my eyes fixed on hers. "Even before Astrid died, you were the only one playing."

"No, you're wrong," she growled, but, as her words died away, it seemed as though the truth had finally sunk in. "You don't know anything about me."

With Penelope at my side, we were half-way to the door before Suzanne spoke again.

"Who *are* you?" It ate away at her to not be in possession of every last fact. She was a woman who lived for control and we'd ripped it clean away.

I stopped beside the dining table to answer her. "I'm just the nanny."

She was up on her feet and charging towards me, her eyes shot through with despair.

"No you're not." Her voice was one long screech. "Tell me who you are!"

I smiled and kept walking, then threw my reply over my shoulder as I walked through the door. "Don't worry, you'll soon find out."

Chapter Twenty-Five

"So…" Penelope began as we hid away in a corner of the kitchen while Ramesh put the last touches to his grand feast. "Does this mean that Suzanne's the killer?"

"Nope, sadly not." I was trying to get things straight in my head as she talked to me.

"Does it mean she's not the killer then?"

I let the question mix in with all the other thoughts I had whirling about up there. "No, we can't say that exactly either."

"So then no one did it? Astrid murdered herself? It's not going to be one of those twist endings where the murderer was actually the creepy old caretaker who was sneaking about our houses lighting the fires?"

This was one possibility it felt safe to rule out. "No, I don't think Maggie's involved."

"Maggie?" Ramesh called across to us. "Someone called Maggie rang Howard a minute ago to say that the police are on their way up to us, but the snow is pretty thick so it's going to take a while."

"Thanks, Ra." I suddenly felt a bit guilty for investigating a murder with another assistant right there in front of my regular sidekick, but he was busy stirring a casserole and didn't seem to mind.

Penelope had more questions. "What was all that stuff you made me ask about the books Suzanne has read?"

"'The Prince' by Machiavelli is a famous text which promotes immorality and deceit as necessary tools for advancing your goals. It says that a good leader's focus should be solely on war and I think that Suzanne used it as her bible, or at least as the rules of the game she was playing."

I'm not sure that this cleared much up for Penelope. "I mean, I've heard of it, obviously. But have you actually read it?"

"Nope. If I'm honest, I pretty much only read murder mysteries these days. But I know what it's about."

"How?"

"I'm not sure, I just know stuff." I considered the question for a moment. "Maybe it's because, when I was a kid, Mum didn't let me watch any TV so I read a million books instead. I used to read our set of encyclopaedias, and anything to do with history or science, and I still remember a lot of that stuff – but that was before I discovered Agatha Christie. I've pretty much stuck to crime fiction since then."

I'd started to ramble so Penelope got me back on track. "Okay, so now what?"

It was the most important question she could ask. I had a good idea who the killer was. I had everything I needed to be able to identify them, I just hadn't quite put it all together in my head.

"Now… it's time for dinner," Ramesh answered for me.

"No, Ra. I'm too busy." I stamped my foot like a toddler. "We're only inches away from the truth. Couldn't you give us another half an hour to-"

He had a face like thunder, lightning and a whole hurricane to boot. "Sally Starmer! I have been slaving away in a hot kitchen all day so that you and your friends could have an earth-shatteringly delicious festive meal. I'm not going to overcook my masterpiece just so that you can play detective."

Another piece of the mystery became clear in my mind and I experienced a unique mix of elation and stupidity as I realised that I should have got there so much earlier.

"Ramesh Khatri, you're brilliant!" He looked back at me as if such a comment was glaringly obvious. "You are my closest friend, a better than average actor, a surprisingly excellent chef, a very convincing Freddy Mercury impersonator and a total genius!"

I ran across to him and gave him a massive great kiss on the cheek. He did not look happy about it.

"Is–oh–bel! I have a girlfriend!" I'd rarely seen him look so outraged (that week). "But as it happens, I do have a theory for who the killer might be."

"Well, you have definitely earned a guess." I couldn't wipe the smile from my face.

A clandestine look passed over him and he called Penelope and me in closer. "What if Astrid and Katie were secretly sisters who were separated at birth and-"

I'd heard enough. "I'm going to stop you there as Katie is the most British looking woman on earth and Astrid had a mixture of Japanese,

190

American and, from her name, presumably Swedish blood."

He wasn't giving up. "Yeah, but what if two different sperm donors-"

"Okay, I take it back. You're an idiot." I blew him another kiss to show I didn't mean it. "Come on, Ra. It's time to serve dinner."

Out in the lounge, Kevin had fetched his console to hook 'Zombie Death Squad IV' up to the TV and had kindly let his little brother have a turn. Neither of them looked like they wanted to be interrupted. I watched for a minute until Aidan's zombie avatar had been torn to pieces by a rampaging mob with pitchforks.

Fun fact, I once dated a guy who was really into computer games. He used to make me watch him play and would explain the plots like they were Shakespearean dramas. I'm very sorry to admit that, back in the days of 'Zombie Death Squad II', I would patiently sit there pretending to be interested.

Urggggghhhh, Nigel. Shudder.

I'm happy to admit that the relationship didn't last long and that at least one good thing came out of it.

The meal was announced and even Grantham and Bertie were coerced into the same room – though at far ends of the table from one another. I probably should have paid more attention to the dinner, but I was devoting the full processing power of my brain to fitting the final pieces of evidence in place to prove my theory.

There were new entries to add to the lists in my head, not least Ramesh's hot kitchen and death itself. When the job was done, I discovered that we were half-way through the mouth-watering coq au vin main course – Penelope later informed me that the starter was a salmon pastry roulade and that I enjoyed it immensely.

I had no idea how I'd managed to split my mind like that to be able to function on two separate wavelengths at the same time.

Ahem… Maybe your little old brain lent a hand?

Ahhhhh. Thanks, brain!

To summarise my thought process, I could draw a line through **the letters to Katie, Astrid's affair, the missing murder weapon, Ramesh's kitchen, Machiavelli's 'The Prince' and the size-fourteen boots** on the list of evidence. This told me pretty much everything I needed to know to be able to circle the guilty party and chalk up my final hypothesis.

I came back to consciousness in the middle of a conversation with Howard about whether the movie 'Elf' is equal or superior to 'White Christmas.' (Sorry, Bing Crosby, Buddy beats you hands down.)

"Don't be a total idiot!" I said, far too aggressively and everyone stopped eating to stare at me. "Oh, whoops. Sorry about that, Howard. I just really like 'Elf'."

He looked so sad and shocked right then that I wanted to give him a hug.

I put my head down and concentrated on eating the fancy French dinner in the awkward hush that we'd fallen into. I can't say for sure, but I got the impression that, before my outburst, Howard and I had been the only ones speaking anyway. Even Ramesh was unusually discreet as he served champagne and transported condiments around the table. He wore a smart white shirt and waiter's waistcoat that he'd got on our case in Spain – I was surprised there'd been space for anything so practical in his luggage.

When I found the nerve to look back up again, it was not a pretty sight to behold. Well, the table was. It was gorgeous in fact – with shiny gold candelabras, matching napkins and crackers with sprigs of real holly on – but the faces of the assorted guests told me that, by this point in the proceedings, few of them wanted to be there.

Suzanne and Toffee kept shooting me evil looks from under their colourful paper crowns. Grantham and Bertie looked like they wanted to go for round two and even Kevin and Justine appeared to have had an argument and were sitting far apart. The only cheerful person there was baby Amelia, who was gurgling happily in her highchair.

"Alright," I said, standing up. "That's enough." All eyes fell upon me. "I know this is not the Christmas Eve that most of you were looking forward to, but perhaps there's one thing I can do to make it better."

I reached into my trouser pockets and took out my glasses. As I put them on, several gasps went up around the table. To be honest, as I still had my contacts in, this made everything blurrier.

"Izzy Palmer?" Suzanne said in the voice of a woman who knew she'd been played for a fool. Justine took a photo on her phone and Howard said, "No, it can't be."

Bertie seemed oddly vexed by the trick I'd played. "I can't believe you reverse-Supermanned us!"

"That's right. It is I!" I said, sounding rather too much like a villain in pantomime. "I mean… It's me, Izzy Palmer."

I waited for this revelation to do its job. Toffee looked particularly nervous, Penelope was enjoying my big moment and Grantham had raised his hand like a schoolchild.

"Sorry? Who's Izzy Palmer?"

There's always one!

"Izzy Palmer of the Private I Detective Agency?" I tried but his face remained blank. "I solved the murder of the billionaire Aldrich Porter and brought film star Sammy Akerele's killer to justice? No, doesn't ring a bell?"

Grantham shrugged apologetically. "I'm afraid I don't watch a lot of television."

He doesn't read the news much either, apparently.

"Okay, not to worry. I'm sure you'll get the gist of what's going on."

Bertie was up next with an interruption of his own. "Is it okay if I keep eating?" The answer to my question was irrelevant as his mouth was already stuffed full of food. "We wouldn't want it to get cold."

"Fine, yes. Go ahead." Everyone picked up their cutlery and I felt like I was putting on a dinner theatre murder mystery performance. "Where was I?"

The disruptions had really knocked my concentration and I stared about the room trying to make sense of the scene. I noticed for the first time that there was a single empty space at the far end of the long dining table where Astrid would have been sitting.

"You're Izzy Palmer," Ramesh helpfully reminded me as he topped up my champagne and disappeared back off to the kitchen.

"Right… yeah, that's it. I'm Izzy Palmer and I was hired by Katharine to come here and pose as a nanny because she was worried about her safety. As you all know, Katie has been receiving letters threatening her life. She believed that someone was planning to kill her on this holiday, which is why she hired me. In the end, though it wasn't Katie who was murdered but poor Astrid Spear, her long-term friend and rival."

I froze and waited to see if any of them would react. "Before we begin, I have to tell you that I'm not going to reveal the incriminating evidence I have on each suspect to make it seem like you must be the killer before moving on to the next person."

"Oh, go on," Bertie cried out in disappointment. "I love it when Poirot does that. He's such a troll. Everyone thinks they're going to get banged up but then he shifts the blame to someone else. Brilliant."

"Yeah, go on, Izzy," his brother joined in. "It sounds like fun."

I crossed my arms and let out a huff. "Fine, but don't expect me to put my heart into it."

"That's the spirit." Penelope added her own special brand of cheerleading.

Their demand changed things and so, to make sure I didn't give the poor woman a breakdown, I went over to Katie to whisper a warning in her ear. She nodded her consent so I was free to begin.

"Right, there are a lot of people here, so let me rule out the kids first and Penelope and Rupert too, as they are quite a bit younger than the rest of you and not so integral to the main group of friends. Plus I couldn't find any evidence on them anyway."

Rupert looked seriously put out about this. "That's not fair. I might have killed her. There are plenty of murderers in our family history. Downright rotters we were for most of the seventeenth century in fact. I could have taken after any one of them."

Penelope was next up to make the case for her husband's guilt. "And don't forget the hundred grand Astrid made you invest in that wearable tech company which never got past the start-up stage." She turned to look at me with a frown. "You should probably have found that much out yourself, Izzy."

"That's right." Rupert sounded quite proud of himself. "I should at least be a suspect."

They were becoming a pain and I decided to do something. "Did you kill her?"

He looked a bit embarrassed. "Well… no."

"Good, then be quiet." That shut them up. "As I said, I was going to skip straight to the killer but, let's do things Poirot-style, shall we?" In fitting with the moustachioed Belgian master detective's own brand of suspense, I paused before starting in on my grand finale.

"Astrid was a capable woman with an incredible head for business. She'd started her life in humble origins but won a scholarship to study at the elite Oxford University here in Britain." I thought about adding the fact that some of the scenes from Harry Potter were filmed there, but it wasn't the right moment. "In her first year there, she moved in with Suzanne and Katharine. The three became inseparable friends, but underpinning their relationship was a competitive streak which would come to define them for years after."

It was time for another interruption. "You are aware that everyone in this room knows this part of the story?" Suzanne's tone was layered with spite. "In fact, we're the ones who told you all this in the first place."

I ignored her and carried on regardless. "The rivalry they shared was only enhanced when the girls met the three men they would go on to marry. Of course, this is a murder investigation, not a romance, so things did not go smoothly. Astrid fell hard for Howard who ran in the other direction and got together with Katharine. Unlucky the first time round, Astrid tried again with Toffee but the future admiral was lovestruck and had eyes for no one but his girlfriend Suzanne."

This revelation drew a gasp from Katharine who had always considered Howard's rejection to be the cause of Astrid's past heartache.

"In many ways, it was this rejection which set us on the path to where we are today." I'd finally got their attention and stopped to let the implications of this statement simmer. "Still, Astrid didn't give up. She was third time lucky with a man who charmed her and supported her and who she eventually fell in love with."

Fair enough. The man's wife's just been murdered, the least you can do is leave him his dignity. Nicely done.

"Grantham did not only share Astrid's love of business, but was entirely devoted to his future wife." I took a moment to address the three husbands. "I have to say that the men here today have shown great loyalty to their wives, which makes a change from most of my cases. Though I'm afraid, ladies, the same can't be said for all of you."

There was an awkward rustle and some downturned eyes, but marital strife wasn't really my area of expertise. I decided to leave my place at the head of the table and began my slow walk round to visit a friend.

"Over the years, the competition between these strong, ambitious women became stricter, fiercer and more defined. Suzanne talked about it as a game and it was clear that, as your lives developed after university, the three of you continued to be active participants. Katharine went into the arts, Suzanne academia and Astrid worked her way up through various pharmaceutical companies until she made it to the top of the pyramid, as the director of a multi-national corporation. They each had their own successes and setbacks and no doubt did all they could to undermine their fellow competitors."

I had paused behind Kevin and put my hands on his chair. He glanced over his shoulder uncomfortably and clearly didn't enjoy having a woman twice his height towering over him at the dinner table so I kept walking. "Of these three women, one was terrorised and another is now dead."

"Oh just get on with it." Suzanne was seething by now but I didn't let her heckles get to me.

"It was a conundrum. I couldn't resolve the fact that someone had sent death threats to Katharine but murdered poor Astrid." Katie flinched a little as I said this and I reminded myself to go softly for her sake. "But I shouldn't have got so hung up on the letters because they were just a distraction. I spent most of today trying to figure out who wanted both Katie and Astrid dead, when the only question that mattered was, who wanted to hurt Astrid?" I finally reached my destination at the far end of the table, directly in front of Grantham. "I told you that all three husbands stayed loyal to their wives, but is it possible to be a loyal partner and also your wife's murderer?"

No one answered as Ramesh returned to collect the plates. I'd hardly touched my main course so he drew a box in the air and turned a dial to suggest he'd put it in the microwave for me later.

RESULT!

"Grantham, you told me yourself that you didn't live up to Astrid's high standards. She grew cold and critical before finally tiring of you altogether and taking a lover. You wouldn't be the first man who discovered his wife's betrayal and decided to seek revenge."

The nondescript little man didn't show any sign of having heard me. In his typically understated way he withdrew into himself, his muscles stiffening, his gaze becoming vacant. I left his guilt as a possibility and moved on to the next suspect.

"And what of the lover? What of Bertrand Gravely-Swans, the

196

recently knighted lord of the manor. He was certainly an impressive catch for a girl from Nowhereseville USA. He had wealth, status… I was going to say charm, but that's not quite the right word."

Apparently enjoying the attention, Bertie smiled down the table at me in silence.

"I can only imagine how thrilled Astrid was to laud it over her biggest rival. Suzanne was the only one of you who didn't seem shocked when the truth about Sweet Boy came out. Astrid must have been desperate to reveal how she'd trumped an admiral with a full-blown lord."

I didn't dare look at Suzanne, but returned to the other side of the room to address Bertie. "I doubt you minded, did you, old chum? You must have known that you were just a pawn in their game."

He laughed and his ruddy cheeks wobbled. "It was fine by me. She could use me all she liked."

Understandably, Grantham threw a silver teaspoon down the table at him, which made contact with a satisfying clack on Bertie's skull.

"Perhaps that wasn't the end of it though. Perhaps you wanted more than to be her bit on the side. You could offer so much. You could make her a lady, expand her wealth fivefold, but Astrid had already got what she wanted from you, isn't that right?"

I had hoped to see some reaction from him, but Bertie kept his usual contented smile on his face, so I pressed on. "She wouldn't be the first person to take advantage of you. I saw it the moment we met. You may be a lord and heir to the family fortune, but you've never quite fitted in with this lot, have you, Bertie? You're great for a laugh and to scrounge a few quid off, but not exactly the marrying type, even if you are filthy rich."

I saw a slight wince from him then, the tiniest movement of a muscle in one cheek.

"And at some point, your patience ran out. You were tired of being used by every last person who was supposed to care about you and you snapped. Was that what happened this morning? Did Astrid drop by to give you your Christmas present with the news that it was over between you? Did you follow her outside and give her a surprise of her own?"

That's when it hit him. I was expecting rage and anger, but instead, a single tear descended from his right eye and in a slow, fragile voice, he spoke.

"Sorry, old duck, you've got the wires crossed. Astrid was waiting until after Christmas to tell Grantham that she was leaving. You were right the first time, I was going to make her Lady Gravely-Swans."

This was too much for Grantham and he yelled out a primal scream from deep in his body. It hit me too. I hadn't been expecting a further twist at this stage and, as if to underline the drama, Ramesh kicked the door open and appeared with a plate full of fire.

Chapter Twenty-Six

"Who's for Christmas pudding?" He wore his usual over-the-top smile which disappeared when he saw the serious faces of every diner there. "Sorry, bad moment? I'll be as quiet as possible. You won't even notice I'm here."

I glared at him lovingly and he stood beside Howard to silently enquire who wanted a portion of flambéed dessert.

"Okay," I said decisively, but wasn't entirely sure where to go from there. "Alright… So Astrid and Bertie were having an affair…" This unnecessary repetition caused Grantham to burst into tears and his daughter ran to comfort him. I noticed that none of the revelations had made Justine cry, but then she'd been dealing with her mixed feelings about her mother from the beginning. I was about to continue with the job I was there for when she stood up again.

"You know what, I don't think I need to hear all this stuff." She walked to the other end of the table. "I'm going to take Aidan and Amelia and we'll finish our dinner in the other room." She picked up the baby but didn't leave. "Are you coming, Kevin?"

He looked torn, but presumably wanted to hear the end of the story. "No, you go ahead." He turned back to the action and she sullenly escorted the kids from the room.

I tried to pick the thread back up but it wasn't easy. "Ok, so Astrid and Grantham…"

Luckily Penelope was there to help me out. "No, you've done that bit. Move on to another suspect perhaps?"

"Right, yeah… thanks."

Do Katie next! No, Howard! I can't wait to see you grilling that big cuddly chap, it'll be brilliant.

I didn't like to give in to my brain's whims but Howard was the obvious next person.

"When Katharine first came to see me, she believed it was her husband who had written the letters. She was already on edge from the death of her parents a year earlier and a difficult period of depression and perhaps paranoia after her pregnancy. The arrival of those cruel threats made her believe that Howard wanted to kill her."

The Scotsman didn't laugh the accusation off or give an excuse, he sat there and listened to what I had to say, as Ramesh once again hurried back off to the kitchen.

"None of us imagined that kind and Christmassy Howard would do anything to hurt his wife, but what if we were wrong? What if there was truth behind poor Katie's claims and, just as he intended, the letters made her look crazy?"

I walked past a nervous-looking Toffee to position myself directly in front of Howard. "Do you know what gaslighting is?"

He showed no fear as he answered. "Yes. It's the fact of denying someone's reasonable accusations and suggesting they are mad in order to gain influence over them. The term comes from a very enjoyable horror film from the fifties."

Okay, but is it as good as 'Elf'?

I wasn't expecting such a full answer. "Okay, good. And thank you for that very accurate definition, Howard. I came to wonder whether this was what you were doing to Katie. If you wanted control of her fortune or to take custody of baby Amelia it would have served you well. But, if that was your plan, why kill Astrid?"

Howard did not look comfortable this time, though he was immediately let off the hook when Ramesh reappeared with a jug of homemade custard. He burst through the door, opened his mouth to ask who needed serving then remembered I was busy.

"Seriously, Ra. This is the last time you're coming to one of these things. You always mess them up!"

"I'm sorry, Izzy." He didn't sound it. "But we've both got a job to do." He raised his chin haughtily and took a turn round the table, ladling out the sweet yellow liquid to whoever needed it.

Fairly sure that he wouldn't interrupt again, I moved on to my next suspect. "There was another explanation which I was reluctant to even consider." I turned to look at my employer who once more quaked at my words. "When Katharine first came to see me, she was scared and skittish. She talked about people who were following her and the lengths she'd gone to in order to lose them."

Two more steps and I was back at my place, directly opposite her. "It was hard for me to imagine that this was just a performance, an act, a role she had adopted. But Katie could easily have written the letters to incriminate Howard and distance herself from the crime she was plotting."

I kept my voice low, my rhythm steady. I was laying out the case, not trying to terrify her but still Katharine turned and jerked like she was suffering through a bad dream. "Hiring a detective to look into the death threats you were receiving would be the perfect cover if you were planning to murder an old friend. But this still didn't explain why you would have wanted Astrid dead."

I looked around the faces of my audience. For the large part, they were trapped within the story but Suzanne still regarded me with the disgruntled scowl that had been glued to her face for the last hour.

"After all, you retired from the rivalry you shared with your old friends after your parents died. But more than that, you'd retired from life. You haven't painted since the day it happened, you haven't shown your face on the London art scene and, if it weren't for little Amelia popping up at just the right time, you might never have re-emerged from your seclusion. Astrid meant nothing to you any longer so why would you have killed her?"

My question caused Rupert to tut at the very idea his sister could have been involved, but Katie kept her eyes on me. "From the moment I found the body I focussed on six main suspects. Bertie, Howard, Katie, Grantham, Toffee and Suzanne. But there were more. The kids could have been involved of course, but there was another person whose importance I hadn't considered."

"Rupert!" Penelope said with some glee.

"Penelope!" her husband called back.

"No, of course not." I again had to wonder why those two were so obsessed with the idea that their loved ones were murderers.

"Astrid." Grantham was far smarter than anyone gave him credit for.

"Exactly." I waited for the reaction to ripple around the room. "You suggested the very same thing before the murder; Astrid could easily have been the one sending the letters. Perhaps she really meant to kill Katie or simply wanted to get her back in their petty game, but, whatever the reason, I'd found my motive. In her already distressed state, Katie discovered who'd been terrorising her and decided to do something about it. She learnt of her brother and Astrid's plan to meet early on Christmas Eve and mercilessly stabbed her to tormenter to death."

A heavy silence followed. This was the darkest vision of what could have happened and the atmosphere in the room had hardened. Howard's poor face was wracked with fear, Bertie put his arm out involuntarily to protect his sister and Kevin released a breath that he must have been holding for the last five minutes.

All the nerves had drained out of Katie. As she confidently held my gaze, she was like a different person.

"That's a pretty story you've constructed, Izzy. But how on earth can you prove it?"

Chapter Twenty-Seven

There was another silence. Another torturous, heart-breaking moment of uncertainty before I spoke.

"No, of course I can't prove it." I straightened up to address the room, an irrepressible smile dancing on my lips. "Because Katie isn't the killer and neither she nor Astrid wrote the letters."

Relief abounded, those who'd fallen still were finally free to stretch muscles and relax.

"All the different stories I've laid out up to now were just theories. They were flights of fancy that I considered and dismissed on my path to discovering what really happened out in the snow this morning. One of the reasons I'm good at this job is that I can put myself in the mind not just of a criminal but a crime writer. I've constructed all these plots for you, though sometimes, the truth is even more surprising than fantasy."

Ramesh had been loitering and decided that this would be the best moment to speak up. "Would anyone like some cheese? Or how about the last piece of Christmas cake? Suzanne, you know you want it!"

I saw Bertie raising his hand but I was too quick. "They've all had enough, Ramesh. So be quiet and listen to the rest of the story." I pulled back my chair at the head of the table. "I know that's why you keep coming in here anyway." Without another word, he did as instructed and I hovered behind him to continue with the explanation.

Although the interruption had provided a little respite, tension lingered. It was obvious that the list of remaining suspects had dwindled. The others threw shifting glances down the table towards Toffee and Suzanne as he offered his wife his hand and, for once, she accepted it. They watched me quietly, their muscles taut, their faces harrowed.

"I should never have forgotten the impact a person can have even after they are dead." I had a sudden flashback to my first case; I saw myself laying out the evidence in a similar setting but with far less tinsel around. "As none of my theories quite fitted with what I'd discovered about Astrid, I went back to the beginning and re-examined everything I knew.

"When I woke up this morning, I found Astrid in that perfect snowy vista with a large hole in her back. There was no sign of a weapon and it was only this evening that I understood where it had gone. But once I knew, I had everything I needed to be sure who the killer was."

I stopped and reached past Ramesh to get my glass of champagne. I was thirsty, sure, but I also liked making them wait. "On my walk in the woods with Howard this afternoon, I had the seed of an idea and it quickly grew. I don't want to diminish the killer's achievement – making the murder weapon disappear in a puff of steam is a pretty neat trick – but, honestly, if they'd used a regular knife or gun, I might never have found them.

"You see, Astrid had her back pierced in several places by one of the icicles cut from the edge of the vacant chalet. Whoever wielded it must have sharpened the end and driven it straight into her body with all the strength they possessed. I'm guessing they'd already heated up the oven and simply popped the disposable weapon inside when they were done. At first, I didn't think anything of the hot kitchen and cloud of steam that Ramesh had to deal with but, eventually, the pieces fell into place."

I went over to look at the Christmas tree and a few of the suspects turned to face me. I paused to watch their reflection in a dangling bauble. "There was another big clue at the scene which seemed like a dead end to begin with. A set of giant footprints belonging to the killer and Astrid's far smaller ones, visible alongside. I hoped that I could trace the tracks back to the killer's chalet, but there were wet prints leading into every last building, a fact that again did not seem relevant until much later this evening.

"We found a pair of size-fourteen boots stashed in the entrance of Howard and Katie's chalet. This suggested that, as no one here takes such large shoes, the killer had disguised their footprints, which led me to think they had noticeably small feet. By first writing the letters threatening Katie and then planting the boots, they were trying to pin the murder on poor Howard with his novelty Brussel sprout ties and penchant for Christmas carols."

I turned round to see Howard frown and his wife squeeze his hand in support.

"What a clever murderer, right? Well… maybe not so much. Even the laziest killer wouldn't leave a key piece of evidence in plain sight.

So, unless it was a truly elaborate double bluff, the boots and giant footprints made me even less likely to believe the Taggarts were behind the crime."

I stopped myself then to perform an unconvincing double-take. "Oh, by the way, Suzanne, what size shoes do you wear?"

She looked unwilling to answer at first but finally shouted, "Four and a half," with an aggressive pout.

"Oh, quite small then." I nodded as if reflecting on this fact. I could see how much she hated this whole situation. "Good to know. And actually, as the day has gone by, I've found that I keep coming back to you Winters. First it was Toffee who caught my attention. He'd teased Astrid on the plane about her past infatuation with Howard and I could tell that there was more to the story than he was letting on."

Typical teenager Kevin peered down the table judgementally at his parents as I laid out the case against them.

"After Toffee was accused of being Astrid's lover, a thread of pure rage surged up within him. During our interview, I realised that it wasn't just the suggestion that he'd been unfaithful to his wife that had angered him, but the very idea that he would have slept with Astrid Spear."

I marched up to the table and pulled his chair round to face me. Well, I tried to, but he was heavy and it wasn't easy. Long story short, he actually had to help me a bit, but then... *then*, I was free to look him straight in the eyes as I asked my next question.

"You hated her, didn't you? You hated Astrid because she used to flirt with you whenever she got the chance. She would rub up against you and sit on your lap, right there in front of your wife and children."

"You're right. I couldn't stand her," he replied, with that fury back in his voice. "The woman was despicable."

This was enough for Grantham and he was up on his feet throwing whatever he could get his hands on at the admiral. Chunks of Christmas pudding flew across the table towards us and Suzanne had to pull the man down into his seat with a clatter.

"She's dead!" he wailed. "How can you speak about her like that after what happened?" His words were swallowed up by his tears and he descended into a blubbering mess.

I didn't let up but kept pressing Toffee. "That wasn't the only problem you had with Astrid though. You hated her because you could never be as important to Suzanne as she was. Your wife has spent the last twenty years obsessed with winning a game that you didn't get to play. You worship the ground she walks on but Suzanne has never shown such devotion. She talks about your marriage as a business arrangement, but for you it's a love song and you'd do anything for her."

He snorted then, unconvinced. "So I killed Astrid to get in Suzanne's good books. Is that what you're saying? Please, my sons could come up with a better explanation than that."

I froze, still looking at him, then gave in and smiled. "You're probably right. After all, your wife has brought them up to be warriors, just like her. And, to be honest, Toffee, I never really thought you had it in you."

Are you trying to get on people's nerves tonight?

Yep! I want to see who'll get mad.

"The truth is, you're not really compatible with Suzanne's idea of what a husband should be. She must have thought that, by marrying a naval officer, she'd be getting a fighter but as you told me yourself, you're more of a pen-pusher."

I straightened back up and looked across at his wife. "No, it wasn't Toffee who killed Astrid. As both he and Suzanne proudly told me, she's the one who has the makings of a killer." I froze and waited to see if she would react before delivering my verdict. "The blame for everything that has gone on here today should be placed at Suzanne Winters' door. If it wasn't for her, Astrid would still be alive."

I saw Grantham tighten one hand around his fork so I quickly ran around the table to put myself in the spare place between him and my chosen culprit.

"No," I told him, putting one hand on his shoulder and prizing the fork free with the other. "You don't know all she's guilty of yet. Just wait a little longer."

Katie let out a sob then and buried her head in her hands. I'd warned her before this started that it wouldn't be easy to sit through but at least Howard was there to comfort her. He wrapped her up in his muscular arms and it was good to see that the trust between them had returned.

Suzanne meanwhile was shrivelling up before us like a grape left in the sun. There was acid in her veins and her eyes shrank down to two tiny dots as I laid out the evidence.

"Let's go back, one final time. Back to last year when poor Katie was in an accident. There was a party, a drunken driver in front of her, a sudden crash and both her parents were killed. But you were on hand to play the good friend."

"I did what I could for her." She'd skipped any quiet, moody stage and started in on the shouting already. "I tried to help her when she needed me."

I was about to correct her when someone beat me to it.

"You tried to destroy me!" Katie screamed. "You twisted my words and made me believe that I'd killed my parents. You actually convinced me that I'd turned the car intentionally so that they'd die. You broke me down and stole my confidence, all in the guise of friendship. All for the sake of a competition that you should have grown out of when we were twenty."

Even Toffee looked disappointed in his beloved wife right then and I figured I'd pile a bit more shame on Suzanne (it's a private detective's prerogative).

"It wasn't enough that her parents had died, bruised and bloodied right beside her, you wanted your victory over Katie to be absolute. I don't know the rules of your game, but it's clear that the only way to win was to destroy your opponent. And that's why you killed Astrid."

For all the judgement directed her way, Suzanne wouldn't give up. "I didn't kill her, you moron."

I kept on. "Everything I discovered told me how arrogant the killer was. Murdering someone in a secluded spot when there were so few other suspects who could be blamed. That took guts or desperation and I think you have a unique combination of the two. It's not just this week that shows it. It's the way you live your life, the way you raise your family. You said it yourself, you're a warrior; you believe that the end always justifies the means. You are a killer."

"I was speaking theoretically and you know it." All eyes were on her as she scrambled for a defence. "I'm an academic. I've studied death and corruption all my life. Evil fascinates me, but that doesn't mean I could murder another human."

I stared at her alone, my focus consumed. "That's not what you said to me earlier. And you certainly weren't far off with Katie. Your mind games drove her to the edge. How long would it have been before you persuaded her to jump from a window or slit her wrists? I can only imagine how proud you would have been to take a life without lifting a finger. Machiavelli would have approved."

She was floundering now, spitting out whatever she could think of to absolve herself of her crimes. "Izzy, you, more than anyone, should know that reading about immoral subjects does not make you a bad person." She glanced back and forth between me and her husband. "I didn't kill her. I didn't kill Astrid."

Her screeching voice rattled the cutlery and candelabras and I waited one... two... three... seconds before putting her out of her misery. "I know you didn't. But it's because of you that she's dead."

A loudly inhaled gasp came out of my assistants at the end of the room. Ramesh and Penelope sounded like kids in a haunted house, but I blocked them out.

"Perhaps your interest in evil is only academic, but if you bring up a child with the same philosophy, they may find it more difficult to draw the line between theory and practice. You didn't kill Astrid, but your son Kevin did."

I pointed down the table to the now empty chair where he'd been sitting one minute earlier.

Oops!

Chapter Twenty-Eight

"Where's he gone?" Grantham screamed, as he'd been a bit distracted by what was going on at our end of the table to worry about what some kid was up to.

"He slipped out," Howard replied. "I assumed he'd gone to see Justine."

"Wait," Toffee said, still wrapping his head around the idea that his son was a cold-blooded killer. "You said it wasn't one of the kids."

"Yes, but Kevin is sixteen, he's hardly a kid. He's old enough to join the army, old enough to get married and old enough to be tried as an adult for murder."

Suzanne was having trouble breathing as the truth set in. "How can you be sure he did it? What possible evidence have you got?"

"He's the only one who's been in the vacant chalet and Rupert told me that the giant footprints went into every house." I was up on my feet already.

Toffee raced to his son's defence. "That proves nothing."

"There's no time to explain all the other evidence. But if you think about the boots, the letters, Machiavelli's 'The Prince', 'Zombie Death Squad IV' and everything that happened last night you should get to the truth."

"Come on, we have to find him." Rupert had pulled his chair back, Penelope was not far behind and several others followed as I ran from the room to the lounge where Justine, Aidan and Amelia were playing sweetly together.

"Where did Kevin go?" I asked them and our sudden appearance clearly startled Justine.

"He... he went outside. He's been acting weird all afternoon. I don't even want to talk to him if you do find him." Pulling baby Amelia right in close to her, she suddenly looked much younger.

"Tell them where he's gone, darling. Kevin's done something terrible." Grantham had come to stand beside me and his daughter's eyes flicked over desperately to him.

"He's been hanging out in the empty chalet. The one on the end of the row. Maybe he's gone there again."

"Thank you, Justine," I said as her father sat down to comfort her.

Incidentally, I take it all back. I'm glad my first kiss was with Gary "Why are your breasts so small?" Flint and not Kevin "I'm planning to murder your mother" Winters.

It felt like we were a crack military unit as we suited up to go outside. I was joined by a whole troop of assistants, some more welcome than others. Ramesh, Penelope and Rupert were there, along with Kevin's abysmal parents.

Ooh, that's a bit judgemental, Izzy. Until you have kids of your own you can't know how hard it is.

Sorry, but I reckon I'll do a better job than they have.

I suppose the bar is pretty low. Estate agent, erotic dancer, British Prime Minister – pretty much anything is better than teen killer.

Kevin must have worked out how to turn off the main lights as, when we got outside, the village square was dark. As if this wasn't spooky enough, there was a ridiculously scary Christmas song that I'd never heard before coming out of the speakers. It went:

> **"Little children who have been naughty,**
> **Should, tonight, be scared.**
> **Santa's coming, they'll soon be caught,**
> **He'll catch them unawares.**
> **Yes Santa's coming a creeping**
> **Down your chimney pot,**
> **To catch all the naughty children**
> **Whether they like it or not!"**

"Oh my goodness," Penelope shrieked as the chorus repeated. "Is that supposed to be Christmas music?"

"It sounds more like the soundtrack to an Eastern European horror film." Ramesh hit the nail on the head.

"Look!" I pointed at the furthest house. The windows were all shuttered but we could make out a flashing light coming from the gap under the door. "He's definitely in there."

> **"He's creeping, he's creeping!**
> **He's coming to see you tonight.**
> **All of the very bad children,**
> **Are in for a very big fright."**

210

As we walked across the square, and this new verse of terror settled into my head, I whispered to Ramesh. "All of a sudden, I don't find the idea of Father Christmas sneaking into my house in the middle of the night so sweet anymore."

Suzanne took this opportunity to discuss who was to blame for Kevin's psychotic behaviour. "I still think this could be some kind of misunderstanding, but I'd like to point out that I am not his only parent. While I may have exposed him to certain adult concepts that he clearly wasn't ready for, his father being away for months on end playing about on boats can't have helped."

Toffee did not agree to disagree. "Oh, please, Suzanne. You're the one who gave him Sun Tzu's 'The Art of War' on his ninth birthday. Are you really trying to suggest any of this is my fault?"

"Well, I'm sorry for not infantilising our children, but studies show that a lot of the problems we have in our society today are caused by-"

"For goodness sake." The admiral was really shouting as we reached the far chalet. "Our son is a murderer and you tried to emotionally brainwash your best friend. *We* are the problem with our society today. No one else – it's us!"

"Guys." Rupert was calm and kind of cool as he sized up the entrance. "Keep it down." He was in stealth, soldier mode. He opened the door and pointed with two fingers to tell Toffee to go in. I'm pretty sure that, if he'd had any shoe polish, he'd have spread it on his cheeks to look like Rambo.

"Kevin?" Suzanne peered into the lounge. "Mummy and Daddy are here."

There were no lights on inside except for the frenetic strobing flash of the Christmas tree. It was like walking into a night club, which I find scary enough at the best of times. Ever the gallant officer, Toffee went in first. He stepped through the door, but instantly slipped over and fell flat on his back.

"Kevin!" He screamed and I could hear a small chuckle travel down from somewhere up above us.

Suzanne peered at the floor beneath her husband. "There are toy cars all over the place." Her eyes darted about in an attempt to make sense of the gloomy scene. "Do get up, Toffee. You're not helping anyone just lying there."

He let out a stifled moan. "I… I think I've done my back in."

"Seriously?" Suzanne was not the kind of person you'd want looking after you when you're sick.

We carefully tiptoed around the cars and through the lounge towards the staircase. No one spoke. With every flash of the pale yellow Christmas lights, my nerves grew.

"Watch out!" Penelope screamed as we reached the bottom step, but it was too late.

An extra-large can of tomatoes spun down from the floor above, landing with a sniper's precision on the top of Suzanne's head. She swayed on the spot like a punch-drunk boxer, before collapsing to the floor.

Rupert had already begun to mount the staircase as another object swung down towards us on a cord. With his military instincts, he got out of the way just in time, but put his hand out to grab it and instantly regretted the decision.

"Arghhhhhhhhhhhh!" he screamed and I winced as I caught sight of what he was holding. "Ow! Ow! Ow!" Poor Rupert went flying back out of the house to plunge his hand into the snow and the red-hot iron dangled in space between Ramesh and me.

"Izzy, do you realise what this is?" my friend said before I could. "Kevin Winters is reverse-Home-Aloneing us!"

We turned to one another to scream but then a thought occurred to me. "Actually, is he reverse-Home-Aloneing us? Or is this a straight-up 'Home Alone' scenario?"

He considered the question as another can fell perilously close to my foot. "Surely it's in reverse as he's the baddy and we're the good guys breaking into-"

"Sorry, you two." Penelope interrupted. "Can we talk about this later?"

"Sure."

"Yep, good idea," we said over one another.

"Thank you." Penelope was all business. "Now, how are we going to get upstairs?"

Ramesh had a bright idea. "Maybe there's a laundry chute we could climb?"

"In Britain?" she asked. "I've never seen such a thing outside of

American movies. What about scaling the roof to get through one of the outside windows?"

"Merry Christmas, you filthy animals!" Kevin shouted down. He timed the words to land at the same time as a clutch of Christmassy paperweights. They rained down noisily and would have done some serious damage if we'd been any closer.

"Don't be an idiot, Kevin." I doubted that reasoning with the homicidal teenager would do much good, but it was worth a try. "There's no getting out of here. The police are already on their way."

"Yeah? Well I doubt they'll take me alive." He seemed proud of this idea. "How did you know it was me?"

"I saw the icicle you'd cut off the side of this chalet. It didn't mean much on its own but when I remembered that Ramesh's oven was on this morning and the kitchen was steamy, I put it together. You were the only one I'd seen coming in here, and the other pieces fell into place through the day."

He paused, presumably thinking over the tiny margins that had led to his downfall. "What pieces?"

"Well, for one, your feet are small for a boy of your age. I figured that would be the kind of thing a teenager might be sensitive about and could have made you think of disguising your shoe size in the first place. What are you? A five?"

"I'm a five and a half." Rupert had told me this already, but it was easy to rile Kevin up. "And Mum says I might still have a growth spurt."

Penelope made the international gesture for *you keep him talking*, and decided to try her luck by slowly ascending the staircase.

I did as instructed. "There was a sense of over-confidence to the whole thing too which reminded me of the boys in my class at school. I mean, using a sharpened icicle and then melting it in the oven. It was all too clever, like whoever had come up with it thought they'd landed on the perfect crime."

"It would have been perfect..." He hesitated then. "If I'd got away with it. Go on, what else?"

Penelope made it up the first two stairs as I answered Kevin's question. "'Zombie Death Squad'!"

"What about it?"

"I had a boyfriend once who loved those games and when you

213

wrote the letters to Katie you used the scariest lettering you could find, which just happened to be from your computer game magazines. But you messed up, you used whole words instead of individual letters and when I saw you playing the game tonight I realised where I'd seen the word *death* in the letter we found in Amelia's room."

"Oh, I knew I shouldn't have used my magazines but Mum and Dad read everything online these days and they were all I had."

He tutted at himself then and Penelope kept climbing those stairs. She tiptoed up them in a ridiculously over the top manner but it was working. Kevin was too focused on my explanation to notice.

"Once again, though, you were trying to be too clever. You sent the letters to hide the fact that it was Astrid you wanted to kill and to shift the blame onto Howard. But no killer would have gone to such lengths if they wanted to avoid getting caught."

"Damn." He laughed like I'd told him a joke in the playground at lunch break. "Rookie mistake, eh?"

"Yeah, you won't be making that one again." *Not in jail he won't.* "When I first saw you kissing Justine in the snow, I thought it was so sweet and impulsive, but then the necklace you gave her made me realise it wasn't quite so spontaneous as it seemed. You must have organised this whole thing weeks in advance, all because Astrid wouldn't let you go out with the girl you liked."

He smirked at this like he was watching a character get slaughtered in one of his video games. "It wasn't just that. I genuinely hated her. She was evil to Justine and always flirting with my dad, so she deserved to die." I didn't expect to hear any remorse in his voice, but the casual way he spoke showed me that, for Kevin, it wasn't even a moral decision. Astrid was just an obstacle that he needed to remove. "But how did you know it was me? Justine could have been in on it too?"

Penelope had got to the first landing and was getting ready to rush up the final stretch of stairs. Ramesh clung onto my arm as we watched.

I took a deep breath and continued. "I did consider that Justine was involved, but the two of you have had very different upbringings."

"What's that meant to mean?" He didn't like this and his anger finally flared.

"You read Machiavelli before you were ten, right?"

"So?"

"Your mother taught you that life is war and nothing should stand in your way of success." I glanced down at Suzanne lying unconscious on the floor but couldn't feel too bad for her.

"What if she did?"

I caught Penelope's gaze as she psyched herself up for the charge up the last few steps. "You were her prince, Kevin. You were the future leader she was preparing for the crown but there was one thing she forgot to teach you."

"Oh yeah?" he said and tossed down a can of drink in our direction without bothering Penelope. "And what's that?"

"This isn't the sixteenth century." I nodded and the Queen's second cousin got the message to go. "These days, great leaders are better off loved than feared."

"That's possible," Kevin conceded, "but 'Any man who tries to be good all the time is bound to come to ruin.'"

My new friend let out a war cry as she stormed forward, only to come up against a large wooden chest, which hurtled down the stairs to squash her. If she hadn't jumped over the bannister at that exact moment, she'd have ended up a human pancake.

Kevin's appropriately maniacal laugh came down to us as Penelope scrambled to safety. "You guys give up? Or are you thirsty for more?"

"Oh, Kevin," I said with false admiration. "Quoting Machiavelli and 'Home Alone', you are so mature."

Penelope, Ramesh and I regrouped closer to the exit.

"What about if we all rush him at the same time?" she suggested. "He can't have had time to set up many more traps."

"Have you seen 'Home Alone'?" I demanded and she looked all perky and interested.

"No, I haven't actually. Would you recommend it?"

Inevitably, Ramesh got sidetracked. "Oh, you must watch it. It's about this boy who has to protect his home from criminals at Christmas after his parents go off on holiday without him."

"That does sound funny!"

"I'm waiting!" the mini-psycho shouted from upstairs.

It was Ramesh's turn to come up with a plan. "What about we try climbing up the roof outside and getting in through a window?"

"That's what I said about half an hour ago!" Penelope sounded a bit put out.

I had a better idea. "How about we learn from 'Home Alone' – which I have watched at least forty-seven times – and do what the two criminals should have done as soon as they got their first bruises?"

Chapter Twenty-Nine

We pulled Suzanne and Toffee's battered bodies back outside and barred the front door with the large plank of wood that fitted on the front of each chalet. The shutters around the house were already locked and there was only a small window at the top of the house that Kevin would have been able to escape through if it hadn't been thirty feet off the ground.

We probably looked a bit too pleased with ourselves as we stood together in the snow, in front of the well-secured house.

"You're all locked up, Kevin." Rupert was lying at his wife's feet, with his hand cooling off from where the demon child had given him a third-degree burn. "You aren't going anywhere until the police get here."

"There is one thing I can do," a little voice came back from the top of the chalet.

"Oh yeah." It was Penelope's turn to underestimate our enemy. "And what's that?"

"I can shoot my way out."

Fragments of broken glass rained down as the barrel of a rifle emerged from the top window. His first shot landed harmlessly in the snow but forced us to run for cover.

"Please, Kevin," Toffee shouted up from the spot where we'd left him. "Don't do anything stupid with that gun. You'll shoot your eye out!"

"You know, this isn't really my thing," I said to Ramesh as we cowered under the eve of the communal chalet. "I'm more of a *stay at home and read mystery novels* sort of person than a *get shot at in the snow* one."

"Where did he even get that gun from?" Ramesh complained and Kevin's prone father did his best to answer.

"We got it for his birthday." He groaned, as his back was obviously still hurting. "He promised he'd only use it for hunting."

"And you believed him?" It was my turn to feel a little outraged. "Do you know your son at all?"

Toffee sounded genuinely upset with himself. "At least it's only a three-round cartridge. Get him to fire off a few shots and, if you're lucky, he won't have any more ammunition."

"Yeah, course. Easy." Ramesh employed his most sarcastic voice but Rupert clearly didn't catch on.

He picked himself up off the floor, had a quick word with Penelope then ran straight into Kevin's line of sight. There was a bang and Rupert shouted, "That's two!"

It was Penelope's turn next. I couldn't believe how brave everyone was being. I was happy to wait for the police to turn up, but not this lot. She followed her husband's path through the snow, pausing for a second in the middle of the square then sprinting off again. A puff of white powder sprayed up where she'd just been standing.

"That's three!" Rupert screamed. "Go, Izzy go!"

Wait, what's he talking about?

I have no idea. No one told me anything. But... I think I have to do this.

Oh, please no. You're not going to be heroic again, are you?

I was already packing snow into my hand, ready to run.

Wait, Izzy. Before you go. I just want to say that, all this time we've spent together, I've loved every minute of it.

There was no time to thank my brain for her service as my moment had come.

I ran out from the side of the chalet and straight into the open square. As I got to the spot where I could see him best, I turned, pulled my arm back and threw my perfectly compacted snowball through the air. I could see just enough of Kevin's head over the window ledge as he reloaded. My well-timed projectile sailed through the space between us in a neatly curving arc. It was just like the snowball scene in 'Elf' – when Buddy hits a bully dead-on from fifty feet away. Except, of course, mine was nowhere near its target and fell with a wet splat against the wall of the chalet.

I watched Kevin train his rifle on me, just as Rupert popped up to throw a large rock straight at him. It hit the murderous sixteen-year-old plum on the side of the head, as the former soldier had intended, and the rifle fell harmlessly to the floor.

"Izzy, you did it!" Penelope sang, running out from under the overhanging roof to embrace me. "You were the perfect decoy!"

It was hard to take this as a compliment.

Ramesh was next to join us, as Rupert had put his hand back in the snow. Even without him, it was a joyous celebration. We jumped about excitedly, the three of us together with our arms around one another, until we could jump and yell no more. The smiles on our faces were wide enough to make our jaws ache and everything seemed right with the world.

Then, right when we didn't need them anymore, the police turned up in a massive snowplough. They drove into the village square with their headlights illuminating the scene.

"I'm Alfie!" the driver put his head out of the window to declare.

"Archie!" the guy on the passenger side added.

"Arnie!" a final cousin or brother or whoever yelled from inside the cab.

"Sorry we're late," Alfie continued. "Would you believe, we ended up at the other Christmas village down near the loch?"

The other guests appeared from the main chalet and Howard came forward to deal with the policemen. An ambulance arrived soon after to bandage up Rupert's hand and Suzanne had come around by this point but was taken off to hospital for observation. With the emergency lights shining back off all that snow, it felt like the end of 'Die Hard 2'.

It wasn't the Christmas Eve I would have chosen for myself. We all had to give statements, more officers came from Inverness to deal with the crime scene and they still had to talk Kevin down from inside the house, in case there were any more booby traps. But, in the end, when Toffee and Kevin had been taken away by the police for questioning and I'd offered to look after Aidan for the night, the chaos died down.

At midnight, I was the last one out in the square to watch the first white flakes of the new day falling to earth. 'Let it Snow, Let it Snow, Let it Snow' rang out from the village sound system and I looked up to the heavens, happy to have fulfilled nine-year-old Izzy's biggest wish of all.

Snow on Christmas Day for the very first time in my life. I'd been dreaming of a white Christmas since I was a kid and it had finally come true.

Chapter Thirty

I tried to be extra nice to Aidan that night. He really was a sweet boy and I hoped that he was young enough to overcome any negative impact his mother's insane moral teaching had had on him. To distract from the fact his brother was going to prison for murder, we built a gigantic den of cushions in the lounge and Ramesh, Justine, Amelia and I (i.e. the remaining children) all slept inside it under big, fleecy blankets.

When we woke up the next morning, it felt like a proper Christmas. I maintained my usual routine of sitting in front of the TV in my pyjamas and watching the original cartoon of 'How the Grinch Stole Christmas'. It actually made me feel more grown up to watch it with some kids for once. I was thirty now, with my own business and a one hundred per cent crime-solving record – far too old to be watching kids' shows on my own.

Tell me you don't mean that!

No, of course I don't. We'll never be too old for classic cartoons.

After Ramesh outdid himself with another delicious breakfast, it was time for Justine and her dad to leave. They were taking Aidan to the city to reunite him with his parents and then deal with all the hell they had to go through for themselves. There's no worse day of the year to spend in a police station, but I hoped that the fact they already knew who the killer was might offer some tiny comfort.

It was quiet at Santa's Glen once they'd gone. The roads had been cleared but Howard had called Jing Jing to say that we didn't need any special entertainment after all. Between meals, we sat around the fire, played with baby Amelia and discussed our plans for New Year. The remaining adults were happy in one another's company and Bertie seemed quite reserved after the revelations of the night before. Our quiet morning was soon interrupted though when Aggie pulled up in her black limo with a celebrity guest inside.

"Mum?" I'd heard the car and gone out to see who it was. "How on earth did you get here?" She didn't have time to answer as there were three dejected middle-aged-to-elderly men with her.

"You won't believe it, Izzy," my father told me.

"I still can't," Greg added.

Fernando was more resigned to their fate and regretfully revealed, "Your mother got us kicked off the cruise."

With her arms out, like she was greeting guests on her very own chat show, Mum came over to explain what had happened. "We didn't get kicked off. It was my manager's plan from the start. He said I need to make a name for myself in order to show the industry I mean business."

"Seriously, Mum. What did you do?" Sometimes you have to take a firm line with parents or they never learn.

"It's no big deal, darling. I just told them that the accommodation they gave me wasn't fit for a ferret, the food was inedible and that, if they didn't put Bu-Bu La Mer in a luxury veranda suite, I'd be calling for my helicopter to pick me up. Luckily they didn't fulfil my wishes and we were airlifted out of there."

"That's not very fair." I have long accepted my role as the mature one in our relationship. "You left them in the lurch."

She waved one flamboyant hand through the air. "Not at all, darling. I had the most wonderful understudy who deserved her moment in the spotlight. If anything, I was helping to develop new talent. And I'm sure this is what I need to kick-start my career. Leave 'em wanting more, that's what I say." She gave a wink, then pulled me in for a hug. "Now, what's for Christmas dinner?"

Mum bustled past me into the house and immediately made friends with everyone inside.

"It's nice to see you, Izzy." Dad had his typical cautious smile on as he gave me a hug. Greg and Fernando queued up to do the same and I felt like I was the celebrity.

Ramesh had dropped his phone in the sink, so he finally had to admit to the remaining members of the Gravely-Swans clan that he didn't have the faintest idea how to cook the gigantic turkey that had been ordered for lunch. If anything, this made Howard happier and I got to look after Amelia one last time while he and his wife were busy cooking.

"You didn't think I was going to leave you *lonely this Christmas*, did you darling?" my mother asked, once she'd grabbed a glass of sherry and settled in beside the roaring fireplace. "You almost messed things up by rushing off to Scotland like that. Ramesh told me there was a spare chalet here, though, so we changed our destination." A wide smile reshaped her pretty face.

"Why didn't you tell me what you had planned?"

Her eyes sparkled in the warm glow that surrounded us. "And spoil the surprise? What would be the fun in that?"

"It's a Christmas miracle!" Ramesh shouted from over at the piano.

That warm, festive sensation buzzed through me as Mum went off for a duet of "I Heard the Bells on Christmas Day". The others dashed about getting everything ready and the smell of roast potatoes and gravy wafted in from the kitchen.

With my favourite Christmas mystery on my lap waiting to be delved into, I sat appreciating the wonderful assortment of people that had come together, up there in the snow. Bertie was hanging extra decorations, as he claimed it wasn't Christmassy enough, Rupert and Penelope were holding the chair, expecting him to fall down, and Baby Amelia was lying on the carpet rolling from one side to another with great joy.

As Mum's and Ramesh's voices blended together to sing, "Peace on earth, goodwill to men," I thought, *yep, that's pretty much it.*

It was a perfect, traditional Christmas. Just a happy wee family, three of my parents, my best friend, an Earl, a lord, a sort of princess and Mum's hairdresser. I couldn't have planned it better if I'd tried.

The End

Wherever you're reading this, we wish you a very merry Christmas, from Benedict, Marion, and Amelie Brown.

Find out how Izzy's adventure began…

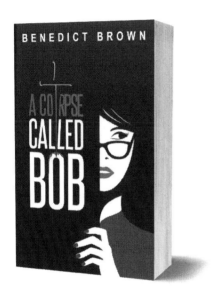

"A CORPSE CALLED BOB"
(BOOK ONE)

Izzy just found her horrible boss murdered in his office and all her dreams are about to come true! Miss Marple meets Bridget Jones in a fast and funny new detective series with a hilarious cast of characters and a wicked resolution you'll never see coming. Read now to discover why one Amazon reviewer called it, *"Sheer murder mystery bliss."*

The next **Izzy Palmer Mystery**
will be available in **spring 2021** at amazon

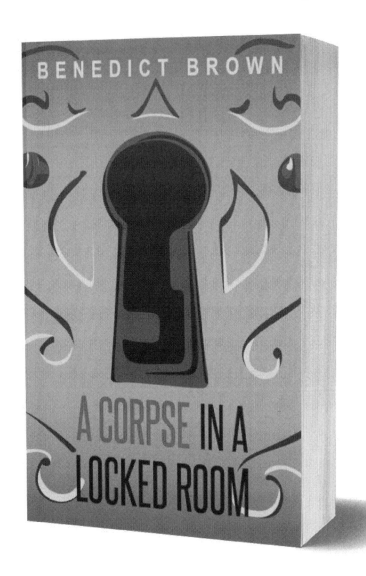

Izzy is heading to a big family party, oops...
someone's going to die.

Get your **Free** Izzy Palmer Novellas...

If you'd like to hear about forthcoming releases and download my free novellas, sign up to the Izzy Palmer readers' club via my website. I'll never spam you or inundate you with stuff you're not interested in, but I'd love to keep in contact.

www.benedictbrown.net

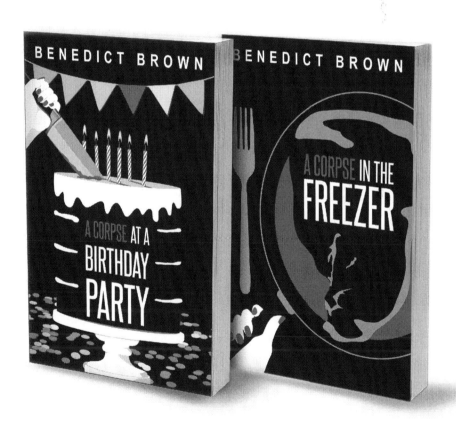

About This Book

I have no hard evidence on this, but I'm going to guess a lot of writers who release Christmas-themed books are doing so because they believe it will make them money. I like money, but that's not why I wrote this book.

I am an absolute Christmas fanatic and to prove this, I'd like to take you through some of my bona fides. When I was seven, I was so happy watching the end of the Bill Murray movie 'Scrooged' that I jumped on our ancient heirloom sofa so hard that the springs broke. (I didn't tell anyone until twenty years later. My mum is still angry about it!)

I own not one but two model Christmas villages. The first is a licensed "It's a Wonderful Life" light-up porcelain collection which I imported bit by bit from the States via eBay. The second has involved far more work. My Lego village now extends to about 20 buildings, a train set and this year will include a motorised funfair and circus area. So, yeah; I **love** Christmas. I've been writing Christmas books as presents for people ever since I was a teenager and it's great that I've finally had the chance to create a more professional effort to add to the festive cannon.

I knew I wanted to set the book in a Christmas village and originally thought it would be up in Lapland but a few readers had been asking for Izzy to head to Scotland, and I liked the British setting, so that's where she ended up. I told my reader team that I would love to write a book that makes people feel genuinely Christmassy the way that 'A Christmas Story', 'The Box of Delights' and 'Miracle on the 34th Street' (preferably the original version) do for me. I hope I've achieved my goal and that some of you will revisit this book during future Christmases.

There's no pre-order for the next book but I have **"A Corpse in a Locked Room"** all planned out and it's going to be a good one. So if you want to find out about new releases and get exclusive novellas whenever I have time to write them, subscribe to the Izzy Palmer Crime Club.

Acknowledgements

Get ready for the sorrys! Dear Scottish people, I know you're not all silly like Artie and Arnie and co. but I grew up watching 'Absolutely' and loved that irreverent comedy and decided to put a few of the Stoneybridge council members in the book.

Sorry to Americans too. I have a lot of amazing American friends and loud-mouthed Astrid is not representative of what I always tell people is the most polite nation on earth. Finally, I have to say sorry to Mahatma Ghandi and his descendants. No matter what Ramesh and Penelope might claim, I have no doubt that his glasses were genuine.

Thank you as always to my wife and daughter for accepting me as I sang Christmas songs in September, and to my crack team of experts – the Hoggs (**fiction**), Paul Bickley (**policing**), Karen Baugh (**marketing**) and Mar Pérez (**dead people**) for knowing lots of stuff when I don't. Thanks to all the fellow writers who have helped with this one too, especially Pete, Suzanne, Rose and, of course, my friend Lucy Middlemass, who still functions as Izzy's brain in my own head.

I also have to thank my wonderful readers. I love hearing from you and have had some brilliant conversations with lots of interesting people this year, so feel free to get in touch if the urge takes you. And please keep leaving positive **reviews on Amazon.** They really help!

I set up a team of advance readers, through my mailing list, who have spent the last month working with me to get this book into shape. It has helped immeasurably and has been such a fun process too so thank you a million times to…

Rebecca Brooks, Joseph A. and Kathleen Martin, James Woodworth, Ferne Miller, John Vaudrey, Craig Jones, Melinda Kimlinger, Deborah McNeill, Emma James, Chet Novicki, Mindy Denkin, Namoi Lamont, Linda Kelso, Katharine Reibig, Pam, Sarah Dalziel, Clare Hogg, Linsey Neale, Kate Newnham, Sarah Brown, Karen Davis, Taylor Rain, Brenda, Christine Folks McGraw, Terri Roller, Margaret Liddle, Esther Lamin, Tracy Humphries, Lori Willis, Anja Peerdeman, Liz Batton, Allie Copland, Susan Kline and Suzanne Lalor.

About Me

Writing has always been my passion. It was my favourite half-an-hour a week at primary school, and I started on my first, truly abysmal book as a teenager. So it wasn't a difficult decision to study literature at university which led to a masters in Creative Writing.

I'm a Welsh-Irish-Englishman originally from **South London** but now living with my French/Spanish wife and presumably quite confused infant daughter in **Burgos**, a beautiful medieval city in the north of Spain. I write overlooking the Castilian countryside, trying not to be distracted by the vultures, hawks and red kites that fly past my window each day.

I previously spent years focussing on kids' books and wrote everything from fairy tales to environmental dystopian fantasies right through to issue-based teen fiction. My book **"The Princess and The Peach"** was long-listed for the Chicken House prize in The Times and an American producer even talked about adapting it into a film. I'll be slowly publishing those books over the next year on Amazon.

"A Corpse For Christmas" is the fifth Izzy Palmer novel and number six **"A Corpse in a Locked Room"** will be coming in the new year. If you feel like telling me what you think about Izzy, my writing or the world at large, I'd love to hear from you, so feel free to get in touch via...

www.benedictbrown.net

Printed in Great Britain
by Amazon

57685769R00137